Death of a Prince

Death of a Prince

Susan P. Baker

Five Star • Waterville, Maine

This novel is a work of fiction. Names, characters, places and incidents are either the product of the author's imagination, or, if real, used fictitiously.

First Edition
First Printing: April 2005

Published in 2005 in conjunction with Tekno Books and Ed Gorman.

Set in 11 pt. Plantin by Christina S. Huff.

Printed in the United States on permanent paper.

Library of Congress Cataloging-in-Publication Data

Baker, Susan P.
Death of a prince / by Susan P. Baker.—1st ed.
p. cm.
ISBN 1-59414-268-8 (hc : alk. paper)
1. Lawyers—Crimes against—Fiction. 2. Attorney and client—Fiction. 3. Fathers—Death—Fiction. 4. Galveston (Tex.)—Fiction. 5. Trials (Murder)—Fiction. 6. Women lawyers—Fiction. I. Title.
PS3602.A588D43 2005
813′.6—dc22 2004029574

Dedication

With love for my children, Susan and Tara.

In memory of Judge Joe Kegans,
a fine lady, a fine judge, and an inspiration.

Acknowledgments

I would like to express my appreciation to the following for their assistance in the development of this manuscript: Galveston Novel and Short Story Writers Club, Susie Fletcher, Sandra Gardner, Nancy Otero, and, as ever, my husband, John Hunger.

Chapter One

Sandra Salinsky stomped the brakes on her Volvo S60 a moment after she spotted the yellow crime scene tape. What in the hell could have happened between the time she left the party at Phillip Parker's beach house the night before and this morning when she arrived to have brunch? And why hadn't Stuart called her immediately? Although her first inclination was to do a quick U-turn and flee in the other direction, Sandra shifted into first gear and eased up the drive to a City of Galveston police unit that blocked the entrance. Putting down her window after the dust from the oyster shell road settled, she called out to the uniformed cop. "Hey, Gonzales, what's going on?"

"Sorry, but you can't pass, Miss Salinsky." Jorge Gonzales, a former divorce client of hers, leaned over her window.

She nodded at the Parker house and the police in the distance. "Somebody get hurt after I left last night?"

"You a friend of Attorney Parker's?"

"Sure. Known him since I was a kid. He's my mother's best friend." She tried to see past Gonzales at what the other police officers were doing. At the entry to the cul-de-sac, two people leaned over a deck at the first house and watched. Across the small canal, she could see others standing in their yards. The scene hadn't quite reached circus proportions, but looked like it was only a matter of time. "I'm supposed to have brunch with Stuart Quentin, his partner."

"I don't guess it would hurt to tell you, being as how you was a D.A." His unwavering eyes met hers. "Attorney Parker is dead."

"Yeah, right." She thought he must be kidding, but he didn't smile. "You mean it?"

He nodded. "You were here last night and you didn't know?"

"What was it, Jorge? A heart attack? A stroke? No, y'all wouldn't be here if it was that."

"A fall, Miss Salinsky. He fell off his balcony."

"No way." Sandra stared at his tanned face for some sign that would betray those words but found nothing. Heat radiated throughout her body. She twisted her long hair up for a minute, hoping a breeze would dry her damp neck. All the blood seemed to have rushed out of her head, leaving her woozy. Turning the air-conditioning up full blast, Sandra directed the vents toward her face. In a moment's time, many of the ramifications of Phillip's death ran through her mind, including the possible effect it would have on her mother, Erma Townley.

"I'm just giving you the official version until the medical examiner says different." His mouth wore a grim line as they continued to stare at each other.

Realization settled over her like the oyster shell dust on her car. "I need to go inside. I'm not feeling well."

Shrugging, he said, "Let me ask the lieutenant." He stepped away and spoke into the tiny transmitter attached to the epaulet on his shoulder. When he turned back, he said, "The lieutenant wants to see you."

"Thanks." She gunned her engine.

"But you got to leave your car outside the gate. Pull it over to the side in the grass there." He pointed to a place on the far side of Phillip Parker's driveway. "The lieutenant don't want people all over the property disturbing the scene."

She followed his instructions, locked her car, and hurried toward the house. Just getting out and walking, she began to feel a bit better. It was probably just the island's heat and humidity. Searching through her purse, Sandra found a barrette and clipped her hair up as she walked toward the crime scene.

She didn't see how Phillip could be dead. He'd been so full of life the night before, celebrating a great victory. But wasn't that what people always said? He can't be dead, why I just saw him the other day.

Lieutenant Dennis Truman, in plainclothes, conferred with two uniformed officers, one male and one female. While Sandra waited, she eyed the blanket-covered body that laid half-on half-off the concrete patio under the house. Flies circled in the still, breezeless air. A sweet, sickly smell wafted from the honeysuckle that covered the awning.

Phillip's left arm, which sprawled at a right angle to his body, protruded from under the blanket. His pudgy fingers were drawn up like the claws of a frightened cat and were embedded in the deep pile of grass.

She edged closer and stared down at his hand. It looked alien. Immediately she realized that his two-carat diamond pinkie ring and his diamond Rolex were missing. She had known Phillip almost all of her life and certainly well enough to suspect that his jewelry had been stolen. He never removed it except to go swimming in the Gulf of Mexico.

Stepping onto the grass, Sandra looked up at the balcony to see if he could have fallen and landed where his body lay. It was three stories up, his master suite on top, as high as a widow's walk. Sandra brushed her hair out of her eyes. No way. Phillip had never gotten so drunk or rowdy that he wasn't in control of his faculties, at least not at any party she'd ever been to, and she'd been to more than a few. When she'd left the night before, he didn't seem any different than at any other time. He would never fling himself over a balcony railing.

Sandra stooped over the body and lifted the blanket. Just to confirm the identification of the victim, she told herself. So she could tell her mother. Right. But inside, she knew she needed to satisfy her morbid sense of curiosity.

When she got a look at Phillip's body, she saw one of the worst corpses that she'd ever seen. That included all the ones she'd had to view during her stint in the district attorney's office. It was hard to tell if it really was Phillip. His mouth was a gaping, blood-encrusted hole. One side of his face was mostly bloody mush. Gray matter had oozed through a gash above the brow. His nose was all but missing, flattened to the bone. A dried pool of auburn blood lay like a flat pillow under his head. The breast pocket of his open dressing gown hung by only a few threads. Underneath, he was naked.

"What the hell are you doing?" Dennis Truman knocked the blanket out of her hand. "You're not with the D.A.'s office anymore." Truman was a thick-bodied black man with skin the same color as a full-time surfer's. About forty-five, he had a square-shaped head, chocolate eyes, graying closely-cropped hair, a strong chin, and a suspicious mind.

Dennis and Sandra had a long history. They'd been friends when she'd been in the prosecutor's office, having worked on many cases together. When she left to go into private practice with her mother, to do defense work, they'd argued; he'd called her a traitor. They didn't see each other for a long time, neither seeking the other out. When they finally ran into each other at the courthouse, their conversation had been stilted. Even after a lunch together and some discussion about it, the relationship just wasn't the same. Now, several years later, Dennis still wasn't over it, though they occasionally got together for a meal.

Even with their history, Sandra didn't like anyone to think they could push her around. She pulled herself to her full five feet ten inches and faced him as she brushed off her knee. "I just wanted to confirm his identity. God, what a mess. Somebody must have been really angry."

"Didn't you see that yellow tape? I could charge you with tampering." He grunted something else, but it was unintelligible.

"Gonzales said you wanted to see me. If that's not the case, I'll just go upstairs." She turned to leave.

"Get back here, Salinsky. I said I wanted to talk to you, but I didn't mean you could trample the crime scene." He grabbed her arm. "What do you have to get all pissed off about? I'm the one who caught you tampering with a corpse, not the other way around. Get over here and sit down." Truman led the way to a cast-iron patio table and chairs.

"So you don't think the fall killed him?" she asked. "Was he drunk? He seemed okay when I left. Maybe he was drugged. I don't think that kind of damage was done to him just by falling off the balcony."

Dennis glanced toward the street. "I'll wait for the verdict from the M.E. That's his job. Mine is just to investigate. What are you doing here? Someone call you to defend them?"

"What?" she asked, surprised, and shook her head. "No. Supposed to have brunch with Stuart."

Dennis glanced at a slim notebook. "That would be Stuart Quentin?"

"Yes, sir." She crossed her arms and stared at him.

"Want to tell me what went on here last night?"

"Could we do that upstairs? I think I'm having a heatstroke." She pushed away from the table to try to catch a little breeze, her chair making a loud, metallic, scraping sound. It was a still, dank day. Her shorts and blouse stuck to her body. The roar of the surf in the distance would have been soothing under other conditions but echoed loudly in her ears. Dennis wasn't faring much better. Rings of sweat under the arms, moisture across his forehead, and his apparent bad temper told her that he wasn't experiencing the most pleasant day of his life either.

"I'll be going up as soon as the medical examiner gets here. Right now I'm going to stay down here to protect the integrity of the crime scene." He glared at her. "You can give me a statement after I interview everyone upstairs."

"Dennis, that could be several hours. I need to get to the office. What do you need to know?"

"Can't be helped." He slipped his notebook into the breast pocket of his shirt.

Sandra had not planned to spend her day out there. She had a ton of work on her desk that needed to be tackled after what would have been brunch, but might now become lunch. "They were celebrating because Phillip won that asbestosis case against the county. Stuart Quentin asked me to join them out here last night. By the time I arrived, there weren't many people left."

"Fine. You can fill in the details when I get around to you."

"C'mon, Dennis. I have a shitload of work on my desk."

"Tell you what. You can go upstairs, and when I'm ready for you to give a statement, I'll let you know. Only don't discuss this case with anyone while you're up there."

Sandra felt her anger mounting. She pushed back her chair as hard as she could, hoping the noise irritated him. With a glance over her shoulder, she walked around to the enclosed staircase.

"And that's what you get for messing with a crime scene," Truman muttered under his breath at her departing back.

Cool air enveloped Sandra as she opened the door. Her damp clothes felt sticky. Her skin was hot to the touch. Her mouth dry, she headed for the kitchen and a glass of water. The mixed aroma of frying bacon and cigarette smoke permeated the atmosphere.

Raymond Rivers, an associate of Phillip's, and Kitty Fulton, Raymond's girlfriend, sat on the sofa. Kitty's face was buried in Raymond's shoulder; his arms encircled her. Their shorts and T-shirts looked like they'd slept in them. "He's in the kitchen," Raymond said before Sandra got a chance to ask about Stuart. Raymond looked despondent, his face pale with red blotches, his hair disheveled like he'd just gotten out of bed. Kitty's soft cries were like that of a mewing animal.

Everyone at the party probably had some small affection for Phillip. His death would alter all of their lives, some in small ways, others in significant ones. Since Raymond was an associate, Stuart would probably keep him on. Sandra couldn't figure out Kitty, though. She didn't know her very well and didn't think Kitty had known Phillip very long.

She didn't see Lizzie, Phillip's long-time girlfriend, who practically lived with Phillip. Bubba Carruthers, the caretaker, lounged in an easy chair in front of the television. He was in the process of lighting a cigarette from the stub of another when she spotted him. Their eyes locked as he puffed away. Cigarette smoke hung overhead like ghostly wisps. After stubbing out the butt, Carruthers leaned back, his eyes following her.

Sandra had never liked him. She couldn't stand it when his weasel eyes scanned her body. It gave her goosebumps. She turned her head away as she reached the kitchen.

Stuart stood over the griddle on which at least a pound of bacon sizzled. He didn't seem to be paying much attention to it.

"You look like hell," she said. Normally he was better groomed than ninety-five percent of the population. His gray-tinged, curly brown hair stood on end. His shirt and shorts were as wrinkled as Raymond's and Kitty's. He wore no shoes. Deep shadows enveloped his eyes.

"I had planned to sleep in," he said as Sandra stood on her tiptoes and kissed him on the cheek. His unshaved whiskers tickled her lips. He had coffee breath.

She filled a glass with tap water and drank it down quickly. "Who discovered the body?"

"Bubba. He'd already called the police when he came up here hollering and waking up everyone."

"Well, you had to get up anyway."

"Yes, but not that early." He rubbed his eyes. "And I would have liked a shower. I went down there and saw Phil and came back and got a blanket. Did you take a look at the body?"

"Pretty gross."

"I didn't care if the cops liked it or not. Lizzie was hysterical. I didn't think he should just lie there like that with flies crawling all over his face."

"You don't have to be so descriptive."

"Sorry." He chased the bacon around on the griddle with a barbecue fork.

Sandra felt an inexplicable urge to laugh, but didn't. It was one of those awkward times when nothing but laughter will relieve the tension, although she feared any laughter on her part would quickly turn to tears. Though true she'd never liked Phillip, she knew how badly her mother would feel when she found out. She slipped her arms around Stuart's waist. They stood watching the bacon for a few moments.

Stuart buried his face in her hair and drew a deep breath. "Umm, you smell good."

"I did until I sat downstairs and talked to Dennis Truman."

"The lieutenant? You know him?"

"Only for a hundred years."

"He question you?"

"Not yet, but he's going to. I pissed him off by looking at the body, so he's making me wait until after y'all give your statements."

"Sounds like he knows you well."

"Very funny. I tried to give him my statement, but he wouldn't listen. He's waiting for the medical examiner and then he'll be up."

"He gave us strict orders not to discuss the case until he returned," he said into her hair. "I could use a shower and a shave first. Would you mind?"

"Finishing breakfast?" She shrugged. "For how many?"

"Everybody, I guess. You can ask them." He handed her the barbecue fork. "Thanks, Sandy." He leaned down and planted a kiss on her mouth.

Sandra wondered how long it would be until there was a follow-up to that kiss, and then realized that she should feel badly for thinking of sex when Phillip lay dead on the grass outside. She smiled at Stuart's back and said, "While you're at it, clip that hangnail. You just snagged my silk blouse."

"Sorry," he said over his shoulder.

She watched his tall frame as he went up the stairs. Physically, they seemed a good fit. She liked spending time with him. He was a talented lover. She just didn't want to make the relationship legal. He didn't seem to understand that. He'd been doing some serious hinting lately, but it was out of the question. One of her husbands had divorced her for being a workaholic and neglecting him and their child. She wasn't ready to be the recipient of the same behavior. She didn't need a permanent relationship with a man like Stuart, who often seemed to have trouble fitting her into his schedule. She made a good living, loved living alone in her condo, and didn't need to be married to be happy. It had taken her a long time to learn that. Stuart didn't yet realize that she wasn't about to change her mind and arrange her life around him.

She turned the bacon, reduced the heat, and started to go talk to the others when she again thought of her mother. Erma and Phillip had been best friends ever since Sandra could remember. In fact, one of her earliest memories was of Phillip coming to the house to what she now called her mother's "Salon," a regular bullshit session that took place in their living room, which in the early years had been on the other side of the wall from her mother's law office.

Fearing that her mother would find out about Phillip and suffer another heart attack, Sandra realized that she had to alert her. But how? Drive over there? Telephone? On Galveston Island, bad news traveled faster than a sexually transmitted disease in a red light district. If she didn't notify Erma quickly, it might come from someone else. She couldn't risk the fifteen-minute or longer drive. It was a Saturday and the seawall would be full of tourists driving like they were on a Sunday stroll. Reaching for the phone, Sandra hoped that she could break it to Erma gently and crossed her fingers that her mother wouldn't have a relapse.

Chapter Two

Erma Townley snuggled in her feather bed and pulled the duvet over her head. In her sleep, something annoyed her, but she resisted rising to consciousness to figure out what it was. It pulled her to the surface and released her several times until finally she stuck her head out into the refrigerated air to get a sense of it. Not the smoke alarm. Nothing burning that she could smell. She wiggled her legs and arms. Her limbs seemed to be working. There—that sound again. The goddamned telephone. Erma lay there, hoping it would cease and desist. She counted nine rings. Finally, she pushed up her eye mask and, blinded by the morning light, groped for her baby blue princess telephone. Whoever it was would be so sorry. "This better be goddamn good," she growled into the receiver.

"Erma, it's me. Sorry to wake you," Sandra said. "I have the misfortune of being the bearer of bad news."

Erma pulled out an earplug so that she could hear better. "Sandra? That you? What time is it?" She cleared her throat. "Feels like the middle of the goddamn night."

"It's almost eleven. You still in bed? What did you do last night? You left the party early enough."

"None of your damn business. Let me get my eyes halfway open." She pulled out the other earplug, plopped both of them on the bedside table, and struggled to a sitting position. "Now," she cleared her throat again, "what the hell is so important that you have to call me on a Saturday morning?"

"Something you'd rather hear from me than through the grapevine."

Erma reached for her cigarettes and lighter. She pulled a green crystal ashtray the size of a dinner plate closer to the bed, stuck a cigarette in a holder, and lit up. Expelling her first deep draw of the day, she said, "Sandra, I'm waiting."

"Are you smoking? You know the doctor said you're not supposed to be smoking."

"Goddamnit, I'm sleeping peacefully, enjoying a Saturday morning in my own bed, minding my own business, not hurting anybody, and am awakened to the incessant ringing of the telephone reminiscent of the years and years and years that I practiced criminal law and made bail bonds, which I would like to blank out of my memory, by the way, and now after you've got me good and awake, you don't want to tell me why you disturbed me? I ought to turn you over my knee like I did when you were a little girl and tan your hide. Now, for the last time before I hang up, Sandra Salinsky, what is it?"

"It's just with your heart—"

"Do I have to crawl through this telephone—"

"Mama—it's Phillip."

Erma felt her heart palpitate. She rested her cigarette in the ashtray, scared that she would hear something that would cause her to drop it on the bedcovers. It seemed like people were always calling with bad news. But it couldn't be bad news about Phillip. His health was good. He just had his physical last month. He'd told her about it when he'd executed his new will and left it with her for safekeeping. Could he have been arrested? That was it. Sandra was a criminal defense attorney. It couldn't be jail, though. They wouldn't keep him in the jail. He had always contributed large sums of money to the sheriff's re-election campaign. He would have been released on his own recognizance. Perhaps he'd done something stupid, or it was a mistake. Sandra had been called to help him out. Sandra was silent on the other end of the phone. Erma forced a laugh. She didn't want Sandra to know that she was frightened. "Phillip? What the hell kind of crazy thing has he gone and done now?" She picked up her cigarette and took another drag, but put it back down in the ashtray.

"Mama . . . he's dead."

"No. Shit. My Phillip? Phillip Parker? He was fine when I left last night."

"I knew I should have driven over to tell you in person. Are you all right?"

"Goddamn. Wait." Her throat clogged up. She coughed and swallowed. It wouldn't do to break down. After breathing deeply, Erma said, "How do you know? I mean, how do you, Sandra Salinsky, know about it? How do you know it's him? There must be some mistake."

"Are you crying? Will you be okay? Should I come into town and stay with you?"

"Goddamnit, answer me. How is it that you know? Why were you called?"

"I wasn't called. I came out here to have brunch with Stuart. The police are here."

"Police. You're at Phillip's house?"

"Yes, the beach house. The police were here when I arrived."

"What happened?" Erma asked.

"Are you okay? Want me to come over?"

Erma coughed again. "I'm just fine. You know how it is when you get to be my age, honey. You get up every morning and check the obits to see if you're still alive. Now spill it. How'd he die?" She gritted her teeth as she waited to hear what had happened to her best friend.

"At first blush, it looks like he fell off his bedroom balcony and hit the concrete patio face first."

Erma grunted. "I don't think so."

"I'm just telling you what it looks like. I've seen his face. It's a mess."

"What do the cops say? Who's doing the investigating? Who called the police, anyway?"

"It's Dennis Truman. Bubba found the body. I think he called the police."

"Truman's a good man. What does he think?"

"He's not saying anything. He's just collecting information. I have to give a statement. I wouldn't be surprised if you didn't have to, also, since you were at the party."

Erma grunted into the phone. Her poor, poor Phillip. It wasn't exactly the way he'd thought he would go. But does anyone go the way they'd choose? "Has the M.E. come?"

"Not yet, I don't think. Dennis is supervising some uniforms downstairs protecting the scene. I'm upstairs with everyone else."

"Oh my God. Lizzie. How is she?"

"Don't know. Pretty hysterical, I hear. She's in one of the bedrooms and hasn't come down. I'm hoping she'll have breakfast with us."

"Poor girl." Erma took a deep breath again. Death was a part of life, though she wasn't ready for him to go. He hadn't been ready to go, either. But there was nothing she could do about it. She needed to get up and get moving. There was a lot to do now. There was his will and estate to contend with.

"I can't for the life of me figure out why he would never marry Lizzie," Sandra said.

"That's rather moot now, Sandra. You need for me to come out there?"

"No. I just thought you'd like to know before the whole

world found out. The cops are going to question everybody here. Afterwards, I'm going to the office to work on a couple of things. Unless—you sure you don't want me to come over there?"

"I'm not a child, Sandra. If you want to come over, come. Otherwise I'll be fine."

"Well, if you need me, I'll be at the office later. If people start calling you, or if the press starts bugging you, call me."

"You're okay, aren't you, honey?"

"Yes, Erma."

Erma knew Sandra never really liked Phillip, but she'd known him for so many years, it must have had some effect on her to see his dead body. She never could figure out why they hadn't clicked. Phillip had been coming to the house since Sandra was a child. And once he and Erma had become good friends, he had provided much-needed referral fees from personal injury cases Erma had sent him, which had helped keep her law practice afloat and allowed her to support her daughter after Sandra's father had left. Well, that was water under the bridge.

"I've got to go. I promised Stuart that I'd cook breakfast and I need find out what everyone wants. Are you sure you'll be all right?"

"Quit blathering about me. It'll take more than one more friend's death to get this old bag down. I'll be fine. You just holler at me later and tell me whatever else you can."

"I'll call you as soon as I get away from here." Sandra hung up.

Erma put the phone down and stubbed out her cigarette. Phillip was dead. She stared at nothing for a few minutes. The phone rang again. "Hello."

"Erma? It's Jill. Sandra called me. You okay?"

"Goddamnit."

"She just wanted me to check on you. I'm sorry about your friend. If you need anything at all, remember I'm right next door."

"If I need a nursemaid, you'll be the first person I call, Jill, okay?"

A chuckle came across the line. "That's what I thought. Goodbye."

When she hung up, Erma tossed the covers on her king-sized four-poster bed aside and slid down until her feet touched the deep pile rug. Her long, cotton nightgown fell to the ground as she slipped it off and reached for her bathrobe, which hung on the end of the bed. Sticking her feet into woolly clogs, Erma reached for her cane and crept toward the bathroom, twisting her body to get the kinks out as she went. It was hell getting old, but ending up like Phillip was the alternative. She wasn't ready for that yet. Turning on the water in the tub, Erma stepped over to the washbasin and stared at herself in the mirror for a moment. Yes, she was still alive. After she washed her face and brushed her teeth, she poured oil into the tub and turned the water down so that it would fill more slowly. Then she picked up her cane again and walked haltingly toward the stairs. Perhaps she shouldn't have bought a two-story house. The stairs were becoming a challenge. Of course, she hadn't thought about that when she'd found her house.

Erma lived in the East End Historical District of Galveston Island. She had purchased the house years before Victorian homes had become the rage. She had gotten it cheap and spent large sums on lavish refurbishing, money she wouldn't have had, she reminded herself, if Phillip hadn't turned those cases she'd sent him into gold.

She had converted the second floor into a large master suite and two smaller bedrooms with a Hollywood bath, one of which used to be Sandra's room. The first floor contained a kitchen, a breakfast nook, a dining room, a library, a sitting room, and a formal living room. She'd thought about making one of the downstairs rooms into a master suite now that she was getting older. It would probably take twenty or thirty thousand dollars, but money wasn't a problem anymore. She just hadn't made the decision yet.

She hadn't told Sandra, either, or Sandra would have nagged her and nagged her about it. Telling Sandra was tantamount to confessing that she was getting too old or feeble to mount the stairs, and she wasn't about to do that. But it would be nice to have her bedroom downstairs. That way, when she couldn't sleep in the middle of the night, which had become increasingly a problem since her heart attack, she could go out to the screened-in verandah that ran along the south and east sides of the house and enjoy the salty breeze blowing from the Gulf of Mexico.

When Erma reached the bottom of the stairs, she stopped to get her breath. Phillip was dead, but her house looked normal. Everything should look different somehow. She proceeded into the kitchen, where she got the coffee out and put everything together in the newfangled coffeemaker that Sandra had gotten her for Mother's Day.

After she turned it on, Erma leaned heavily on her cane as she walked to the kitchen table and sat down. Carefully leaning the cane up against the side of the table, she put her head on her arms and wept.

Chapter Three

Phillip Parker's house was three stories on stilts, including the master bedroom suite and bath on top, from which he supposedly fell. Furniture groupings sectioned off the main floor. Guest rooms filled the second floor.

Kitty and Raymond huddled in a conversation pit area. Several large leather sofas ringed a huge, square, marble coffee table. As Sandra approached, Raymond whispered to Kitty. She sat up, wiping her eyes. She was a big-breasted blond who engaged in weight training. Although she was quite beautiful, Sandra thought Kitty would be more appealing if she'd let her hair go natural and shed some of the makeup. Now, Kitty was sans cosmetics. Dark rings encircled her red, swollen eyes. Raymond didn't look great either. Even with his glasses, it was easy to see that he hadn't had a good night's sleep.

"Looks like I'm cooking," Sandra said. "Bacon, scrambled eggs, and toast. Anything else and you fix it yourself." She studied both their faces for a moment. "Want some?"

"I guess so," Raymond said. "If it's no trouble. You, dear?" he said to Kitty.

"I don't know if I could eat anything," she said and began sobbing again.

Raymond pulled her to him. "A couple of eggs for her, Sandy."

"Okay. Where's Lizzie?" she asked as she headed toward Carruthers.

Raymond peered over Kitty's head. "In one of the second-floor bedrooms. Stuart checked on her earlier, but she was so hysterical he couldn't deal with it, so he just closed the door. I doubt if she'll eat anything."

"Okay. I'll look in on her when everything's finished." Without getting close to Carruthers, she called to him. "Bubba, you want some scrambled eggs and bacon?"

He looked at Sandra and said, in a slow, labored monotone, "Yeah, I guess so, Miss Sandra. You want me to cook it?"

Feeling repulsed at the thought of his hands on her food, Sandra said, "No, thanks. I've got it covered. I'll holler when it's ready."

She went back into the kitchen and checked on the bacon. It was creepy how everyone seemed to be in shock. Good thing Stuart and she weren't in what she called "the sleeping together publicly" stage of their relationship, or she would have slept there and been acting strange, too. As she pulled a carton of extra-large eggs and some cream from the refrigerator, it occurred to Sandra that each person probably wondered which one of the others had killed Phillip. She wondered, too. If there hadn't been any way for an intruder to gain entry to the house, it had to be one of them.

Sandra broke open a dozen eggs, beat them, and dumped them into a large frying pan. In between stirs, she toasted bread and piled it high on a plate. When the eggs were almost cooked, she turned off the flame and gave them another stir.

"I feel a lot better," Stuart said as he entered the kitchen.

"Good, you can finish up. I'm going up to see Lizzie."

"I wouldn't if I were you. She's not fit to talk to."

She grimaced. "I can't just leave her there. I'll be back in a few minutes to eat with you."

Tapping lightly on the door to the bedroom Stuart had pointed out, she called Lizzie's name several times. Getting no response, she tried the doorknob and found it unlocked. Lizzie lay on a queen-sized bed in the dark, a washcloth draped over her eyes. The room had a too-familiar sour smell. It reminded Sandra of the aftermath of drunken college parties.

"Lizzie, it's Sandy. All right if I come in?"

Lizzie muttered something unintelligible.

Sandra closed the door behind her. "Let me freshen this for you." She took the washcloth from Lizzie's forehead into the bathroom and ran cold water over it. On the opposite side was another door. Opening it, she saw it was another bedroom with another queen-sized bed, dresser, TV, clock radio, and a lamp on a night table. The bed was neatly made. An overnight bag rested on the floor next to the door. Who had spent the night in the adjoining room? Stuart? She brushed aside a twinge of jealousy. She didn't know what had happened the night before, but it was unlikely that Lizzie had been contemplating throwing over multi-millionaire Prince Phillip for her Stuart. Yes, she did think of him as hers. And she wondered why Lizzie was in one of the downstairs bedrooms instead of upstairs in the master suite.

Taking the washcloth back to Lizzie, Sandra folded it into a rectangle and placed it over Lizzie's eyes. Lizzie's pale face and skin seemed more wrinkled than usual. Her nose and chin were red. Her strawberry-colored hair was so matted that it looked like flowerless pigweed. She wore a silk teddy and was covered only partially by a sheet.

Sandra straightened the bedclothes and folded the coverlet at the bottom of the bed. Pulling up a chair, she spotted a bottle of vodka on the floor within arm's reach. She realized that the glass of clear liquid on the nightstand was not water. "Do you want to talk?"

"I just want to sleep." Lizzie slurred her words.

"Have you slept at all?"

"A few hours."

"What happened?"

"We had a fight."

"What about?"

Lizzie pursed her lips. "I don't want to talk about it."

"What are you doing in here?"

"I couldn't stay with him. He threw me out."

"What time was that?"

Lizzie pulled the rag from her face. "Why the Spanish Inquisition?" Her swollen eyes wouldn't open all the way. Clearly, she'd been crying for hours.

Sandra couldn't tell Lizzie that she wondered whether she'd murdered Phillip. "I'm just concerned about you, that's all. Would you like to come down and have breakfast with us? I scrambled some eggs."

"I think I'm going to be sick," Lizzie said, holding the washcloth to her mouth.

"Here, let me help you." Sandra supported her by the shoulders as Lizzie staggered into the bathroom and collapsed on the floor next to the toilet. Sandra lifted the lid. Lizzie heaved and hugged the bowl.

Sandra felt her own stomach roil and tried to ignore it by searching for some clean washcloths. When Lizzie was through, Sandra tidied her up and helped her back to bed.

Hoping to catch a small breeze to clear the odor out of the room, Sandra pushed open a window. The ocean rippling against the bulkhead a few hundred yards away might soothe Lizzie to sleep.

"Be sure when we get upstairs that you look in every room for bloodstained clothes."

Sandra recognized the lieutenant's voice outside, below the window. So they definitely suspected one of the people who had spent the night.

A woman's voice said, "But we don't have a warrant. What if they won't let us examine their stuff?"

"You let me worry about that. You guys just do as I tell you. Don't let any of them pack up without you seeing what's in their gear."

"Yes, Lieutenant." A man's voice.

"With what happened to that man's face, somebody's gotta have blood—" Truman's voice became unintelligible as they apparently walked away from the window.

When Sandra turned back to the bed, Lizzie had her hand wrapped around the glass on the bedside table.

"You've had enough of that, girl." Sandra took it from her.

Lizzie looked as though she might cry. "But I've got a splitting headache. Can you get me something for it?"

"Lizzie, what are you going to do, drink yourself to death? Face reality. Phillip is dead."

"Shut up! Just shut up!" Lizzie closed her eyes, covered her ears with her hands, and lay back down on the pillow.

Sandra took the bottle of vodka and the glass into the bathroom and emptied them. She shook out three painkillers. She wasn't much at nursing, but she wanted to help Lizzie if she could. It took a little persuasion to get them down her with a glass of water. She only hoped they wouldn't make Lizzie any sicker on top of all that vodka.

Lizzie lay back on the bed. "I just want to die."

"You'd feel a lot better if you ate something. Killing yourself isn't going to help matters." Sandra knew she probably wasn't saying the right thing. She was better at legal arguments than nurturing but felt she had a moral obligation not to leave Lizzie in this condition. Who would look out for her now that Phillip was dead?

Lizzie covered her eyes with the back of her hand in a classic martyr pose. "What am I going to do without him? How am I going to live?"

Phillip had been dead only a few hours. Sandra had thought Lizzie mourned him. Now it sounded like she mourned his money.

"I'm sure he made provisions for you, Lizzie." Sandra really had no idea, but it would be only logical and she wanted to reassure Lizzie.

Lizzie pushed up the cloth. "I don't know of any. And look at me, Sandy. I'm not young anymore. I'm thirty-seven years old. I've been with Phillip for ten years. My hair is fading; my skin is getting wrinkled. Who would want me? Even Phillip was growing tired of me." She burst into tears. "What's going to happen to me?"

Sandra stayed long enough to make sure Lizzie wasn't going to regurgitate the painkillers. She didn't think Lizzie would commit suicide, at least not until she found out what was in the will. When Lizzie wouldn't stop crying, Sandra gave up and went back downstairs. Stuart had gathered everyone and was playing host. He, Bubba, Raymond, and Kitty sat in a row at the long glass table in front of the picture window. They were eating, but their faces looked like someone had hypnotized them.

When Sandra sat down next to Stuart and tapped him on the arm, he shrugged. She stared at them. One must be the killer—either that or the woman upstairs. Which one? "Is the food okay?" she asked no one in particular.

"Fine," Raymond answered in a monotone.

"The eggs aren't rubbery? Sometimes I cook them too

long and they're rubbery. Cooking is not exactly my long suit." Sandra looked at the congealed mess on her plate and suddenly lost her appetite. She chewed on a piece of toast while she decided what to do.

Stuart patted her arm just like she'd seen him pat an old lady client's once. Kitty turned red-rimmed eyes on her for only a moment. Bubba was totally unresponsive. She wanted to jump up and object, but there was no one to rule. She waited a few minutes to see if anyone else was going to attempt conversation. Failing that, Sandra asked, "So did anyone hear or see anything last night after I left that would give us any clues as to what happened?"

Tears streamed down Kitty's cheeks. As she patted her face with her napkin, her eyes darted at Raymond.

"We went to bed right after you left, Sandy," Raymond said.

"Well, I was hoping that's what Stuart did. Alone, I hope?"

"Definitely," Stuart said.

"Okay, so someone has to know something." She glanced at each of them again. "Bubba, you didn't hear anything?"

His eyes slid slowly in her direction. "No, ma'am." He shoveled some food into his mouth and chewed slowly as he stared. Washing the food down with a slurp of coffee, he said, "Cleaned up the joint a little and went downstairs to bed." There was scrambled egg caught between his teeth.

"It's pretty amazing that someone could be busted up practically into little pieces outside in the yard and no one inside the house heard a thing. Didn't anyone hear any screams or any hollering?"

"You forgot that all the bedrooms are on the opposite side of the house and one floor down from Phillip's suite," Stuart said.

"Oh, that explains it." Sandra still thought someone should have heard something, but decided not to press the point. She was ready to get out of there. "Well, the cops are coming upstairs in a few minutes. I suggest that each of you be prepared to give them a detailed statement of what we did last night, especially what you did after I left."

"And I thought I told you not to discuss this case when you came upstairs," Dennis Truman said from behind her. "I ought to run you in."

Sandra wondered how long he had been standing there.

"I'm getting a little tired of you, Miss Salinsky."

"Dennis, I—"

"Shut up. Just shut up."

Stuart stood. "Now look here, Lieutenant, I—"

"You sit down, Mr. Quentin."

"Yes, sit down, Stuart," Sandra said.

"Salinsky, get your ass outside on that porch. I want to talk to you." He went out the glass door and left it open for her.

Sandra had seen Dennis angry before. She wasn't worried. She only hoped that Stuart would calm down and keep out of it. She patted his arm. "I'm a big girl. I can take care of myself." No sense in everyone getting even more worked up. She went outside onto the porch and closed the sliding door. "I apologize, Dennis, I was wrong."

"You sure as hell were. What do you think you're doing? You can't just come into a crime scene and act like you're still with the D.A. Damn, Sandra."

"I said I was sorry."

"You gotta let me do my job without interfering. Now I'm going to take your statement and then you get the hell out of here."

"Yes, sir." She leaned against the banister, the wind

blowing her hair across her face.

"I'm not playing with you." Truman frowned and pulled out the slim pad of paper he'd had earlier. "Right now, I have Bubba Carruthers, Kathryn Fulton, Raymond Rivers, Stuart Quentin—your boyfriend?"

"I guess you could say that."

"And Elizabeth Haynes." He glanced back at his paper. "And Robert Earl Bradshaw, the off-duty cop that was assigned to Mr. Parker last night, is waiting for me down at the station. Anybody else around when you were here?"

"A few, but they'd all left before I did. Everyone else was fixing to go to bed."

"Why didn't you stay?"

Sandra laughed. "That's really none of your business, Lieutenant."

"You and the boyfriend have a fight?"

"Hey, since when is my personal life public property?"

"Okay. Okay. What was going on when you left?"

She shot him a sidelong glance. "I told you. Everyone was fixing to go to bed. Bubba was cleaning up. He lives downstairs, you know." She pointed toward the underneath of the house. "He's the caretaker. Phillip closed that in and made it into an efficiency apartment a few years ago."

"Yeah, Bradshaw told me that much. Salary and a place to stay. Pretty good deal if you can get it."

"Phillip could afford it. It's not like he wasn't insured, but with the constant string of beach house burglaries, he just didn't want to deal with all the hassles. What's another thousand or so a month to someone like him?"

"What do you know about Carruthers, anything?"

"He's kind of a slime. I don't know where Phillip dug him up. Twenty years ago I would have said he was probably a client of Erma's, but not any more. You might ask Erma later or else Lizzie. She'd probably know."

"Elizabeth Haynes?"

"Yes. Phillip's girlfriend." The impact of what had happened started to really sink in. Life without Phillip Parker. Was he really lying downstairs, dead? As hardened as she'd become as a felony prosecutor and later a defense attorney, the deep sense of sadness she suddenly felt surprised her. Perhaps talking to the police made it seem more real.

"Okay," Dennis said, "so Carruthers is cleaning up. I assume that he comes downstairs as soon as he's finished. That leaves—"

"Well, Stuart and me, but I was heading home. Kitty and Raymond. Raymond is an associate of Phillip's. Was, I mean."

"How long was he with the firm?" Truman studied her.

"Raymond? Couple of years, I think. Nice guy. Worshiped the ground Phillip walked on, for some ungodly reason."

Truman, nodding, made notes. "Think he's capable of murder?"

"Everyone is capable of murder, Dennis." Sandra stared at him a moment. "Look, it doesn't take a genius to know that Phillip probably didn't fall off the balcony. He sure as hell didn't jump, not with his millions and the new fame the asbestos case would bring him. He was an egomaniac. Wanted to be like Joe Jamail."

"The so-called Texas Tort King?"

"Yeah, Jamail, who seemed to make millions and millions off every case he touched, hence the allusion to King Midas. Phillip called himself the Prince of Personal Injury, though Jamail's fortune dwarfed his."

"Oh, poor guy. How many millions less did he have?"

"I have no idea." Sandra smiled.

"What're you smiling at?" Truman leaned back, his elbow on the banister, and stared at her.

"I knew you thought he didn't fall."

He shrugged. "So what? A moron could have figured that out. What about Kathryn?"

"Kitty?" Her turn to shrug. "I don't know that much about her. She's been dating Raymond for a while. They appear to be in love. She's some kind of a model."

"She makes a lot of money herself?"

"I'm sure she must. I don't really know her that well. We don't socialize, if you know what I mean."

"Something wrong with her?"

"Well, she's not exactly a mental giant, Dennis. We don't have a lot in common. I mean, she's a clotheshorse. I'm an attorney."

"And a snob."

She fanned herself with her hand. "Aw, big shit, so what else is new?"

He shook his head. "Tell me about Stuart."

"Stuart?" she smiled. "Well, he's probably got an IQ exceeding one hundred and fifty. Can take one look at a situation, analyze it, and draw conclusions in a matter of moments. Did he push Phillip off the balcony? I doubt he'd be capable. He's pretty mellow, participated in all that peace stuff at the federal courthouse during the beginning of the Iraq thing. Works his butt off, morning, noon, and night. Hardly enough time for anything else."

She had been thinking of their sex life but didn't say so. When it was there, it was very, very good. The man seemed insatiable. But it was the frequency that was the issue between them, or rather, the lack thereof. He seemed to be less and less available lately. Not that any of that was relevant to what Dennis Truman wanted to know.

Dennis grinned. "Sounds like a personal problem."

She started away.

He pulled her back. "Okay. Your personal life is off-limits. For now. So is Stuart Quentin an associate, too?"

Sandra crossed her arms. "Partner, bought in last year. But I have no idea what their partnership agreement says. He couldn't possibly be getting an equal share. Probably some stock. You'd have to ask him. Brought a bunch of lucrative cases with him."

"You sure you aren't just prejudiced in his favor?"

She ran her hands through her damp hair. "No. I definitely am. Don't go by what I say."

"And that leaves Elizabeth Haynes."

"Yes, Liz. Lizzie. She and Phillip have been together for eons. She's mad about him. Was mad about him. I always thought they'd get married, but . . . Anyway, why would she harm the man who lavished money, jewelry, cars, etcetera on her for years? You know they have his and hers Mercedes, don't you?"

"Lifestyle of the rich and famous—"

"Exactly."

"Where do you fit in, Miss Salinsky?"

She grinned. "Just a working girl trying to make a buck."

Truman laughed. "And trying to catch a husband?"

"No, thanks. I've had two and that's enough to last any woman a lifetime."

"Is there anything else you think I need to know?"

She thought of Phillip's naked body, including his naked hand, and shook her head. "Can I go now?"

"I guess, but in the future," Dennis pointed his pen at her, "you'd better remember what I said about messing in crime scenes. One of these days you're going to go too far."

"In the future, I hope I won't be at any more crime

scenes," she said. "Adios." She saluted Truman and turned to go back inside so she could tell Stuart goodbye.

"Tell that Raymond Rivers to step out here," Truman said.

All heads turned her way when Sandra entered. "Raymond, he wants to see you next. I'm out of here y'all. If you need a criminal defense lawyer, you know where my office is."

Stuart turned an angry face toward her. "Is that supposed to be funny?"

"I guess not." She leaned down and pecked him on the cheek. As she headed for the stairs, the door below opened. It was the medical examiner, a fellow who greatly resembled Hollywood's version of Moses. She met him at the halfway point on the stairs.

"Leaving so soon, Sandra?"

"Yes, Hank. Already told the cops what I know, except for one thing. Have them check on the missing watch and ring. The decedent's missing watch and ring. He always said he'd never be caught dead without them."

Chapter Four

Late the following afternoon, Sandra worked at home finishing a set of interrogatories designed to irritate the hell out of her opponent in an immensely ugly divorce case. It was payback for the nasty things he'd implied about her client at the hearing on temporary orders. As soon as she finished running spell check, she hit the print button so she could see a hard copy before she faxed it to the guy's law office. Her laser printer hummed loudly as it kicked out the thirty questions. She had just time enough to go to the john and fetch a bottle of water.

When she returned, Sandra proofed her work and faxed it over. That would serve the S.O.B. right. That's what he got for leaving his fax machine running over the weekend. When he arrived at his office on Monday morning, her surprise would be waiting for him. She laughed and felt maniacal as she turned her own fax machine off. After preparing copies for her client, addressing the envelope, and reviewing her to-do list to make sure she'd completed everything she'd brought home, she shut down her computer. After all, it was Sunday.

Sandra punched in Stuart's home number but got no answer. She tried his office and cell numbers again. She'd been phoning all afternoon. A client had dropped off five pounds of extra-large shrimp. After a dinner Stuart had treated her to recently, not to mention the hot dessert, she thought it might be nice to reciprocate. Besides, Stuart was a whiz at grilling shrimp. She was best at gulping them down. He still didn't answer. For someone who kept hinting at permanent commitment, he sure seemed to make himself scarce at times.

Gathering up her portable phone and a bottle of water, Sandra went out onto her balcony, slid onto a plastic chair, and wove her toes into the wrought iron railing as she admired the rolling waves. The sun had begun its descent, but it still wasn't cool outside. There wouldn't be a significant drop in temperature until the following winter. Usually the island skipped fall entirely, except for hurricane season, and went directly from hot, damp summers into cold, damp winters.

A strong south wind whipped strands of hair around her face, where they stuck to beads of perspiration that broke out almost as soon as she set foot outside. She didn't mind. She wasn't planning to move from that spot until well after the sun went down, when she'd take a quick run on the seawall and a splash in the pool before it got too dark.

One of the reasons she had decided to buy the condo was that she enjoyed periods of solitude on the balcony where she could watch the brown pelicans soaring inches above the waves in search of dinner or see the dolphins breaching just over the breaker line. She also loved to sprawl out on a chaise lounge with a good read and sip wine.

Eleven stories below, a line of cars headed toward Sixty-first Street and then the causeway off the island. Every Sunday each summer was the same, miles of cars exiting, people returning to the big city. As she watched, she saw a black BMW coming fast from the east. It pulled into the parking lot below. Kitty Fulton drove a black beamer. Sandra hung over the balcony to see who it was. A blond woman jumped out, glanced over her right shoulder, then over her left, and hurried toward the front of the building.

Inside her apartment, Sandra pulled a brush through her long black hair and twisted it up into a knot. Her curiosity was about to get the best of her.

Opening the door at the first knock, Sandra found a surprised and breathless Kitty on the other side. Her hair was in a French twist. She wore a black suit, a prim white button-front blouse with a large oval, silver, antique brooch at the throat, and white spike heels. Tears filled her bloodshot eyes.

"Come in." Sandra held the door wide. "I saw you from the balcony." She pushed the door closed. "What're you doing dressed to the teeth on a Sunday afternoon?" Sandra briefly thought about the T-shirt and shorts she wore. She wasn't much for dressing on the weekends. The weekdays were another story. She spent a lot of money on clothes. She was a firm believer that any lawyer who charged several hundred dollars an hour ought to look like it, even though a lot of her friends never dressed up unless they were in trial.

Kitty twisted her purse in her hands. "Can I talk to you?"

"Sure. Sit down." She pulled out one of the barstools and went around into the kitchen. "Want something to drink?"

"Got a beer?"

As Sandra retrieved a can from the refrigerator and a mug from the freezer and set both on paper cocktail napkins, she studied Kitty. The woman was dressed to the nines all the way down to her fingernails, which looked like they cost every bit as much as her own. Opening the can of beer with a top popper, she went back around the counter to sit next to Kitty, anxious to hear why she was there.

Kitty poured the beer expertly down the side of the mug and took a long swallow. Afterward, she expelled a deep breath. "Oh, that's good. It's so hot out there."

"You could have gotten a beer at a bar."

"I'm sorry. I feel like such a hypocrite. I am a hypocrite.

Sandy, you've just got to help me." Kitty banged the mug on the counter and burst into tears.

Kitty's makeup rolled down her cheeks. After a moment, Sandra thought about finding some Kleenex and loped into the bathroom for a box. When she returned, she pushed it at Kitty and asked, "Did you and Raymond have a fight?"

"You don't understand." Mascara formed two vertical lines down her face like clown makeup.

"Tell me, then."

"I . . . killed him. I killed Phillip Parker!"

Sandra slid off her barstool. After a moment, she put an arm around Kitty. "You don't know what you're saying." Kitty sobbed into Sandra's shoulder as Sandra walked her to the sofa and sat her down on one end with the box of tissues.

Kitty smeared the mascara across her cheeks and blew her nose. Her breath came in short gasps. "It's t-t-true. I've b-been in church all day praying over it." She reached for another tissue and blew her nose again. Taking a couple of deep breaths, she said, "I had to tell someone. I just couldn't keep it to myself any longer. If I go to the police, Sandy, will you defend me like you said yesterday?"

"Hold on. I—I was just making a joke yesterday." Dumbfounded, Sandra stared at her. Kitty would have been her last choice for murderer of the year. This had to be good. She loved a juicy murder case. She couldn't wait to hear her story and then call Erma. Erma. Phillip. Her mother's best friend. Shit. Well, the least she could do was hear Kitty out. She held up her hand. "Slow down a minute, will you? I've got to think."

"I just thought that if anyone could get me off, Sandy, it would be you. I—I've seen you and you're good."

Was Kitty just trying to flatter her? Did she really want Sandra to defend her or did she have some other motive?

Kitty appeared sincere. Sandra knew she was good. She just didn't know whether Kitty really knew it. Perhaps Kitty wasn't as dumb as she appeared to be. "Whoa, Kitty, slow down girl. How about you tell me what happened, and then we'll go on from there."

Kitty bit her lower lip. "You mean the whole story? Everything?"

"Well, sure. If I'm going to help you, I'll need to know it all."

Kitty's breath came unevenly. She wiped her nose again and settled back into the sofa. "Okay, Sandy, if you think it will help. Only I don't know where to start." Her face puckered up once more.

Sandra brought Kitty's mug of beer over to the coffee table. She hoped the alcohol would make it easier for the younger woman to talk.

"Thank you." She gulped down a couple of swallows and patted her mouth with the crumpled tissue.

"You know, Kitty, you don't have to be afraid of me," she said. "People tell me all kinds of things. Everything's confidential. I can't reveal what you say to anyone."

"You didn't say you'd represent me."

"Doesn't matter. Even if I don't, I still can't tell anyone what you said."

Kitty sniffed and nodded and watched Sandra's face.

"I want to represent you, Kitty, but I'll have to hear you out first. It's only routine. I never agree to represent someone until I hear his or her side of the story. No lawyer would."

"Well . . ."

"What you say remains confidential," Sandra repeated. "Whether I take your case or not. Or whether you decide you don't want me or, heaven forbid, fire me later. Is that what you're worried about?"

Kitty licked her lips. She rubbed them together and nodded. She reminded Sandra of a nervous little kid. "I didn't know. I've never had to hire a lawyer before. My husband hired the one for our divorce. I just signed the papers."

"I didn't know you'd been married." As she listened to Kitty, she had the most tremendous desire for a cigarette. She found herself groping the coffee table for a package of them before she remembered that she had quit years ago. Sandra sucked air into her mouth and exhaled a couple of times. She smiled at Kitty, who she thought looked at her peculiarly.

"Ten years ago. I got married when I was eighteen. This sounds weird, but I think I married him because we were already doing it. Having sex." She swiped at her nose again. "We had gone together for two years and had been doing it for most of that time. I felt so guilty. We got married the week after my birthday. That's why my name is Fulton."

"Oh." Sandra wasn't sure what Kitty's marriage had to do with the murder, but she nodded and feigned interest to keep Kitty talking.

"Having a different name seemed to fool my father, though I didn't mean it to. He didn't recognize me. I guess because it had been so many years. Of course, I look a lot different. See, before he left, he called me Kathy. I told my teachers in kindergarten that I wanted to be called Kitty and it stuck. My mother didn't like it. She always called me Kathryn."

"To get back to Phillip's death—"

"Just a minute. I'm getting to that."

Sandra drew back. Kitty made no sense, but Sandra decided to let her go on since she seemed so determined.

"My mother was heartbroken when I married so young. It didn't last more than a year and a half. It seemed to me that

Mama had been sickly ever since Daddy left us. She died when I was twenty, and I promised myself then that I'd find the bastard and make him pay."

Kitty's voice had grown vehement. Sandra decided "Uh-huh," was all she would say. She was anxious to hear how all this seemingly irrelevant information about Kitty and her mother was going to fit with her killing Phillip.

Kitty pushed her shoes off and hiked her feet up under herself like Sandra had done. She smoothed her skirt over her knees and pulled a throw pillow into her lap. "I didn't know how I intended to make him pay, Sandy. I didn't mean to kill him. I just wanted to talk to him."

Phillip had been Kitty's father, Sandra realized. She almost laughed at her own stupidity. No wonder Kitty rambled on. "Would you mind if I got a legal pad to make some notes? Just to keep all this straight in my head?"

Kitty nodded. "Okay." She reached for her beer as Sandra leapt from the sofa and dashed into her office.

Sandra could feel the adrenaline spurting into her veins like drugs into a junkie's. She would have to take Kitty's case, even if it meant a knockdown, drag-out fight with Erma. The defense of Phillip Parker's daughter for his murder could very easily be the case of the century. Grabbing a legal pad and a pen from atop the file cabinet in her office, Sandra ran back into the living room. She tried to smile encouragingly at Kitty as she sat cross-legged on the opposite end of the sofa, Indian style. "Go ahead," she said, concealing her glee as best she could. Head down, Sandra scrawled notes as fast as possible, recording what Kitty had already told her. They'd be going over it many more times before trial, but initial impressions were always important.

"I used most of Mom's life insurance to bury her. I sold the furniture. We lived in a rented house. I went to New York to be an actress. I held the starring role in my high school play my junior and senior years. The money from the furniture and stuff didn't last long. I read for a lot of parts but only got a few walk-ons. So I decided to see if maybe I could model a little. That's how I came to live in Texas."

Sandra glanced up. "What's how you came to live in Texas?"

"Oh. I made a lot of money in New York as a large-sized model, but I didn't really like it, you know? Life is real hectic there and a girl like me from Tennessee is used to a slower lifestyle."

"Just out of curiosity, what size are you?" Kitty wasn't her idea of the type of people who should be modeling for August Max Woman or Lane Bryant.

"Oh. Ten to twelve." She feigned a smile.

Sandra didn't always win the struggle to stay a size twelve, but she didn't consider herself large-sized. Tall people just wore a larger size, that's all. "Go on."

"Well, someone told me that I could make money in Dallas and that the pace wasn't quite as bad as New York. After I landed my job there, I moved down here to Galveston and bought my condo near Gaido's Restaurant up on the seawall because I always wanted to be near the water." She flashed a quick smile. "And I like that giant crab they have out front." She wiped at her eyes again with the wadded-up tissue. "I still do some magazines, too. I usually fly to my assignments."

"You were looking for Phillip all that time or did you know where he was?"

"No, I didn't start looking for him until I moved to Dallas. I needed money to support myself—that was the main thing at first. But my mother had told me years ago that he had come to Texas."

Sandra shook her head. "No—I'm confused. Explain to me what happened with Phillip."

"When I killed him, you mean?"

"Before that. What happened to him and your mother? They were married, right?" Sandra tapped her lower lip with her pen. These days, you never knew whether a person's parents had been married or not.

Kitty started fanning her eyes with her hand. Sandra saw that she was close to tears again. She nudged the Kleenex box over to Kitty's side of the coffee table.

"I'm sorry, Sandy. It's all I've been doing for two days now." She blew her nose; her chin quivered.

"You're going to be okay."

"It's not that. This whole thing has brought back so many memories. He was so ugly to me, Sandy. He made me feel so worthless." Kitty broke down and started sobbing.

Sandra, who still didn't have a handle on what Kitty's emotional state was all about, didn't feel that she could do anything but hold Kitty's hand and wait for the tears to subside. Sandra had thought she was hardened to tears after so many years of divorce, child custody, and criminal cases, but she found herself responding to Kitty by wanting to cry herself. She didn't yet understand what Phillip had done to this young woman, but figured it must have hurt her very deeply. Sandra squeezed Kitty's hand and patted her knee and finally got up and moved to Kitty's end of the sofa and ran her hand up and down her back and hugged her. That always seemed to work with people. She muttered inane phrases and wished Kitty would stop crying so she could finish her story.

A few minutes later, Kitty began taking gasps of air in an apparent attempt to settle down. Lifting her head from Sandra's shoulder, Kitty pulled a few tissues from the box.

"You going to be all right now?"

Nodding, she blew her nose several times and wiped her eyes again.

Sandra began to wonder if perhaps Kitty needed psychological help. It was something she would discuss with her if she decided to take her case. If nothing else, she would never be able to put Kitty on the witness stand if Kitty couldn't tell her story without breaking down. The risk that jurors would think her mentally unstable would be too great.

Kitty stared hard at Sandra as she made her next statement. "He left us when I was about five. As far as I know, we never heard from him again."

So that was why she was so hurt. How could Phillip have abandoned his only child? "You mean he never supported y'all?"

Kitty shook her head. "I don't think so, else why would Mama and me have been so broke? She was a teacher, but they didn't get much back then, and especially in such a small town."

"She could have gone after him for child support in the divorce."

"I know, Sandy, but I don't think Mama ever divorced him. She didn't have the money and she wouldn't have wanted anyone to know about what had happened. She told people he was dead. Sometimes I think she believed it herself."

"Maybe he divorced her after he got here."

"Maybe. I looked through all her papers after she died. If she got any, she must have destroyed them."

Sandra shook her head. "There are ways to get divorced without ever telling the other party. It's not exactly legal, but it can be done." She stared at Kitty. "Maybe he never let her know." Or, she thought, maybe they never did divorce and that's why he never married Lizzie. Damn. Just wait until Erma heard that.

Kitty shrugged. "I don't know, Sandy. It really doesn't matter though."

It mattered more than Kitty knew, but she wasn't going into that yet. "Do you know why he left? Were they having bad financial problems or fighting a lot? Was he an attorney then?"

Kitty shook her head and stared down at the pillow in her lap. "It was because of me."

"Oh, Kitty," she said, "children often believe they're at fault in their parents' separation but they aren't. I'm sure they just didn't get along for some reason."

"No, you don't understand." Kitty raised her eyes to meet Sandra's. "He didn't want a child. I heard him say so. He left because of me." She bowed her head and sobbed.

Reaching for Kitty's hands, Sandra grabbed them in her own and squeezed them. "It wasn't your fault. You were a child. How old were you—four? Five?"

"Five when he left. At first Mama thought he was dead. He wrote her a letter telling her he was going to kill himself. After a few years of not hearing from him again, she went to Social Security to draw death benefits and found out that he was still alive. I don't know how she found out he had come to Texas. She didn't tell anyone, though; she kept pretending that he was dead."

Sandra shook her head and scooted closer to Kitty on the sofa, slipping her arm around Kitty's shoulders. "God, Kitty, there had to be more to it than that. Your mother never told you why he really left?"

"After Mama died, I found some papers. I think my father was being investigated for taking money that didn't belong to him. All I can figure is that he couldn't deal with that and having a child, and left us." Kitty bit her lower lip, as if to hold back a scream. She started breathing in short gasps.

Sandra patted her shoulder. "It's okay, Kitty. You're a survivor." She hugged her real hard and then released her. "You need to try to maintain control so we can finish this, and then honey, we're going to get some help for you. Okay?"

Sandra was trying to sound strong and cheerful, but she felt sick inside. How could Phillip Parker have done such a thing? She'd always thought he was an asshole, but this proved it. She wondered if her mother knew. Impossible. Her mother never would have developed a relationship with the man had she known. And what would she do about telling her? If Sandra represented Kitty, Erma would be helping with the defense. She'd have to know. But first, Sandra needed to get the rest of the story and decide whether she would represent the girl or not.

Picking up her notepad and pen, Sandra said, "Tell me how you went about finding Phillip."

Kitty sniffed again and wiped her nose. "It really wasn't difficult, but I didn't do it myself. About three years ago, I hired this firm I saw an ad for in Houston. They're investigators, but they use computers. They said they could find almost anyone in about twenty-four hours if the client could supply a driver's license number, or former driver's license number, Social Security number, or credit card numbers. I had found my father's Social Security number in those old papers of my mother's."

"They found him in twenty-four hours?"

"Less than. Actually, the guy admitted he already knew where my father was, but he charged me for his knowledge. I wasn't much for reading newspapers or I probably would have found him myself."

"Scumbag," Sandra muttered under her breath. "So then what did you do?"

"I had the investigators dig up everything they could find on him. You know what I just thought about, Sandy?"

She shook her head.

"They didn't find a divorce or they would have told me. I wasn't worried about it then. I just wanted to figure out how to approach him. I wanted to talk to him. I wanted to see if he was sorry for abandoning us."

"You didn't want to make him pay anymore?"

"No." She shook her head again. "I don't need the money."

"Are you sure? The police are going to ask you that."

"I'm sure. You see, after I got saved, I prayed over it. I forgave my daddy a long time ago. I just wanted to talk to him."

"So why didn't you just call him?"

"I didn't think he would talk to me. The investigators told me he always surrounded himself with people. So I decided to try to meet him socially. I got information on his employees and then I met Raymond, and . . ." she shrugged.

"Raymond doesn't know?"

"Oh my gosh, no." She ducked her head. "I hadn't planned on dating Raymond."

Sandra stopped short of saying that she hoped Raymond wouldn't dump her after he found out her original motive. "Is that true?"

Kitty nodded and looked as if she were about to cry again. "Do you think he'll think I don't love him? That I was just using him? That's what Phillip said."

Sandra signaled time out. "Wait, Kitty. Don't start crying again." Not when she was getting to the good part. Not that all of it wasn't good. She felt slightly overwhelmed by the whole messy story. "Calm down and tell me what happened Friday night."

Kitty breathed deeply. "Well, you know we were all celebrating. I'd met him several times, but there never seemed to be an opportunity to be alone with him—to talk to him without others overhearing."

"But there was on Friday?"

"Yes. He invited me up to his room. He hit on me, right in front of Raymond, too."

"Tsk tsk." That sounded like Phillip. In all the years she'd known him, she'd never seen him actually abandon Lizzie for someone else, but she'd seen him hit on young women all the time. How did Lizzie put up with it? "So Raymond knew you were going up to Phillip's room?"

"No. I didn't tell him. I waited until he was asleep and then I tiptoed out. He'd never have let me go, even if he had known Phillip was my father."

"Did anyone else see you go up there?"

"I passed Lizzie on the way up. She most definitely had the wrong idea and muttered something mean as we went by each other. She was carrying a bag and heading for one of the empty rooms. Her face was all red like she was really mad."

"So what happened after you got into his room?" Sandra had moved back to her spot on the other end of the sofa, so she turned around and propped her bare feet on the coffee table, her legal pad balanced on her lap.

"It was just terrible. He wasn't dressed. He must have planned to have sex, because he was in his robe. To make a long story short, we went out on the balcony and he was putting his hands on me, groping me, and I was trying to talk to him and when I said he was my daddy, he flipped out."

"What? What'd he do?"

"He just went berserk. He called me names and said I was lying, trying to get money out of him. He said I was using Raymond. We struggled. Then he seemed to believe me and said I had come to ruin him. Why hadn't I stayed away? I don't even remember why, now, but somehow he fell over the balcony and I was holding his hand and holding him . . ." She closed her eyes.

"Until he fell?" Sandra chewed on the end of her pen as she listened to Kitty's story.

Kitty nodded and covered her face with her hand. "It was just terrible. I leaned over to see what had happened to him, and he started screaming cuss words at me."

"You mean he was still alive?"

"Oh, yes. He was going to have me arrested, he said, for blackmail, and on and on. I didn't want to listen to him so I ran back to my room and got undressed and got under the covers. When Raymond came in, I just told him that I couldn't sleep and had taken a walk."

Sandra got up and began to pace up and down the living room. If what Kitty said was true, someone else had killed Phillip Parker. There were four other possibilities. Then another thought struck her. "Kitty, what were you going to do next?"

"That night?"

"Yes. If Phillip was still alive and he was hollering that he was going to call the police, why did you go to bed? It doesn't make sense."

Kitty shook her head. "I can't explain it, Sandy. I just thought that I'd be safe with Raymond. When the police didn't come after awhile, I fell asleep."

"And Raymond never left the room?"

"Not while I was awake."

Sandra crouched down in front of Kitty so that they'd be face-to-face. She could smell the beer mixed with Kitty's perfume. She recognized it as Chanel No. 5. "Now, this is important, Kitty. When did you first find out that someone had bashed in Phillip's face?"

Kitty grimaced. "They did?"

She looked so sincerely repulsed by the idea and at the same time so surprised at that revelation, that Sandra clapped her hands and laughed. "You didn't know?"

"No one told me. How bad was it?"

"Well, let me say this, anyone who saw the body couldn't help but notice."

Her nose scrunched up like she had just smelled something rotten. "Musta been bad then."

Sandra watched Kitty for a moment. She knew she was innocent. She didn't care what the reviewers had said about her role in the high school play, she couldn't be acting. "Okay, young lady, I'll represent you. But we've got a lot more talking to do. For starters, where had Raymond gone when he got back to the room after you did?"

Chapter Five

"For heaven's sake, Mother, she couldn't have killed him," Sandra yelled into her cell phone. "He was still screaming bloody murder when she ran away."

"So she says. What do the police say?"

"We're meeting Dennis Truman in a minute. I called him before we left my place."

"You mean you're driving your car while you're talking to me? I've told you how dangerous that is. Pull over."

"It's okay, Erma. I do it all the time. I've got that hands-free setup."

"Pull over or I'm hanging up."

"All right. Give me a minute to change lanes. Okay. All right, there's a spot. Some surfer kid pulling out. Hang on while I parallel park." She drove for about two blocks before she spoke again. The seawall was still highly populated with joggers, walkers, bladers, and bicyclists, but on-street traffic was clearing out now that the weekend tourists had headed for home. "Okay. You there? Hello?"

Erma said, "That blessed car phone scares me to death. I swear you're going to get killed talking to people while you're driving. How many times do I have to tell you to park before you make a phone call? A person would think you were a teenager the way you act sometimes, Sandra."

"Could we get back to the subject at hand?"

"Sandra, I've got to tell you. I'm not real pleased about

this. Goddamnit, he was my best friend and my daughter is going to represent his killer?"

"Quit saying that. Quit saying she's his killer or I'm going to hang up. I told you she didn't do it, Erma. Why can't you just trust my instincts? If you could talk to her, you'd see."

"Humph." She muttered something incoherent.

"Well, you haven't heard the good part and if you don't act right, I'm not going to tell you."

"What the hell did you call me for?"

"So you'd know why I was going to be late for Sunday dinner," she said. It was a lie. She had forgotten Sunday dinner until just that moment. Good thing she hadn't gotten a hold of Stuart. Sandra wanted Erma to calm down before she went over there. With her heart condition, Erma didn't need any more excitement.

"Humph. What good stuff?"

"That'll just give you something to think about, Mother. I've got to hang up. Kitty is supposed to meet me and she's probably almost there by now."

"You parked the blessed car. Tell me now."

"No. I've got to go. She'll be scared if she gets to the police station and I'm not there."

"I hate it when you do that. It better be good, Sandra."

"Oh, it is. See you later." She laughed as she hit the end button and turned onto Twenty-fifth Street toward city hall and the police station. The south wind had grown stronger. The palm trees in the esplanade that dissected the four-lane street for the next seven blocks swayed in the wind. Out of nowhere, dark clouds began to sail overhead as the sun began to set. A salty mist settled on her car as she drove into the parking lot.

Lieutenant Truman waited outside. It was his day off, but the desk sergeant had agreed to find him when Sandra told her what she wanted. Kitty had parked in the city manager's spot. Sandra pulled next to her and together they followed Truman up the stairs. She had to shun a feeling that she was accompanying Kitty to the gallows.

The Galveston Police Department occupied the back of city hall. The front part of the building looked like it should be in the historic register. It was home to the city manager's office, council chambers, and other parts of city administration. The back half of the building was modern-looking and housed the police, the central fire department, and the municipal court.

They followed Truman past the holding tanks and the clerk's office, up the stairs, past the courtroom, down a hall to the left, and ended up at a large office with back-to-back desks. It could have been any office in any police department in any city of the world. It was more worn out than a cop who'd been on a ten-day stakeout. The air was permanently infiltrated with the aroma of stale coffee and cigarettes. Two minutes after arrival, Sandra found breathing difficult.

Pulling up a couple of metal chairs beside his desk, Truman motioned for them to sit. Kitty looked like an actress with opening night jitters.

"It's all right," Sandra said in a soft voice. "He just needs you to tell him what you told me; then he'll type it up and you can sign it. Then you can go home." She saw Truman cut his eyes at her. She knew what he must have been thinking, but he hadn't heard what Kitty had to say yet. He couldn't charge her after he heard her statement.

Truman rolled a printed form into the typewriter and hit a few keys. "I need to read her the Miranda warning, Miss Salinsky," he said when he stopped typing.

"That's okay. I've already explained her rights to her."

"No. I have to." He shrugged.

Sandra stared at him for a moment. "Kitty, he's going to read you your constitutional rights. It's just routine." She didn't know why he insisted when he could have had the two of them sign a waiver, but it was easier to give in than to quibble.

Truman plucked a business-size card from the center drawer. "You have the right to remain silent—"

Kitty burst into tears.

"Go ahead, Lieutenant," Sandra said as she fished in her purse for a tissue. She had the feeling they were going to be there all evening, alternating between talking and weeping.

Truman started over and read the whole card in his deep, melodious voice while Kitty sobbed. Sandra studied the yellowed ceiling tiles and wished she hadn't quit smoking; a long draw on a strong cigarette would have tasted good about then. When Truman was through, he put the card back in his desk and sat silently staring as she tried to get Kitty to stop crying.

Just when Sandra thought she had her under control, in walked the first assistant district attorney, Edgar Saul, who was enough to scare the bejabbers out of anyone. It was her bad luck that Edgar would be the one to catch Kitty's case, that it was his weekend to be on call. Still, that didn't mean that he would be assigned to it. But she was kidding herself. If Edgar wanted to prosecute Kitty, the file was his for the taking.

Kitty drew in a sharp breath. "Who is that?"

"The chief assistant district attorney."

Her fingernails dug into Sandra's arm and she whispered, "Omigosh. He looks mean."

Edgar was probably the meanest-looking man alive, except for a crazed rapist she had prosecuted. The rapist had looked like something out of everyone's worst nightmare. Edgar Saul looked like, and was, the prosecutor from hell.

His skin appeared to be the color and texture of erasable bond and was pockmarked. He had teeth so large and lips so thin that even when he was smiling, which was seldom, he looked like the big, bad wolf. He had a hooknose, eyes as dark as a moonless night, and bushy black eyebrows. His black hair was styled in a crew cut. He was so tall and so thin that if he turned sideways, the raindrops would miss him.

During trials, Edgar wore well-cut suits, button-down collar shirts, bland striped ties, loafers, and a pair of large, circular glasses, but even those failed to humanize him. Still, juries seemed to love him. His conviction rate was ninety-nine percent, a better record than that of the district attorney himself.

Edgar had a reputation for living his job. It was more than a career to him, more than a profession, more than a way to earn a living. Edgar Saul wasn't a lawyer who happened to prosecute. In the same way that a Siberian is a race of tiger, to Edgar, prosecutor was a race of human. As Edgar Saul rounded the first row of desks and headed in Sandra's direction, she saw that the intensity he emanated even from a distance frightened Kitty. She whispered to Kitty, to try to calm her down.

Sandra had worked with Edgar for three years but, even so, had never become entirely comfortable around him. Though she wasn't afraid of him anymore, she had a healthy respect for him. She saw it as her job to make both Dennis Truman and Edgar Saul understand that Kitty was not the perpetrator. She would show them with the facts that Kitty should be eliminated as a suspect, which would help them narrow the field.

"What do we have?" Edgar asked after the formalities of handshaking. He positioned himself behind Truman and studied the sheet of paper in the typewriter.

"We were just getting started," Truman said. "Pull up a chair."

Kitty had switched from digging her nails into Sandra's arm to digging her nails into her own palm.

"Miss Salinsky advised her client that it would be in her best interest to come down and make a statement," Dennis Truman said. "Are you ready?"

Sandra thought she spotted pity in Truman's eyes. His back was to Edgar Saul. Dennis had suddenly seemed stiff, more formal. She figured it was due to Edgar. In spite of his conviction rate, Edgar Saul's harshness didn't win him any popularity contests with the cops.

With Sandra's coaxing, for the following hour Kitty related the events to the two men: one black, one white; the former, human and responsive; the latter, apparently subhuman and unresponsive; both officers of the law, both players in the human drama that would continue to unfold in the days to come like the pages of a pop-up story book.

Once she began, Kitty controlled herself a great deal better than she had at Sandra's condo. When she was through, Sandra allowed Kitty to answer their questions. Truman read the statement back to her. Kitty signed it. Edgar Saul and Sandra sat nearby.

Edgar pushed back his chair and beckoned for Truman to follow him. While they conferred on the other side of the room, Sandra said, "Don't worry, Kitty. Since he was alive when you left the balcony, I don't see how they can possibly charge you."

"But what if they do?" Kitty whispered. She squeezed the balled-up, shredded tissues Sandra had given her when they first arrived.

"Then I'll have my work cut out for me." She patted Kitty on the arm. Standing up, Sandra stretched. Her backside was getting numb from sitting on the metal chair for so long. "Not to worry, kid. I won't let them hurt you." She stared into the other woman's eyes and hoped she could keep her promise.

"That district attorney hates me," Kitty said.

"He hates everyone."

"But he really hates me. Did you see the look in his eyes?"

"No, honest to God, he looks like that all the time."

"If they charge me, will he be the one that represents the government against me?"

"I hope it won't come to that."

"But could he?"

"Yes. But first of all, I hope they won't charge you. Secondly, I hope he won't be the one. Thirdly, I hope we never go to trial. Ad infinitum."

"Whatever that means, me too, Sandy. But I'm awfully scared."

"I know. Who wouldn't be?"

They both stared at the men. Edgar crooked his finger at Sandra. Taking a deep breath, she squeezed Kitty's shoulder and walked over to where they were talking.

"I'm going to have to charge her with manslaughter," Edgar said in a low voice.

"What? You can't do that." Sandra looked at Dennis.

Dennis shrugged and stared over her shoulder.

She lowered her voice to a fierce whisper. "He was still alive. Didn't you hear anything she said?"

"Yeah. I heard her say that he abandoned her and her mother when she was a small child—and I'm not unsympathetic, if it's true. Then she said he wanted to have sex with her the other night and she killed him for it."

"For heaven's sake, Edgar. Don't you get it? Someone else killed him after he hit the ground."

"That's bullshit and you know it."

"What's the autopsy say?"

"Too soon," Truman said. "It's not back yet."

"It'll support my theory. I saw Phillip's face. You couldn't get that from a fall."

Edgar stood with his arms crossed. "I'm charging her with manslaughter. Take it or leave it. I'll ask for a ten-thousand-dollar bond."

"Ten-thousand-dollar bond. Are you crazy? That's totally out of the question, Edgar. She's not a flight risk. She shouldn't be arrested, not to mention having to post bail." Sandra looked at Dennis for help, but he stood mute.

"If you cooperate, I'll ask Judge McWheeter to authorize a pretrial release bond," Edgar said. "At least getting out of jail won't cost her a fortune."

Sandra's temper flared. They were fixing to take her client into custody. Not only could she not believe it, but apparently there was nothing she could do about it. The most they offered was a way to walk her through the system and get her out right away. Frustrated, she gritted her teeth. "That's what I get for trying to be the good guy and bringing her down here to make a statement. I could have sat on her and made you figure it out."

"Take it or leave it, Sandra," Edgar said.

She had a strong desire to stick her tongue out at him, or spit, or do something to show him how she felt. "Give me a moment to explain it to her." She started toward Kitty and then turned back. "But don't think I'm giving up without a fight."

His expression unchanged, Edgar said, "I know you better than that."

Perching on her chair again, Sandra said, "I'm sorry, Kitty. They're charging you with manslaughter."

"You mean I have to go to jail?" Her eyes grew large and her face puckered up again.

"Now hold on." She held Kitty by the shoulders and stared at her. "Just for a few minutes. I'll stay as close to you as I can. They agreed not to oppose pretrial release."

"I don't understand any of this, Sandy." Her eyes searched Sandra's face. "Are they saying they don't believe me?"

"Look, they believe it was . . . there are certain parts they believe. Otherwise, I guess they'd be charging you with something worse."

"Like murder?" Her hair had pulled loose from the French twist and stood out on the back of her head like a rooster's tail feathers.

Sandra nodded. "They think he died when he hit the ground."

"Oh my God. So they do think I killed him. Am I going to get the death penalty?"

"No, of course not. If you'll just calm down a minute, I'll explain it all to you." Sandra pulled up a chair opposite Kitty's.

Kitty looked like a recalcitrant child. "I'm sorry."

"Forget it. Now listen. Just because you're being charged with something doesn't mean you're automatically convicted. That's what you've hired me for. Manslaughter is a second-degree felony. It's not a death penalty charge."

"What could I get?"

"We'll worry about that later."

"No. Now. Tell me what I could get."

"It's punishable by . . ." Sandra closed her eyes and recited the penal code from memory. "Two to twenty years and/or a ten-thousand-dollar fine."

"Twenty years in prison?" Kitty's voice was loud and high pitched. Sandra was sure they could hear her on the mainland.

"Now I'm not going to let that happen." She felt herself growing impatient. "Come on, get up. Lieutenant Truman will drive you to the county jail. I'll follow. Mr. Saul is going to call the judge and get him to authorize your release on a pretrial bond. We can pick up your car later."

Kitty stood. Her shoulders slumped. Her suit was as crumpled as she looked. "I don't understand."

"Your bail—instead of a bail bondsman, you're going to get out much cheaper through the county pretrial release program, where you just have to pay a little over a hundred dollars."

"I don't care about the money," she said. "I didn't do it." Kitty looked beaten.

"I'm sorry, honey. It's the best I can do right now. As soon as we get you squared away, we'll start working not only on your defense, but I'll try to figure out who really did it. Okay?"

"Okay. I know you know what you're doing, Sandy. I trust you."

The sweet expression Kitty wore for a moment was like a knife in Sandra's stomach. Talk about feeling guilty. She couldn't have felt worse if she'd killed him herself. She called out to Truman. "Let's go."

Truman did five minutes' worth of paperwork in the police department booking office next to the holding tank, and then he put Kitty in the back of his car. Sandra followed him in her Volvo.

Sunday evenings at the county jail were literally a scream when weekend drunks were hauled in. The cells smelled like vomit and salt. Sand covered the floor from the swimsuits and bare feet of young people arrested for disorderly conduct, minor drug charges, or driving while intoxicated. It was a loud, noisy, and unruly crowd, but the upshot was that, with all of the commotion, it was a less frightening place than in the quietly intimidating atmosphere of the off-season.

Sandra left her car on the street while Truman, since he was a police officer, parked in the sallyport and took Kitty through the locked side door. Sandra was well-known at the jail. Normally, lawyers showed their state bar ID cards at the bulletproof window and the deputy buzzed them through. Sandra waved at the deputy behind the glass.

The buzzer for the first door went off immediately. As soon as it shut behind her, the lock of the iron-barred door in front of her clacked in her ears. Pulling the heavy door open, she swung through it, her nose immediately assaulted by the smell of ammonia from the mop water with a faint scent of fresh vomit. Her eyes watered. She spotted Kitty at the far end of a long counter. Catcalls and whistles rang out from the cells. Kitty's appearance had created quite a stir. Sandra quickly wrote the date, time, and her name on the lawyer's sign-in sheet and hurried to Kitty, who continuously smoothed down the wrinkles in her black suit.

There was one other woman in sight. She sat alone in the soundproof interview room. Sandra recognized her as a prostitute. When she'd first begun private practice, she'd been appointed to represent the woman on a misdemeanor. Small and fair, Ruth had been better looking than most of the locals. She had come from a good family, but cocaine use had forced her into the streets. Sandra inclined her head as Ruth's eyes met hers.

Dennis Truman spoke to the desk sergeant, who nodded to Sandra as she walked up. "You all right?" she asked Kitty.

Kitty smiled. "Lieutenant Truman is real nice. He said he'd try to get them to take me to a room by myself to book me."

"They'll probably agree. I don't think they'd get much cooperation from any of these guys if you were stuck on the bench with them for a couple of hours." She indicated the young drunks lining the walls and cells, waiting to be processed in or out.

Kitty's smile was the first she had seen since the party on Friday night. Sandra had forgotten how attractive Kitty could be. Her eyes crinkled. Her face lost its pitiful look.

"You're going to be okay, kid." She rounded Kitty and leaned over to hear what Truman and Sergeant Jiminez said.

"ID is going to come get her and process her in their office," Truman told her.

"I appreciate that, Dennis. Thank you."

"You can take her on back," Jiminez said, pointing. The ID sergeant strolled around the corner.

Truman, Kitty, and Sandra followed the other sergeant to an office where they could be alone. As soon as Kitty was settled, Sandra went outside and phoned Raymond, explaining what had happened. It didn't take a lot of coaxing to get him to agree to meet them when Kitty was released. Returning to the office, Sandra found that the sergeant had just finished fingerprinting Kitty.

Kitty rubbed at the black ink on her fingertips with a brown institutional paper towel, a stricken expression on her face. Two Polaroid photographs lay on the desk next to the fingerprint card. One was a frontal view; the other, a profile. In spite of the tendrils of hair that framed her face, in each of them Kitty looked stark. Scared.

"Judge McWheeter called pretrial," Truman said. "As soon as we're finished here, they'll take an application and then you can take her home."

"Thanks, Dennis. You about finished, Sergeant?"

"Let me read back what I have in the computer to be sure it's correct, and then you can go to pretrial."

Kitty sat in the chair next to the sergeant's desk while he reviewed the data with her.

"Well, that's all for me," Truman said, reaching for the door.

Sandra held out her hand. "You'll call when the autopsy is in?"

Dennis took her hand. His was big and warm. Made her realize how cold hers was. "Sure," he said. "In fact, I'll call the M.E. tomorrow and see if they can hurry it up."

"Listen, Dennis. Thanks for being so good about everything. I appreciate the way you handled her. You couldn't have been nicer."

He waved her away. "No problem," he said awkwardly and pulled the door open.

"I'm sorry to have bothered you on your day off, but I thought you'd want to be the one—"

Nodding, he said, "Talk to you tomorrow. See you, Dan," he called to the sergeant as he went through the doorway.

Sandra stood over Kitty as she waited. She was anxious to get her out of there and even more anxious to discuss the case with her mother. It would take a bit to calm Erma down, but once she got past her personal feelings about the matter, Erma would be Kitty's greatest ally, Sandra just knew it. In spite of her old-fashioned ways, Erma had one of the finest legal minds in the state when it came to criminal law. Though the trial work now fell to Sandra, they reviewed and picked apart each case until they had thoroughly analyzed every facet. Erma also read the law for pure entertainment. As a result, her mind was a wealth of legal information. Sandra couldn't have picked a better law partner than the one to whom she had been born.

As soon as the sergeant was through with Kitty, Sandra led her back down the hallway, past the prisoners who again became more than unruly, and to the Pretrial Release office. Theirs was a one-page application, legal-size. All Kitty had to do was fill out the form as to her name and address, list three references, her work history, her criminal history, Sandra's name as retained counsel, and they were out of there. Fifteen minutes later, Sandra delivered Kitty to Raymond, who ushered her down the stairs and into his car before the one reporter who hung around on weekends could figure out who she was. Trying cases in the newspapers was not Sandra's style.

Heaving a huge sigh of relief, she rubbed the ache in her neck; the muscles felt like tightly twisted ropes. Bugs circled the corner streetlight in the dark. The area around the county courthouse and jail was deserted. In the morning, three hundred jurors reporting for jury duty would be looking for parking in two hundred spots. The humidity was at least a hundred and fifty percent.

As she dragged herself back to her car, Sandra began to wonder who had finished off Phillip Parker if it wasn't Kitty. The way she saw it, there weren't that many suspects. She only hoped it hadn't been Raymond, in whose custody she had just placed her client.

Chapter Six

Erma vaguely heard the front door open and close. She had dragged herself out of bed later than usual, her energy having evaporated during the night. She remembered having eaten a meal sometime during the day, but not what. She remembered having spoken to her daughter on the telephone, but the details of the conversation escaped her. She remembered sitting down in her favorite chair in the living room, but she didn't know how long she'd been there. Everything in her mind seemed to be disappearing into a black hole.

"What are you doing dressed like that?" Sandra asked. "You look like you're wearing widows' weeds."

"CNN Headline News" blared on the television in the living room. Erma looked from the screen to Sandra. "When did you get here?"

"About ten minutes ago. I let myself in and used your bathroom. I walked right in front of you. Didn't you see me?" She took the remote control from the side table and turned off the TV. "Are you okay?"

Erma said, "You look like shit. Did you go down to the jail like that? You could have at least put a dress on."

"Next time I walk a client through, I'll be sure to tell them that my mother won't let me go until I put on a dress."

"Goddamnit, don't get sarcastic with me. I never went out when I was your age without looking like a lawyer. People won't hire you if you look like a pig. They want someone who looks like they're an expensive mouthpiece, a professional."

"Yes, Mother. I know how frightening I look without makeup. I know I shouldn't do legal business in shorts, a T-shirt, and running shoes. You've told me a hundred million times. In the middle of the Kitty-crisis, I just didn't think about looking like a professional mouthpiece."

"Aw, quit patronizing me." Erma got up slowly from her Queen Anne chair, trying not to let Sandra see that she was having difficulty. She picked up her highball glass from the floor beside her chair and hobbled toward the kitchen.

"So, are we still having dinner?" Sandra asked, following.

"You're hours late."

"I know. I called you and explained everything, remember?"

"I'd ask you for a note from your mother except, goddamnit, I am your mother."

"Not funny, Mother."

"Call me Erma. It makes me feel so much younger."

"Okay, Erma. Are we still having dinner? I'm very hungry and would appreciate something to eat. We could talk about the case at the same time."

"The case." Erma glanced at her daughter as she set the glass down in the sink. "Sit down over there," she said, indicating the kitchen table.

Sandra complied. "What are we having?"

"I've already eaten." Erma pulled a plastic-wrapped plate of food from the refrigerator and plopped it onto the dinette table in front of Sandra. Wilted lettuce and tomato peered out from under a smear of French dressing. A layer of fat covered small, red potatoes and a chicken breast.

"You're punishing me. I can tell," Sandra said. "Could you at least warm it up in the microwave?"

Erma grunted her assent and picked up the plate again.

"Ha, so you're using it now. It only took you two years."

"You're using it now?" Erma mimicked Sandra. "I most certainly am not. I went over to the Wal-Mart and got one of those where you just turn the lever to the amount of time you want to cook. The fancy one you gave me I donated to the women's shelter."

Sandra rolled her eyes. "Whatever, Erma. Scrape the salad off the plate and that congealed fat from the chicken and potatoes before you microwave it, okay?"

"Is that a comment on the weight of the evidence?" Erma said. "Ha ha. Joke's on you." She pushed the salad into the sink.

Sandra frowned. "You're not making sense. Are you drunk? I saw the glass you put in the sink. You've been drinking."

There seemed to be a big ball about to burst inside Erma. She kept her back to Sandra, wanting to be as strong for her as she had always been. Opening a lower cupboard door next to the sink, Erma leaned over and pressed a button on the compact microwave that had been concealed inside. The door popped open. Making a big production of standing out of the way so that Sandra could see, Erma slid the plate inside and slammed the door.

"Mom," Sandra said, "I'm glad you're adapting. I'm glad you're using any microwave. It didn't have to be the one I gave you."

Erma stood facing away from Sandra, not replying, her eyes squeezed shut.

"I apologize for the crack about being drunk. I know you're trying to follow the doctor's orders. Let's not fight."

Erma heaved a sigh. The bell rang on the oven. Opening the door, she poked at the chicken, pushed the plate back inside, and started the process again. "How's Melinda?"

"You really are aching for a fight, aren't you? Rather than talk about your granddaughter, why don't we discuss Kitty?"

"That murdering bitch—"

"She didn't do it. If you'll just listen for five minutes, you'll understand the situation."

Erma sighed again. Breathing deeply was hard sometimes. A good sigh could be an accomplishment. She turned to Sandra. "I can't believe that you agreed to represent her without discussing it with me, Sandra Salinsky. It's not like this case is a routine criminal case. Phillip was my closest, dearest . . ." her voice began to crack.

Sandra jumped up and ran over to Erma. "What's the matter with you? Are you crying?"

"I demand an explanation, goddamnit. You can't just take a case like that without my consent."

"You are crying," Sandra said. "So his death finally got to you. Thirty-six hours, not bad."

"I'm angry, that's all. You should have spoken to me first. I'm not crying, crying. I'm just angry crying."

"It's okay, Erma," Sandra said and put her arms around her mother. "Everything is going to be okay." Her chin rested on the top of her mother's head.

Erma pushed at Sandra's arms, but Sandra held tight. Erma sighed again. If she could keep on sighing, she might feel better. The bell rang on the microwave. "There's your dinner."

"Mother, it's okay to be sad that Phillip died."

"Was murdered by that bitch."

Sandra dropped her arms. "She didn't do it. If you'd just let me explain. Erma, he was her father."

Erma, who had leaned over to get the plate out of the microwave, stood straight up. "I knew it. I knew there was something about that girl."

"Oh, so you did, did you?" Sandra smiled.

Erma nodded and reached for the plate again, using a cup towel for a potholder. "But that doesn't mean she didn't kill him." She shuffled over to the table and dropped the plate onto the placemat. "Now eat."

Sandra obediently sat back down and picked up her fork. "So you'll listen?"

Erma poured Sandra a glass of iced tea and pushed a spoon, a lemon slice, and sweetener toward her. Her chest felt tight. She tried sighing again but with no success. "All right. What have you got?"

Sandra swallowed a large bite of chicken and launched into the events of the day. When she got to the part about Phillip deserting his wife and child, Erma realized that Sandra was right, Kitty would have to be his daughter. No one else in the world knew about that. She grunted and nodded and gave Sandra a look that dared her to ask what she knew. Sandra continued with Kitty's story.

"So what makes you think she didn't run downstairs and finish Phillip off?" Erma asked.

"She didn't know his face had been smashed in. I don't know, there was something about her reaction when I told her that said she hadn't done it."

"Could she have been acting? Could you have wanted to believe her so badly that you took what she said at face value? No pun intended."

Sandra glanced at her mother and shook her head. "Give me a little credit, Erma."

Erma nodded. "I do."

"You knew he had a daughter and never told me, didn't you?"

"I know a lot of things that I've never told you about a lot of people."

While Sandra waited for Erma's response after she'd brought her completely up to date, she got up to refill her iced tea.

Erma, her arms crossed about her chest, her feet by then propped up in a chair she'd dragged over next to hers, chewed on her lower lip and stared into space. She had always wondered what Phillip would do when his daughter came looking for him. Now she knew. She wasn't real proud of her friend but had always accepted him, knowing his shortcomings, just as he had her. Pity it had turned out the way it did. Now it was time to fulfill a promise she had made to him. Now it was time to look out for his daughter the best she could, just as he had agreed to do for Sandra if things had turned out differently. She turned her attention to Sandra. "I tend to agree with your evaluation of Kitty."

Sandra nodded, opened her mouth to say something, apparently thought better of it, and took a swallow of her tea instead.

"Did you get a decent retainer?"

Sandra nodded again. "Twenty-five thousand."

Erma broke into a smile. "That's my girl."

"She's got it. Models make more per hour than the average lawyer."

"There ought to be a law against that." Erma cleared her throat. "You're not going after a plea bargain, are you?"

"No way. I'm convinced that his fall was purely an accident. I'm going to fight this all the way to the court of criminal appeals, if I have to."

"It just seems like you've been doing an awful lot of pleas lately," Erma said.

"Court appointments. Most of them are too chicken-shit to go to trial if I can get them a good deal. Even the one from last Friday. I knew I could beat it, but the offer was eight years and he insisted on taking it." She shrugged. "He said he'd done stuff he hadn't gotten caught for, so he might as well take the deal. Stupid son of a bitch."

"So you'll try this?"

"Oh, yes. I hope it won't come to that. I hope the autopsy will show them that it couldn't have been Kitty and they'll start searching for whoever really killed him. I'm sure going to need your help on this one." She grinned at her mother.

"You can't expect the cops to do the logical thing. They may really believe she ran downstairs and finished him off. By the way, did anyone check her hands?"

"For what, blood?"

"Blood, scrapes, anything that might have indicated she wielded something hard enough to," she winced, "damage the bones in someone's face?" Normally blood and guts didn't bother Erma, but this was her friend. She wouldn't have wanted to be the one to identify the body.

"Damn it. I didn't think of it. I didn't notice any abrasions. I don't think they did at the jail either. And Dennis and Edgar never said a word."

"Why would they, when you handed her over on a silver platter?"

"Are you being critical of me, Erma dear?"

Erma grimaced. "Let's just say I would have done things a little differently. But it's your case. You do what you want."

"Don't start that. I'm serious when I say I'm going to need your help. I want your help. What do you say?"

Erma cocked her head. "Might be fun. I know that normally I'm pretty hands-off with your criminal practice, but this might just prove to be a barrel of laughs." She smiled.

Sandra said, "Especially if we can kick Edgar Saul's rear end all the way across town, but Mother my sweet, just remember whose case it is and who's calling the shots."

"If I forget, I'm sure you'll remind me. By the way, you might be interested to know that I'm going to set up a time for the reading of Phillip's will."

"You've got the will?" Sandra sat up straighter and stared Erma in the eye. "That means you are Phillip's estate's attorney and possibly even his executrix. How could you not have told me that? I never came across a file with his name on it. Where did you keep it?"

"This isn't twenty questions," Erma said, feeling more than a little pleased with herself.

"I can't pretend I'm not surprised. You don't tell me about being in charge of Phillip's estate and then you get miffed because I take Kitty's case without your knowledge? I guess that makes us even. What's in it?"

Erma laughed. "Would you be interested in being present when I conduct the reading?"

"Would I be interested in being there? So you're going to do it like in the movies? With all the drama? You're enjoying this, aren't you? Come on, Erma. Did you already know all this stuff? Did you know that Kitty was his daughter before today? Tell."

Erma knew that she had about the best poker face west of the Mississippi. She'd honed it for years. Besides drinking with the guys, in the old days she had been the only woman welcome at their poker games. They were Thursday nights because no one had to pick a jury on Fridays. All they had to do was show up at docket call. They drank and stayed up all night playing poker, dragging themselves before the court at 9:00 a.m. on Friday, knowing that the worst the day would hold would be a few pleas of guilty either after docket call or after lunch. Almost any attorney, no matter how drunk on Thursday night, could handle that.

Erma spoke as if she hadn't heard Sandra. "If you're interested, I'll keep you posted. It seems to me that the most appropriate place would be at his law office, but I'll have to see if his staff has any objections."

"Are you going to tell me or not?"

"Not, dear."

"You look like the proverbial cat. Every time I see that smile I find out later that you had something up your sleeve."

Erma got up from the table and ran the water in the sink, flushing the salad down the disposal.

Sandra brought her plate and handed it to her mother. "I'll bet Lizzie is in for a bundle. She deserves it after what she put up with from that son of a bitch. Is Lizzie going to get the bulk of the estate? How much is it? Several million? Several hundred million?"

"You can give up guessing, because I'm not even going to give you a clue," Erma said, putting her face, her lips firmly pressed together like a stubborn baby's, up to Sandra's.

"You old shit. You never intended on telling me, so why did you bring it up?"

"By the way, Stuart called. He said he's been looking for you all evening. Said he left a bunch of messages on your answering machine."

"Okay. You just have your fun." Sandra got her napkin and utensils from the table and handed them to her mother. "I'm going to call Stuart." She punched numbers into the kitchen phone.

"Hi. I'm still at Erma's." Sandra looked over her shoulder at her mother and whispered, "Meet me in thirty minutes. And don't be any later. I'm pretty tired tonight." She hung up.

"You don't have to whisper on my account," Erma said. "I know you're not a virgin." She dried her hands and sat back down at the table.

Sandra smirked. "Ha ha. If you've got Phillip's will, I guess you're the executrix of his estate," she said. "And if so, when is the funeral?"

"What did Stuart want?"

"Me. I'm going to have to run. Could you at least tell me when and where the funeral is?"

"The memorial service will be at Memorial Methodist Church on Wednesday afternoon, if the body's released. The cremation will be at McCaskill Brothers on Tuesday night. No one else will be there, darlin'. You needn't come."

"Oh, don't be like that. I'll come keep you company." Sandra gave Erma's shoulder a squeeze. "I really have to go now, Mother. I'm very tired. Seeing Edgar Saul gave me an adrenaline rush, but now I'm drained." She kissed the top of Erma's head.

Erma smiled. "You're right. We can discuss this later. You go on home and get laid and then get a good night's sleep."

Dropping to one knee in front of Erma, Sandra said, "Hey, you let me know if you want me to go with you to pick out an urn or coffin or whatever you do in these situations. We can leave from the office tomorrow. I'll drive."

Erma patted Sandra's cheek. "I was going to go after lunch. They'll need a coffin pretty quickly after the body is released, but in cremations it doesn't have to be fancy." She let out a long sigh. "I think they have only a couple of choices." She swallowed several times in quick succession, trying not to make a fool out of herself.

"Hey, Erma. You want me to stay with you?" Sandra stroked Erma's hand. "I can see Stuart anytime."

Erma shook her head. "I really don't mind being alone. In fact, I'm going to bed as soon as you leave. I'll be all right." Pulling her hand away, Erma said, "You go on now."

"Okay." Sandra stood up, her knee creaking like an old

person's. "You take it easy tonight. Get some rest. I'll let myself out."

Erma watched Sandra's departing back. As soon as the door closed, she got another highball glass out of the liquor cabinet, poured herself two fingers of bourbon, stuck a cigarette in the cigarette holder hidden in the cabinet, lit it, and strolled haltingly out onto the back porch to her rocker. She'd be goddamned if any doctor was going to tell her how to live her life.

Chapter Seven

As she left, Sandra knew that Erma felt Phillip's loss more than she wanted to let on. They had been the closest of friends since Sandra's childhood. The first time he had come over with a check for them for a referral fee on a personal injury case Erma had sent him, he and Erma had sat up late in the evening talking and laughing. Erma had been as carefree as Sandra ever saw her. The referral fee was a great deal more money than her mother got as a retainer in a criminal case in those days. The two of them had danced around the room like a couple of leprechauns in the forest, for Phillip had been almost as short as her mother.

Sandra's chest constricted with the pain she felt for Erma; it was just a hint of what she'd feel someday when Erma died. She chewed on her lower lip as she drove up to the beachfront, not wanting to think about her mother being gone from her life. When she stopped for the red light at Nineteenth and Seawall, Sandra saw that the boulevard still swarmed with tourists in spite of the hundreds who had left earlier. Yes, it was summer, tourist season. It was good for the economy; the shops would pay more taxes; unemployment would be down for the summer. Still, she had a yearning to put her foot to the floor and just let her car go all out through the often bumper-to-bumper vehicles. The neat thing about winters in Galveston was that there was much less traffic. She could race down the West End in her S60—something it was designed to do. When she'd bought the car, the newspaper reporter she'd been dating told her she was stupid, that there was no place she could go where she could experience what the car could do, that she was just wasting her money. She bought it anyway and dumped him. It was worth the battles in municipal court over the tickets she got to enjoy the surge of energy as she blasted westward at high speeds on dark winter evenings. Even though it was several years old, the Volvo still moved like it was just off the factory line.

Now, in the height of the summer, she was stuck between slow-moving vehicles. Breathing deeply, she watched couples stroll along the boulevard. Runners were interspersed throughout the route, their legs strong, long, and lean. Surfers and other kids clustered in several sections, taunting each other. It reminded her of her teenage years. Some things never changed.

As soon as she got to her condo, she parked behind the security fence, set her alarm, and darted inside to the elevator. Changing into her swimsuit, Sandra poured herself a glass of wine and headed for the pool. She hoped the chlorine would wash the jail's ammonia smell off her skin. Hurrying back down, she dove into the deep end. When she came up for air, she began the crawl. Stiff from sitting all day, her muscles needed a workout. She flipped over and backstroked a few lengths, staring up at the cloudless night, the stars and the partial moon her only audience. When she tired, Sandra floated on her back. She could have stayed in the pool for hours had she not reached one end and seen Stuart standing above, peering down into her face. He wore a muscle shirt, jogging shorts, and running shoes.

"When I couldn't find you, I suspected you were down here." He smiled as he crouched down on the edge and held out her wine. "Ready to get out?"

"More ready for you to get in." She sipped some wine and handed it back to him.

"You know that's not going to happen." He stood.

Treading water, she stared up at him. "I would never let you drown, Stu. I told you I was a Water Safety Instructor when I was a kid."

"Do we have to go over all this again?"

She smiled. "I know something we could do in the shallow end that would be of absolutely no risk to you."

He glanced around the deserted area. "Yeah, right."

"No one would see us. No one ever comes down here at night except me."

He smiled. "Come on, Sandy, get out, will you? It's getting late."

She could hear the impatience in his voice, so she caved. She pulled herself up and took the towel from him, patting herself dry. "I don't understand why you won't let me teach you how to swim." Slipping her feet into her sandals, she said, "I'm good at it and have a lot of patience."

"I don't understand why we have to keep going over all that," he said and cut her a look that said end of discussion.

They walked back in silence. She didn't understand a person being afraid of the water. Especially living on an island. She also didn't understand why he wouldn't at least try. And a part of her wanted to know what his fear was all about. Maybe someday he would trust her enough to confide in her.

When they got inside, she ran a hot shower. Stuart had done his miles before he came. They stepped under the flowing water to the sounds of New Age music, "Songs from a Secret Garden," one of her favorite albums. Stuart pulled her against him and caressed her back. She stroked his hair, then his neck, and responded hotly to his kiss. What they started in the shower, they ended in her bed. Stu was one of the best lovers she had ever had. And a good kisser.

She had gone out with a lot of men, been married to two, and more than anything else she liked a good kisser. If they were good at that, they could learn the rest.

When they parted, she pulled the sheet over her and leaned her head on his shoulder. "Whew, I'm exhausted."

Stuart kissed her wet hair and wrapped his arms around her shoulders. "You want to talk about it?"

She told him a bit of what had happened with Kitty. "There is still so much that needs sorting out in my brain. It all happened so fast."

He nodded. "I missed you today."

"I'm sorry. I tried to get you earlier, but when Kitty came over I lost all track of time. I guess I could have called you from the jail but didn't think about it."

"Um. County jail?"

"Yes. God, it stinks worse on Sundays than it does on weekdays. Ammonia mixed with vomit, urine, sand, and salt. Yuck."

"I don't know how you can stand doing criminal law."

She smiled. They'd discussed that before, too. "At least it keeps me awake."

He chuckled and slid his finger up and down the bony part of her jaw.

She laughed, too. "And I adore times like these when I have an innocent client. Criminal defense lawyers live for the times they can right a wrong." She stared into his eyes. "We get fired up." She laid her head back down on his chest and said as an aside, "Especially if we've been paid well."

"You're so bad."

"I know." She laughed again.

"So you think Kitty's innocent? I thought she confessed."

"She had a part in it, but I don't think she finished him off." Sandra sat up to swallow some wine and pull the comforter up over the sheet.

In the middle of the night, when she awoke and had trouble getting back to sleep, Sandra got up and went into the living room. It was then that she noticed the light blinking on her answering machine and listened to the messages.

"It's me, Stuart. Call me when you get in."

"It's me again. Did you forget we were going to get together? Call me."

"Missus Salinsky, this is Jeffery Stubaker. I just came back from the grocery store and caught my wife loading up a moving van. I called the police. I hope that was the right thing to do. If not, please call me at home. My number is seven-four-one-one-seven-zero-zero. It's five o'clock."

"It's me. It's six thirty and I still haven't heard from you. Call me, Sandy. I'll try you at your mother's."

"Mom? It's Melinda. Why didn't you call me this weekend? Daddy said you're probably busy with Grandma, since he saw in the newspaper that Mr. Parker died. Anyway, please call me and let me know if I'm coming to visit you next weekend. If not, I want to do something with my friends."

Guilt plucked at Sandra's conscience. She had barely thought of her daughter for several days. Even though she'd given custody to Melinda's father, she often missed the child like crazy and wondered if she'd done the right thing. Then something like this past weekend happened and Sandra was reminded of why she had agreed to it. Jack was a far better parent than she could ever be. At fourteen, Melinda was turning out well. She was beautiful, intelligent, affectionate, and well behaved, except for those times when she was as irrational as any other teenager.

Sandra chastised herself. First chance she got, she would

call and set up a visitation time. Hitting the rewind button, she pushed Melinda to the back of her mind and returned to bed.

Though she occasionally complained that the space in their historical cottage was cramped and that it was old-fashioned, Sandra had to admit that the Law Offices of Townley and Salinsky were conveniently located. Being two blocks south of the courthouse, they walked to court in good weather while other attorneys circled the block looking for parking, in particular during jury weeks when the parking garage filled up early.

Their law library/conference room took up most of the second floor loft. They had a large kitchen and bathroom in the back of the house on the first floor. Individual offices were sandwiched between the reception area and the kitchen. The front door opened into a waiting room: polished wood floors, sofa, two chairs, area rug, coffee table, and a receptionist's desk. The coffee table was laden with magazines, the same as any self-respecting lawyer's office, only instead of *Texas Monthly* and *Field and Stream*, they had *Texas Monthly* and women's magazines like *O* and *More*. Sandra had considered sticking something a little more risqué out there, but Erma had overruled her.

They were still arguing over having a receptionist. Erma thought they could have a high school girl in one of those work programs part-time. Sandra thought they didn't need the headache and the responsibility of having a kid around. Currently they were at an impasse. With the exception of a telephone extension, the front desk remained vacant.

The back half of the large, rectangular room held a huge antique desk, hutch, credenza, the latest in computers, and a laser printer. Their secretary, a woman in her late fifties who played the computer keyboard like a concert pianist on a baby grand piano, fit with them like a crucial piece of a puzzle. Although she had worked for them for only eighteen months, to Sandra, Patricia was like a favorite aunt. Her predecessor, Marguerite, who had been with Erma since the beginning of time, had suffered a stroke and moved to Biloxi to live with her daughter. Sandra had selected Patricia while Erma mourned Marguerite. Sandra liked her because Patricia had treated Erma respectfully no matter how rude Erma got during the interview, replying to her questions with a "Yes, ma'am" or a "No, ma'am." If the woman could put up with Erma in her worst moments, Sandra knew she'd be great with clients. Besides, Erma had driven away the other applicants.

It also hadn't hurt that Patricia loved operating a computer, knew current word processing and bookkeeping programs, and liked dunning clients for fees. All Erma and Sandra had to do was review the contract with the client and fill in the dollar amount. Patricia discussed fee arrangements and followed up on them later as well. She was every attorney's dream.

While a jewel work-ethic-wise, Patricia's appearance went wanting. She had crinkly blue eyes, freckles over a narrow nose, full lips, and a body that looked like a bread plate. To top that off, no matter what she wore, she looked like a Goodwill reject.

Monday morning, Patricia and Sandra were alone in the office. Sandra had just finished explaining the events of the weekend. "I don't expect Erma to appear until later in the week since she took Phillip's death so hard. And, Patricia, when she does show up, keep an eye on her."

Patricia grimaced. "I hate being her babysitter, Sandra. You know how pissed she gets."

"Yes, I know exactly how pissed she gets, but neither one of us wants her to die, so we've got to do it. I'll be in my office."

Sandra had just settled at her desk and spread her notes about Kitty's case around her when the phone rang.

"The district attorney's office, specifically your favorite person, Edgar Saul, on line one," Patricia said.

"Hey, Sandra, you got a problem," Edgar Saul said. "Just got a partial autopsy report this morning. It seems I didn't charge your client correctly."

He didn't even attempt to hide his glee. His voice gurgled like a boiling geyser. Edgar rarely showed any emotion, like a sociopath she once knew, so she anticipated bad news. "What are you talking about?"

"You want to come surrender her or should I have her picked up?" Having worked with Edgar, Sandra could picture him putting his hand over the phone and feigning laughter.

"What the fuck are you talking about?"

"Now don't get angry, Miss Salinsky. It seems your girl lied if she told you the murder was an accident."

"Oh yeah?"

"Yeah. According to the preliminary report, the medical examiner concluded that, and I quote, 'the decedent fell on his back but was turned over to make it appear that he fell on his face. The body was dragged to the edge of the concrete patio where the face was carefully placed at a forty-five-degree angle, so it would appear that the face was damaged in the fall,' end quote."

"That doesn't mean that when he fell it wasn't an accident."

"Nah. But my first clue was, according to the M.E., the fact that there were repeated blows to the face and skull with a blunt object. They're still testing to see what material the blunt object left embedded in the skin so we can identify it."

"If you had seen the body, you would have already known that. It doesn't mean that Kitty killed him." Her damp hands shook. "If they're still testing, then there is nothing conclusive."

"Oh, don't be so damn naive, Salinsky. After your years of experience, I expected more from you than that. Your client was angry because her daddy abandoned her and, first chance she got, she bashed his head in."

"A person has to be pretty angry to bash someone's head in, Edgar." Sandra thought of her own situation. Her father had done the same to her and Erma. Sandra had trouble holding in her resentment if she dwelled on it very much. Even with her admittedly bad temper, though, she'd never get so worked up that she would murder him. She might say she wanted to kill him, but she'd never really do it.

"Yeah, so . . . wouldn't you be pissed if your father abandoned you?"

Sandra couldn't tell if he was taunting her or not. She couldn't remember whether he knew about her father. They'd worked together, closely together on several cases, but he wasn't the type one confided in, so probably he wasn't trying to get to her, she just wasn't sure. She breathed deeply. It still rankled, nonetheless. "I don't think it's enough to kill somebody over. Fathers abandon their children all the time in this country. It's like a national epidemic."

"Well, face it, this girl got a chance to take revenge, and she did."

She sighed and bit her lip. She knew Edgar well enough to know that there was no arguing with him once he made up his mind. "Can I get a copy of the report?"

"When it's complete. So are you going to negotiate, or are you going to be a hard ass about this thing?"

"Jesus, you're jumping to conclusions real quick, aren't you, Mister Saul?"

"Listen, babe, we've got her dead to rights."

She bristled in spite of the fact that she knew now that Edgar was goading her. "Well, you mind telling me what else the autopsy says, hon?"

"Fractured shoulder blade, dislocated arm. Oh, and this'll kill you, ha ha ha, he's missing his Rolex and his diamond ring. Are we going to have to swear out a search warrant or will you get her to turn those items over when you bring her in?"

"You think she robbed him after she killed him? Come on, get real. The girl's a model, for chrissake. She makes more money than me and you put together."

"Yeah, right."

"Right. Check it out."

"Well, anyway, you going to bring her in or not?"

She burned with frustration. She hated to upset Kitty again. The next time those tears started flowing, they might not ever be dammed. Sandra had never in her life seen anyone cry as much as Kitty. "What are you going to charge her with?"

"Capital murder."

"You're crazy, too."

"Okay, Salinsky. I'm going to lay it out for you only because you used to work here and I have some sympathy for your situation. Here's the scenario: your girl was abandoned by her father—"

"That I already know, Edgar."

"Wait, hear me out. She goes looking for him. Turns out that daddy dear is a wealthy, well-known attorney. Your girl decides, hey, I can get some money out of the old boy if I just tell him I'll tell the world he abandoned me when I was a child."

"Blackmail! Edgar, you're nuts. She didn't need the money." Sandra felt her face grow hot with anger. "And even if that was true, you can't get capital murder from blackmail."

Edgar laughed. "Here's the good part. The cap murder part. Are you ready for this? Wait for it. Wait for it. Retaliation."

"For what?" Sandra looked up. Patricia stood in the doorway. She must have heard her yelling into the phone. Sandra waved her away.

"When Parker refuses her demand for money, he tells her he's calling the police to have her arrested for blackmail. That's when she does the deed. Got it?"

"You're fucking nuts, Edgar Saul."

"You want to go look at the statute? Murder in the course of retaliation—"

"I know what the statute says, smart ass, but you'll never be able to prove your theory. And just where does the watch and ring fit into all this?"

"Easy, when she goes down and finishes him off, disappointed that she's not going to get a big money payoff, she takes the Rolex and diamond pinkie ring as a consolation prize." He laughed again. "We got her, babe."

Sandra wanted to rage into the phone. Instead, she said, "No way. No fucking way."

"How's it going to be?" His voice had grown hard. "Want me to send a car for her?"

Her inclination was to tell him to stick it where the sun didn't shine, but she could tell that he was already angry. She took a deep breath and let it out slowly before answering. "I guess I'll bring her in. What kind of bond are we talking about?"

"No bond."

"No bond? You can't fucking do that."

"I'm getting a little tired of you telling me—"

"At least get the judge to set a reasonable bond, Edgar. Come on. Get a life."

"That ain't my job, Miss Salinsky. Now you either bring her ass in here by noon or I'll send a dozen cars over to her place." He hung up.

"Son of a bitch." She punched the intercom button. She knew he wasn't fooling around, though why he was so adamant that Kitty had to come in right away, she couldn't figure. God, he could be unreasonable when he wanted.

"Yes, ma'am," Patricia said.

"Will you call Kitty Fulton and ask her to meet me here in no less than an hour? Her number's on that piece of paper I left for you to make up the file with."

"You want to talk to her?"

"No. Don't tell her I'm here. Just make sure she understands that it's important that she get here ASAP." She kicked back in her chair and stared at the ceiling. There was no way she could tell Kitty over the phone what her future held. She'd just have to try to get her out of jail as soon as she could. Damn it. Edgar's little trick was going to screw up the whole timetable she'd figured out for Kitty's case.

The county jail was no place for a woman like Kitty. She'd be a mental patient by the time she got out, if she had to spend much time there. Sandra had represented some of the women who had been in jail a while because they didn't have the resources to make bail. Whores and drug addicts. Real murderers. The lowest forms of human life. Scary to look at with their rotten teeth and open sores.

She could remember when she'd first started practicing law and she'd been appointed to represent people on the misdemeanor jail docket. All the women were there for prostitution. One of the male defense lawyers took one look at them, turned to Sandra, and said, "Not in my worst nightmare." An apt description, she had thought at the time.

With the turn of events, Sandra was going to have to drop almost everything else for a few days until she got Kitty squared away. She'd have to get a hearing before a district judge to get a bond set so Kitty could get out of jail. She was also going to ask the justice of the peace for an examining trial. Maybe after a hearing, the justice of the peace would decide there wasn't probable cause. If Edgar Saul was going to be an ass about the case, she was going to have to use every tool she had in her repertoire.

She took out a legal pad and jotted down a new timetable. It was Monday. If Kitty was charged with capital murder that afternoon, then she could file her writ before the courthouse closed. Three days' notice to the D.A.'s office in accordance with the rules would make it Thursday at the earliest that she could have a bail bond hearing. Three days in the county jail. Poor Kitty.

Of course, she was counting on the judge setting a reasonable amount of bail, too. But what if he or she didn't? What if they set it at a mil? Could Kitty make that? She wasn't sure about Kitty's financial status. She didn't know if Kitty owned property or had any more cash. She did know, though, that she couldn't leave anything to chance. She had to prepare as if there would be no bail set. She also needed to file a demand that afternoon for an examining trial. Make the D.A.'s office do some work. She'd be the aggressor. Make them keep up with her. Especially Edgar Saul.

Sliding the heavy wooden pocket door open, Sandra went into Patricia's office. "What're you doing?"

Patricia's fingers flew across the computer keyboard. "Some estate work for your mother." Next to the machine lay a stack of legal-sized yellow paper with Erma's notes written in her almost illegible script.

"Can you drop it for a little while and work on something I need real quick?"

"You know how she is, Sandy. She gave this to me first. If she finds out—"

"I don't think she'll mind this time. It has to do with Phillip's murder."

"What is it?"

"Writ of habeas corpus and a demand for an examining trial. I'd do it myself, but I'm going to have to take Kitty back over to the courthouse."

Patricia grimaced. "I hate it that you have to do your own work sometimes. I'll squeeze it in, and I don't even want to know why you're taking that poor girl to the courthouse. I have a feeling it's not for something good."

"Does Erma's stuff have to be done right now?"

"I guess not." Patricia patted the top of Sandra's hand. "I've got most of your stuff on software anyway. It shouldn't take too long to get it out. How much is the bond?"

"That's just the problem. There won't be a bond." She told Patricia the facts to put into the motions before she returned to her office to brood over the whole Parker mess.

Somehow she couldn't picture Kitty standing over Phillip with a blunt instrument and beating him to death. It didn't seem the sort of behavior consistent with Kitty's personality. Besides, it seemed likely that one of the others would have seen her running down the stairs and out the door to finish him off. And what about blood spatter?

Wouldn't the cops have found some blood on her clothes on Sunday? And wouldn't Raymond have noticed? And would Raymond protect her if he knew she was a murderess? Would he want a murderess for the mother of his children? No. Definitely she didn't believe Kitty had done it. She just had to convince the district attorney's office not to put her to trial. But first, she needed to go through the preliminaries.

A short time later, Patricia ushered Kitty into Sandra's office and slid the door closed, leaving them alone. Kitty took one look at Sandra and shivered.

Kitty wore red spike heels, a two-piece black and white hound's-tooth check suit with a vent halfway up the back of the skirt, red belt, red blouse, red purse, red earrings, and red bracelet. Her lipstick and fingernails even matched the other accessories.

Sandra remembered the old jokes about what's black and white and red all over. Funny what stupid stuff came to mind during serious occasions. "Sit down, Kitty."

"What is it? Is something the matter?"

"You're going to have to spend a few days in jail."

Kitty gasped. She couldn't have looked more horrified if she'd just seen a body rise up inside a casket.

"The medical examiner's preliminary report says that after Phillip fell, someone—uh . . . finished him off and then moved the body so it would look like he fell on his face. I knew that it was going to reflect something like that, but I didn't think they'd charge you like they're going to."

"I—I swear I never touched his body, Sandy. I couldn't have. I went right back to bed. I told you that."

"I know you did. There's another thing."

"There's more?" She glanced heavenward. "What now?"

"I noticed this on Saturday when I looked at the body.

They believe someone took Phillip's Rolex watch and that big diamond pinkie ring he always wore."

"They think I took them? They think I killed him for a lousy watch and ring?" Her voice rose. "If I—I would have intentionally killed him, it wouldn't have been for some stupid reason like stealing his jewelry." She was out of her chair then, pacing off Sandra's office, leaving little round dents in the wood floor with her spike heels. "It would have been because when I was a child, he raped me. He raped me!"

"What? What are you talking about, Kitty?" Sandra went to her and jerked her around to face her.

"Just what I said. My mother caught him with me on my bed with my panties down. There, I've said it. That's why he left us." Rage filled her eyes.

Sandra didn't know whether to feel pity or anger. Kitty had lied to her. "Sit down, Kathryn." She pointed to a chair. "You sit down right there and this time tell me the truth."

Kitty jerked her arm away and flounced over to the chair Sandra had ordered her into. Sitting erect, her face was as bright red as her accessories. Sandra stood over her, fuming. An abandoned child might not be angry enough to kill a parent, but a molested child certainly could be. Damn, she knew this case seemed too easy. She couldn't, just couldn't, let Edgar Saul find out that Phillip Parker had sexually molested his daughter. What a perfect motive for murder. Years of pent up anger and shame, especially if she had never dealt with it in therapy. And she suspected that was the case. It just wasn't talked about as much back then.

"Now you be straight with me this time, Kathryn Fulton. Did you kill your father, Phillip Parker?"

"Sandy, no, I swear—no, I didn't."

Sandra looked into her eyes, wishing she could tell if Kitty was being honest. "You expect me to believe that after you lied to me? Why did you lie to me?"

"I didn't lie. I just didn't think you needed to know."

"I'm your lawyer for chrissakes." Sandra perched upon the edge of her desk. "You let me decide what I need to know from now on, all right?"

"You don't have to get so mad about it. God." She crossed her arms in front of her breasts and crossed her legs at the knee.

Sandra wanted to smack Kitty, except Kitty's body language already told Sandra how defensive and insecure she felt. "Who else knows about this? Does Raymond know? Does anyone else know?"

"Why is it important who knows?"

"Are you going to start questioning everything I'm trying to do here, Kathryn? Do you want to hire someone else to represent you or do you think you can represent yourself? Or do you just want to cooperate with me and hope I can get your ass out of trouble?"

"God, what are you so angry about? I'm the one whose father did stuff to her."

Sandra expelled a deep breath. "Okay." She laughed. "You're right. But don't you realize what this information could mean to a judge or a jury?"

"Yeah, I guess I do, Sandy. I'm sorry. I swear I didn't kill him, though."

"Okay, I believe you." Sandra hopped down and went back around her desk to sit in her chair. "I'm sorry to blow up at you, kid. I'm sorry Phillip did that to you, too."

"Yeah, but it was a long time ago."

"Can you tell me what you remember about it?"

She nodded. Her eyes swept around the room. She nodded again. "I remember he hurt me down there. I don't remember a lot of details, but I remember thinking he peepeed on me. And the day my mother walked in, my parents had a big, big fight."

Sandra's stomach ached just listening to Kitty recite the details. "Did she call the police?"

Kitty shook her head. "He left after that. We never saw him again."

"Humph. And he never sent any support?"

"No. He really did write a letter telling my mother he was going to kill himself."

Sandra made some notes. She was struggling inside herself trying to decide whether she should tell Erma about this. She really didn't want to. "What else do you remember?"

"Couple of times I tried to talk to her about it over the years, but she always said it was best to put it all behind us and forget about it."

"So no counseling for you?"

Kitty dropped her arms and got up. She walked over to a painting of a mother and a child and stared at it. "I went to therapy after she died. After I got some money, I mean." She turned on her heel. "I know I'm not that smart, Sandy, but I knew I had, as my therapist put it, 'unresolved issues.' "

"You still in therapy?"

Shaking her head, she smiled. "Think I should be?"

"You think you should be?"

"Sometimes. The last couple of days I've thought about it—and not because I killed my father."

"Sometimes I think everyone needs to go to therapy."

Kitty smiled again. "When Raymond and I get married, we're going to premarital counseling."

Sandra threw her pen down. "Okay. There's not much time left, Kitty. I have to take you over to the county jail before they come over here and arrest you."

Kitty made a sound like a little squeal of pain. "Can you explain to me why I have to go to jail again?"

"They're charging you with capital murder."

"Oh my God! That's a whole lot different from what you said before. Did you know this yesterday?"

"I didn't think it would happen."

"You didn't think it would happen? You knew about the watch and ring, but you didn't think it would happen? What did you think would happen when the police discovered they were missing? You made me turn myself in when you knew that there was a possibility that they would charge me with murder or this—this—capital murder, didn't you?"

"I guess it's your turn to be angry. If you didn't do anything more than you told me, then you have nothing to worry about."

"Thanks a lot. That, from someone who isn't going to jail. Thanks a whole lot."

Sandra waited. So much had gone on between the two of them that she fully expected to be fired. Not that she'd blame Kitty, but in spite of her apparent deceit, Sandra really looked forward to handling Kitty's case. If she didn't bungle it, it would certainly enhance her reputation.

"You didn't have to make me turn myself in, you know."

"I know."

"We could have waited until they figured out I was in there with him."

"Yes, we could have waited."

"I guess they would have figured it out pretty quickly though." She shrugged. "I mean since Lizzie saw me on the stairs."

Sandra stared up at Kitty. "I haven't figured out why Lizzie didn't say something to them on Saturday."

"I couldn't either." She let out a long sigh. "I can't go to jail, Sandy. I saw some of those people. They were nasty looking."

"You don't have any choice in the matter. We only have a few minutes before you've got to be at the D.A.'s office, so calm down and let me brief you on what I'm going to do. And no matter what else happens, remember one thing. Tell no one about what Phillip Parker did to you."

After she accompanied Kitty first to Edgar's office and then to be booked into the county jail, she paid a call on the superintendent and got him to agree to provide a separate cell and close supervision of her client. After all, if—or rather, when—Kitty was found not guilty of the charges against her, she would become a celebrity, given that she was Phillip's daughter and all. You never know but that a person like that might someday be able to do something for the sheriff who was the superintendent's boss. Elections did come every four years in Texas, she reminded him. And the sheriff would be standing for re-election. And elections did cost a tidy sum these days. And campaign contributions were always necessary. Treat a person right and they were likely to remember it later.

Her next onerous task was to accompany Erma on a coffin-shopping trip. Sandra hadn't had time for lunch but didn't think that she'd be able to choke anything down anyway after being at the jail. How the employees and inmates of the Galveston County Jail could eat while the stench of ammonia filled their nostrils 24/7 was beyond her. She supposed they got used to it, but she found that it was difficult to even smell food, much less eat it, after passing by the mop bucket.

Erma sat at the dinette table in her kitchen. She munched on a salad and thumbed through a magazine. She wore a black caftan and leggings and ballet slippers. Her hair was disheveled, but at least she wore a little foundation, powder, and blush so her face wasn't so ghostlike.

She raised her eyes when Sandra came into the room. "You know, spending a few days at home might just be enough to convince me to retire. It's rather nice sitting here, relaxed, studying recipes." She pointed to photographs of artfully designed food.

"Jesus Christ, Mother, you're not old enough to retire." It frightened her to see that her mother wasn't herself. No eagerness to argue. No vibrant energy. No cussing every other word.

"Yes. Yes, I am. I'm rather enjoying myself, too. Haven't done this in a while."

"You can do it every weekend. Now get up and let's go to the funeral home." She tugged at Erma's arm.

Erma stared into her face. "I could tell you what to get and you could go for me, dear."

"Dear? That's the second time in recent history that you've used that term of endearment. Pun intended. Come on. I need to discuss this case with you. Will you get up? We've got a lot to do." The lines in her mother's face told a story that she was not ready to hear. She had aged significantly in just a couple of days. It was grief, Sandra knew. Erma tried to hide it, but she was sure it ate her up inside. Sandra hoped it would not take over her mother's life. She wanted to make her mother's grief as short-lived as possible.

Erma was the type of person who withered without a cause. As a younger woman, the period of time between major trials had been filled with Sandra's needing her. As they had grown older and Sandra was busy with school activities, Erma had filled the void with her friends. She did things for them. She had been the one who was always there for them. And Phillip had been one of the neediest of her friends, having the largest ego on the Gulf Coast. Sandra could see that Erma was already feeling his loss, the emptiness caused by his death, even though their monthly dinner date was not past due, even though he'd just been gone two days—two days that she ordinarily would not have seen him.

"Come on, Erma," Sandra said. "The least you can do for Phillip is pick out exactly the type of coffin he would have selected for himself."

Using Sandra's arm as a crutch, Erma lifted her body from the kitchen chair. "You're right, Sandra. That's the least I can do. It'll be my one last act of friendship toward Phillip."

She was so pitiful, Sandra felt like crying. But that never had been, and never would be, her style. "So Mom," she addressed her in a way quite atypical of her, "after we get through picking out the coffin, do you think you could help me with Kitty's case? They've now charged her with capital murder."

"What?" Erma glared up at Sandra, her teeth bared like a mad dog's. "They can't charge her with that. Why, she's Phillip's child and she never would have done such a thing, no matter what went on between them twenty years ago."

Sandra wondered whether Erma knew something that she wasn't telling. "Yes, Mother, dear," she said, and held the door open. Smiling at the back of her head, she launched into a description of her conversation with Edgar and the trip to the jail earlier that afternoon. She noticed as they walked to the car that there was a bit more bounce in the little woman's step.

Chapter Eight

Later that night, Sandra lounged on a kitchen stool at Stuart's house and watched him grill shrimp. She'd changed into tennis shoes, shorts, and a T-shirt after dropping Erma back at home and had run for thirty minutes along the seawall. She hated every minute of jogging and did it only because she didn't want to wake up one morning and see the Pillsbury Doughgirl looking back at her in the mirror.

Stuart had insisted she bring the shrimp to his house as soon as she got through running, without stopping to shower and change. She had the distinct feeling, every time he cooked for her, that he was trying to entice her into a more serious relationship. She enjoyed being with Stuart. Since he was so brilliant, their conversations were stimulating. A scholar and a gentleman, he resembled someone out of the old South. Bowing, scraping, posturing—if you will—in and out of the courtroom. And the sex. The sex was very good, though not frequent enough for her. In fact, Stuart was probably better than both of her ex-husbands put together. Stuart put her first and his own pleasure second. The names of the men in the world who did that could probably be written on a pencil eraser. Lastly, he had more staying power than anyone she had ever known. But she didn't want to get married again and had to push her own legal arguments for marriage out of her head.

Watching him prepare their meal, Sandra couldn't quite

articulate why she didn't want to marry him. She just knew that she didn't. The fault must lie within herself. She'd been twice burned.

She had Melinda, so she didn't have a ticking biological clock. Her career had brought her more money than she needed. With her mother, daughter, and law practice, she wasn't especially lonely. She also had a good friend in Patricia and often hung out with other lawyers, both female and male.

The problem, she thought, must be that she didn't especially need Stuart. The status quo satisfied her, at least most of the time. Why did he push for more—for permanency? Did he really want to get into that whole marriage scene when they currently had the best of both worlds?

Stuart snapped his fingers in front of her face. "Where are you?"

She grabbed his hand and let him pull her to her feet.

"You were off in another world again. What's on your mind?"

Slipping an arm around his waist, she laughed. "I don't know. Sorry. Dinner ready?"

He stared into her eyes for a few moments. "Come on. I've already set the table." He'd told her once that he observed all the decorum of a formal dinner even when he dined alone. He thought it made a meal more pleasurable.

Her stomach rumbled when she saw the shrimp, broccoli in a lemon sauce, rice pilaf, and tossed green salad. It was a lot better than the meals she threw together for herself or grabbed at fast-food joints. She couldn't help but wonder what it would be like if they married. Would he cook or expect her to become Little Susie Homemaker? "It looks scrumptious, Stu. You went all out tonight."

"Payback for your cooking breakfast last Saturday. Let's eat before it gets cold."

She kissed his temple where there were a few gray hairs. Slipping around to her side of the table, when he pulled out her chair, she sat down and spread the cloth napkin over her bare legs.

Stuart poured white wine into her glass and stood by like a liveried waiter while she sampled it. When she smiled at him and nodded her head, he laughingly filled her glass, then his own, and took his seat across from her. Tall lavender candles burned on the center of the table. They ate silently for a few moments.

"Speaking of last Saturday, Erma and I picked out a coffin for Phillip today."

"Did she insist on buying the most elaborate one?"

Nodding, she said, "I tried to talk her out of it, but Erma said Phillip would like to have a nice send-off even if he was to be cremated. She bought the most expensive urn as well."

"A pine box would have worked fine for a cremation."

"His estate can afford it, I'm sure."

"I'm sure, too." He picked up his wineglass and stared into it. "Is she pretty heartbroken?"

"Erma?"

"Yes."

"Yes. They'd been friends so long. I think it makes her feel defenseless, like she's next."

"I never could understand their relationship. He could be such a bastard." Stuart smiled at her and sipped his wine.

"I know. The town abounded with stories. You thinking of anything in particular?"

Stuart shrugged and asked, "How's Kitty?"

Sandra swallowed quickly. "Oh, God. I can't believe I forgot to tell you. I guess the coffin bit made me forget. They've arrested her for capital murder."

"Capital murder? How do they figure that?"

"His diamond Rolex and pinkie ring were missing." While they ate, she gave him a brief rundown on what had happened.

"Have they searched his suite?"

"Yes. You know he wore that watch everywhere except into the Gulf. And the ring he never took off."

"What does Kitty say?"

"About the blackmail? Not on your life. And the watch and ring? No way."

"What about the charges?"

"She's pissed, to put it mildly. She told me off in no uncertain terms, but I'm still representing her."

"What was she angry at you for?" Stuart sliced a shrimp in half and bit into it.

"I think partly because she needed to let off some steam and partly because she wasn't thinking. It wasn't any real big deal, except that I thought she was going to fire me and that got the old adrenaline flowing."

"Why do you care?"

" 'Cause I don't want to lose this case. It could be the biggest thing of my career."

"It could also be very dangerous. Have you thought of that?"

"Now you're sounding like Erma and I think she's just jealous."

Stuart reached across the table and took her hand. "Don't be flippant, Sandra. I'm worried about you. You say that Kitty didn't do it. Don't you know what that means?"

She squeezed his hand, pulled hers back, and made a pretense of cutting her food. "Sure. That means that I've got to defend her from Edgar Saul, the prosecutor from hell."

"No. Not that, Sandra. It means the killer is still out there somewhere."

"So? I'm not a threat to the real killer." She stuffed half a branch of broccoli into her mouth and chewed while she avoided his gaze. The trouble with Stuart was that he knew how she worked. He knew that she'd be looking at everyone else that had means, motive, and opportunity in order to cast doubt on Kitty's guilt. She was fighting a losing battle if she thought she could convince him that she was not a threat to anyone else. She was a threat. She knew it. Stuart knew it. Her mother knew it, too. In criminal cases, they practiced law much the same way.

"Who are you trying to kid?"

"Well, there's no reason for them to think that I'm a threat, anyway. I'll just ask a few questions of each of them and maybe I can come up with enough to convince the judge that Kitty couldn't have done it."

"The judge?"

"At the examining trial. I'm going to try to convince the judge not to refer this case to the grand jury. To find that there is no probable cause."

Stuart laughed. "The examining trial. What makes you think—"

"Because I don't think Edgar has enough evidence yet to go to a grand jury. I don't think he'll risk the grand jury no-billing her—ego-wise or otherwise. It would look terrible in the papers, and he'd play hell getting a true bill later from another grand jury." She took a drink of wine. "Besides, can you imagine what I could do in court if he did get another grand jury to indict later? I'd use that like crazy in her defense. No, the way I figure it, knowing Edgar as I do, he will carefully and methodically put all the facts together until he can present an airtight case."

"Then why did he have her arrested and charged with capital murder?"

"I don't know. My best guess would be that Lucien wanted something to tell the press. From what I hear, they've been all over him since Saturday afternoon. There's an election looming, you know. It would be like Lucien to grandstand."

He nodded. "That would make sense."

"See, it doesn't matter if Kitty is released later on. When they really do have the real perpetrator in custody, they can apologize to Kitty. They don't give a shit what happens to her—how she's traumatized over this thing."

"Calm down. You're getting off the subject."

"It makes me damn mad, though. Think about it. If you were Kitty, how would you like to be locked up with all those whores and drug users?"

Stuart frowned. "I haven't been inside a county jail in a long time, but my recollection of it is that it's pretty grim. I take it you're doing all you can to free her?"

"Of course. I've got a bond hearing set for Thursday at ten-thirty in front of Judge McWheeter."

"McWheeter?" Stuart laughed. "Isn't he the one—"

"Yep. He's a real womanizer. I'm hoping he'll feel sorry for her when he sees her, and set a reasonable bond. Edgar got it fixed so there isn't one right now." She munched on another piece of broccoli. The lemon sauce tasted tart and sweet at the same time. She wondered how Stuart managed that.

"This Edgar sounds vicious."

"He is. If you knew him, you'd know that. He told me once that it was better that an innocent man be executed than a guilty man go free."

"So he's the kind of prosecutor that always believes the worst. Sweet guy."

She sighed. "So you've got an idea of what I'm dealing with." She finished off her shrimp and followed it with a swallow of wine. "By the way, have you seen Raymond? How's he taking it?"

Stuart shook his head. "The boy is inconsolable. The murder was bad enough since he idolized Phillip, but for Kitty to be accused has really been hard on him. I think he planned to go to church tonight to pray for guidance."

"And he can't know about the cap murder charge yet, unless Kitty was able to call him from the jail," Sandra said. "Poor guy. He seems so dedicated to her. I wonder . . ."

Stuart got up and began clearing the table. "What?"

"Do you think he knew Phillip had invited Kitty up to his room?" She carried her plate into the kitchen behind him and set it on the counter. Finding a pair of rubber gloves under the sink, she put them on and began rinsing dishes and filling the dishwasher while Stuart cleared the table. It crossed her mind for a moment that they were like old married people. She quickly shook off a feeling of suffocation.

"What are you getting at?"

"Do you think he wasn't really asleep when Kitty went up there? Maybe he woke up and followed her. Maybe he listened outside the door and heard a struggle. Maybe Raymond burst in and saw them struggling and threw Phillip over the balcony."

"I don't think so. Raymond is too slow to anger."

"Why do you say that?"

"Because Phillip abuses him—abused him—almost every day at the office and Raymond never even flinched."

"Like what did he do?"

"Well, during the trial last week, Phillip got so angry at Raymond that he took hold of his ear and pulled him down the hall during a break."

"In front of other people?"

Stuart nodded.

"That makes me sick to my stomach. And Raymond let him do it? What did Raymond do?"

"Nothing. Rubbed his ear and made it even redder if that's possible. Apologized to Phillip for what he forgot to do."

"What did he forget to do? Never mind—it doesn't even matter. That's so disgusting. How could Phillip do that to someone, another attorney? How humiliating."

"Phillip really got out of hand sometimes, Sandy. I often wondered if there was something wrong with him. Medically, I mean."

"Like a chemical imbalance?" She made a mental note to mention it to Erma.

"It would make his behavior more excusable. The way he was," Stuart paused and shook his head, "it's almost intolerable to think that he was that way solely out of meanness. What would make a man so mean? Especially a rich man. A man who didn't want for anything? I often wished I'd seen that side of him before we became partners."

"Maybe Raymond had enough. Maybe Kitty came running downstairs and told him that she'd flipped Phillip over the balcony and Raymond ran outside and finished him off. It would have been the perfect opportunity."

"Wouldn't Kitty have told you if Raymond ran out like that?" Stuart had stacked all the serving dishes and stood next to her at the sink.

"She could be protecting him. Kitty could be willing to go to the executioner for Raymond."

"But, would Raymond let Kitty do it? That's the question. I don't think so."

She chewed her lip. "Maybe he's considering it right now as we speak. Maybe he'll go confess tonight."

"In your fondest dreams."

"No. I'd like it better if he waited until the trial. I could use the publicity."

Stuart put her in a headlock and kissed her hair. "You're terrible."

She twisted out of his arms. "I'm a normal criminal defense lawyer. Always working on her rep. Reputation is everything." She laughed.

"Well, I think if you're staking your reputation on Raymond having killed Phillip, you're in for a lot of disappointment."

"Yeah. I guess he doesn't really seem the type." She put a plate in the dishwasher and turned back to Stuart. Standing on her tiptoes, she looked him dead in the eye. "But what about you? Where were you?"

"Me?" Stuart laughed. "Okay. I confess. I threw Phillip off the balcony when I came to Kitty's aid."

She took the next plate from him. "You could have."

"Yes. I could have. All right. How's this scenario? I couldn't sleep so I was wandering around in the moonlight when all of a sudden I heard an argument from up above and Phillip came flying down. I'm having financial difficulty and saw my chance to steal his thirty-five-thousand-dollar Rolex and ten-thousand-dollar diamond ring, so I clobbered him in the face and took them and then ran up to my room and jumped into bed before anyone saw me."

"Ha ha. Very funny. But you admit you could have killed him, don't you?"

"Sweetheart, based on what you've told me, anyone who was there that night could have killed him." He pulled her to him. She rested her two wet rubber-gloved hands on his chest. "Does it turn you on to think that I may have committed a murder? Does it make you want to come to bed with me two nights in a row?"

Sandra found herself giggling like an adolescent. She'd never admit it to him, but it did give her an oddly euphoric feeling. When it got right down to it, Stuart was a suspect. Not that he could have done it any more than Raymond. But someone had to have killed Phillip if he was killed after he hit the ground. Stuart cupped his hands on her bottom, pulled her up against him, and nibbled on her neck. She pushed him away. "You want to get your kitchen cleaned up or not?"

"You going to come to bed with me or not?" he replied, his voice husky.

She smiled. "In a few minutes." Handing him a sponge, she told him to wipe the table. She got another one and went over the stove and countertops as she thought about all the possibilities she could raise in Kitty's defense. She thought that Lizzie probably had the most to gain, but remembering the way she had been the other day, how could she have done it? Talk about heartbroken. Unless her behavior resulted from her regret at having done him in, as they say. Then there was Carruthers. Her thoughts always came back to Carruthers. Now there was someone who could benefit from a Rolex watch and a diamond ring. He wouldn't have to be a personal slave to anyone for a while if he could sell that watch and ring for half what they were worth.

After she finished wiping down the countertops, she watched Stuart straightening the dining room table and chairs. She enjoyed being with him like that, each of them sharing the household chores. Oh, why were her feelings so ambiguous?

Physically, they were a pretty good match. He had a nice body. His polo shirt stretched across his biceps. At fifty he still only had just a tiny paunch below his waistline. His legs were muscular from his almost daily jogs down the beach. He had just the right amount of body hair—not too much on his chest and back, but a smattering—enough to be really sexy. Why couldn't she make up her mind?

Stuart caught her watching him. His solemn face changed into a bright smile as she switched on the dishwasher and peeled off the rubber gloves. When he returned to the kitchen, she said, "I've been thinking. What do you want to bet that Bubba Carruthers is the killer?"

Stuart tossed his sponge into the sink and dried his hands on a dishtowel. "What do you want to bet that I can make you quit thinking about this case for the next hour or so?" Stuart reached for her T-shirt and began pulling it over her head.

She laughed and reached for his belt buckle. "Want to take another shower together?" Her heart already beat a little faster. She had wanted to go over all the suspects with Stuart and see if he could help her narrow it down since he had been there. There was a lot to do before the examining trial the next week, but she still had plenty of time. The following day she would go out and see Bubba Carruthers. Right then, she had better things to do.

Chapter Nine

Phillip's house appeared dejected, as if it knew its owner would not return. It had an unkempt look as well, not quite as tidy as it had been just a few days earlier. It didn't help that Bubba had parked his pickup on the blanket of Bermuda grass that paralleled the curving driveway from the beginning of the property line all the way to the canal slip.

Then there was Bubba himself. He stood behind the truck, the water hose dangling from one hand, a rag in the other, a smoking cigarette glued to the corner of his lips. When he spotted her, he dropped the rag into a bucket and swallowed from a beer while not removing the cigarette from his mouth. Some trick. If Phillip had been alive, Bubba would never have engaged in such behavior. He never would have even contemplated it. Phillip's regular gardener worked long hours keeping the grass alive during the island's harsh summers. He grew squeamish if people even walked on it, much less parked a vehicle on it.

Sandra pulled her Volvo into the driveway and cut the engine. Bubba acted like he didn't see her, but she knew he had. He pretended to be in his own little world, his radio blaring from atop a table under the house. She wondered how many beers he'd consumed.

"Hey, Bubba!" Sandra waved. She got the distinct impression that he would acknowledge her presence only when he was good and ready.

Getting out of the car, she slammed the door behind her and crossed the driveway until she was so near his truck that he couldn't avoid seeing her. She only hoped he didn't turn the hose in her direction. "Can I talk to you a minute?"

He finally made eye contact. Finishing off his beer, he crushed the can like he'd wring out a washrag, and tossed it against the house where it came to rest next to the faucet with several others. When he came out from behind the truck, she could see that he wore only a dirty white T-shirt and cut-off blue jeans that were brown around the edges. His feet were bare, another thing Phillip never would have allowed. And there was dirt under his overgrown toenails in spite of his standing in wet grass. Dropping the hose, he leaned over the faucet and turned it off. He grabbed another beer and followed her under the house where he sprawled on a bench, his elbows resting behind him on the picnic table.

Lighting another cigarette from the one in the corner of his mouth, Bubba let the smoke wander upward as he spoke. "What can I do for you, Miss Sandra?" His smile was little more than a leer.

If anyone ever appeared to fit the stereotype of a criminal more than Bubba Carruthers, she'd never laid eyes on him. She couldn't help noticing that his teeth were yellow around the edges and gray in the middle.

"Wondered if I could ask you a few things about the other night?"

"Yeah? Like what?" He wore a couple days' worth of beard. A scar ran across the bag under his left eye. Sandra was close enough to see that even though it was eleven in the morning, he hadn't washed the sleep out of his deep-set dark eyes.

"Well, for starters, like where you were when Mr. Parker fell over the balcony?"

"I don't know when he fell over the balcony." His tiny eyes stared past her.

He was so repulsive that she could hardly sit still. The only clean-looking thing about him was his crew cut, and she thought that was because it was so black the dirt couldn't be differentiated from the natural color of his hair.

Averting her gaze, Sandra was thankful that she'd sat upwind. She pondered whether to say anything to him about his behavior—his demeanor and his mode of dress—then thought better of it. In a few days, Phillip's beneficiaries would deal with him. It wasn't her place. She didn't want to criticize him and thus jeopardize whatever information she might be able to get out of him. Glad that she'd had the time to formulate her thoughts before opening her mouth, just as in a careful cross-examination, she hoped to extract as much information out of him as possible. She smiled. What she wanted to do was knock the smirk off his mouth, but she smiled anyway. "You found the body, didn't you?"

"Yeah, but later. Not when he fell. By the time I found him, there was already a skin on his blood."

"A what?"

"You know," he stared at her and grinned, "the blood was thickening up like tomato soup when you let it cool off in the pot, only darker."

"I get the picture." She had the feeling he enjoyed describing that for her. "Is there anything you can tell me about Friday night? Anything at all that you've remembered?"

Clusters of sweat beads clung to Carruthers' upper lip like a jewel-embroidered collar. She wondered whether it was the heat or the fear of someone finding out the truth. Carruthers puffed on his cigarette and didn't answer.

"Maybe we could start from when I went home. Do you remember when I left, Bubba? You were still behind the bar, serving drinks, perhaps cleaning up a bit. What happened after that?"

Bubba shrugged and hung back, his elbows on the table behind him, his legs spread wide. "The party, it pretty much ended when you and Mr. Stuart went outside. I was finishing mopping up behind the bar when Mr. Stuart came back."

She nodded. "So did you come downstairs then?"

"No. Mr. Phillip, he said I could have the leftover food, so I was eating when they started fighting."

"Who?"

"Mr. Phillip and Miss Lizzie. You could hear her screaming at him."

"Who else was around?"

"Mr. Stuart had went into his room. Miss Kitty and Mr. Raymond had went to their room, so it was just me. I was afraid they'd come out and think I was deliberately over-hearing, so I packed up and brung my plate down here."

"You went to bed then?"

He shrugged. "Well, not exactly. I ate and went down to The Cantina. If Miss Lizzie pushed him off, it must of been after two when I got back."

"Wait a minute. Wait a minute. Miss Lizzie pushed him off?"

"Didn't she?"

"You don't read the papers?"

He looked over her shoulder into the distance again. "No, ma'am, Miss Sandra."

"Why do you think Miss Lizzie pushed him off?"

"She was awful mad. She was cussing him and calling him all kinds of names. I just figured she'd had enough of him."

"Enough to kill him?"

"You never know what sets people off nowadays."

"Do you think Miss Lizzie would steal from Mr. Phillip?"

Carruthers' eyes wavered like warning flags in a rough wind. "Like really steal something? Like more than take something without asking?"

"Yes, like money or jewelry or something like that?"

"Is something missing?"

"Do you know of something that is missing, Bubba?"

He shrugged again. "Nothing I can think of right off-hand."

"Did he keep valuables out here?"

Shaking his head, he said, "Not usually. Unless he was going to stay for more than a few days. He carried a lot of cash, though."

"I was aware of that. And he had a dreadful habit of flashing it in people's faces, too."

"Yeah. I tried to tell him once not to do that, but he got mad and swelled up like a blowfish."

"I've seen him do that."

Carruthers laughed. "He couldn't take no joke."

"So what usually was here? What usually were you in charge of?"

"Say, what are you getting at?"

"You want me to be straight with you, you be straight with me. You know what I'm saying?"

"Okay. Okay. Mr. Parker usually kept his old BMW out here. I had to keep it washed and waxed and the tank topped off. And take care of his little Sailfish that he liked to sail around the slip in. He kept the big boat over at the Yacht Basin. There's a mechanic there that looks after it." He crossed his arms and looked at her.

She waited a few moments. "I know that's not the extent of your duties."

"I'm 'sposed to make sure the bar stays full of booze, the wine rack's full, and the freezer always has steaks and fish in it. If I knew for sure he was coming, then there was a list of fresh stuff I had to get from the store."

"Was there a list of hard liquor and wine and beer, too?"

"Yeah. But mostly I went by what was opened. I just bought more of that. He let me have the opened ones for myself."

She was familiar with Phillip's strange behavior. He never liked to use food from open containers. Once a bottle or jar had been unsealed, it would either be given to staff or thrown away. The contents would never pass Phillip's lips. Sandra was sure there must be a psychological name for it. That was one of the things that had always irritated her about him. He was so wasteful.

She found herself remarking to Bubba, "On the few occasions I went out with him and my mother, he made the restaurant staff bring him the unopened containers of condiments for his examination as well as the uncooked cuts of meat so that he could test for freshness." Bubba looked at her sideways, like a bird. She suddenly realized that she had gotten sidetracked. It was hot and humid out there. She needed to get some answers and get back into the air-conditioning as soon as possible before she began to smell like Bubba.

"Did Mr. Phillip leave cash for you to make those purchases or did you have charge accounts?"

Bubba glowered at her. "Neither one, lady. There was a checking account, which he put money in weekly. You know, you're starting to make me mad with your sinuations."

Sandra ignored his outburst. "Let's get back to where you were on the night of Mr. Phillip's death. You say you were at The Cantina on the seawall?"

"Yeah. That's right."

"From when to when?"

Bubba's face puckered up like an old pair of lips. "Don't

know exactly. From some time after you left here till they closed at two."

"Anybody see you there?"

"You know, Miss Sandy, if you'd a asked the cops, they could of told you all this."

"Anybody see you there, Bubba?"

"The barmaid, Sue Ann Lopez."

"Anybody else?"

"They might of, but Sue Ann's the one who brought me my beer."

"What can I expect her to say if I speak to her?"

"That I stayed there until the joint closed."

"Anything else?"

Bubba shifted about on the bench. "Naw."

"And when you got home, was Mr. Parker's body already on the ground?"

"I told you. No." He stood up and put one foot on the space where he'd been sitting, as if to push off. "Anything else?"

Sandra kept her seat, trying to rein in her impatience. "Yes. Are you sure you didn't hear anything after you got home? You didn't hear any more hollering or cussing like before you left?"

Shaking his head, Bubba walked away.

"Now wait a minute," she hollered at his departing back. "You can't have it all your way. Either he died before you got home and you found the body, or he died after you got home and you heard everything and know who did it, or else . . . you killed him."

"You're full of shit." Bubba drained his beer can, twisted it up like he had the other, and flung it back toward the metal bucket. "You ain't got nothing on me, Miss Sandra Salinsky, or you'd go to the police. What did you come out here for anyway?"

Sandra felt a bit frightened but didn't want him to know it. She stood up and stretched. "For one little thing, Bubba. To find out what you stole from Mr. Phillip."

He stepped in her direction and then apparently thought better of it and turned his back on her again. She tried goading him into saying something more, but when she couldn't get anything other than a scary glance, she figured she'd better pack it in and head back to town. Once she was in her car, he stared at her all the way to the street. She lost eye contact as she drove away.

Erma had phoned Lizzie and made a lunch date at Petronelli Brothers. The restaurant was situated in the historic part of town on The Strand, just a few blocks from Erma's home. She allowed the valet to park her car but was forced to rely on her cane to climb the stairs, glad that Sandra wouldn't be around to observe her.

Lizzie had beaten Erma there and was in the bar. She rode a tall stool, stared at her reflection in the mirror behind the bar, and sipped from a martini when her eyes locked with Erma's.

"Goddamnit it, Lizzie, you're not sloshed already, are you?" Erma said as she struggled to get up on a stool.

"Erma. Erma, Erma, Erma." Lizzie leaned over and draped an arm around Erma's neck. "What are we going to do without him?"

Erma patted Lizzie and pushed her back toward her stool so she wouldn't fall off. "Gimme a bourbon straight up, Sam," she said to the brown-headed woman behind the bar. "How long have you been here?" she said to Lizzie and saw Sam's eyebrows shoot up.

"Oh, I don't know. A few minutes."

"Enough to get loaded, I see," Erma said. She swallowed

from the glass that had been set in front of her and muttered, "You couldn't have sat in one of those wicker chairs while you were waiting; you had to climb up here. Thanks for nothing."

"Erma, what am I going to do?" Lizzie took another swallow.

"Well, for one thing, eat lunch." She motioned to the bartender. "Get us a table, will you?"

The bartender walked into the dining room and returned with a waiter, a tall Middle-Eastern Omar Sharif-looking man. "If you would be so good as to accompany me, Ms. Townley," he said, offering his elbow for Erma to hold as she made the difficult transition from barstool to floor. She downed the remainder of her drink and let him guide them to a table. "Come on, Elizabeth, goddamnit, he's not going to wait all day."

Lizzie frowned at Erma and then at her martini. Grasping the stem of the glass as though it were a lifeline, she slid down from the stool onto her stiletto heels. She balanced herself before bringing up the rear.

The smell of garlic hung in the room, as strong a presence as the brocade draperies on the windows. Erma felt hungry for the first time in several days, her mouth watering as they grew close to the food. Once they were settled at a table near the lunch buffet, Erma saw the smear of red lipstick on one of Lizzie's front teeth. It gave her a bloody-looking smile. As she arranged her napkin on her lap, Erma couldn't help but wonder whether just a few days ago there would have been a smear of blood on Lizzie. She had stayed out of Phillip's and Lizzie's lives, out of their business, for years; minding her own was enough for one person. Now there were things that she needed to know.

"That's better," Erma said as she watched Lizzie get settled. "Isn't this an improvement?"

Lizzie wore a pout. "You always thought I wasn't good enough for Phillip, didn't you?"

"Goddamnit, Lizzie, where did you ever get an idea like that?" She glanced at the waiter who stood at her elbow. "I'll have iced tea and the buffet, young man, if you'll be so kind as to fix my plate. I don't think I can get back up just now and it does look so awfully good today."

"It would be my pleasure, Madam. And you?" He looked at Lizzie.

"Water and another martini."

Erma said, "She'll have what I'm having, but she'll get her own food. Thank you."

"What right do you have—"

"Did you drive down here, Lizzie? If you did, then it is my duty as your friend to see that you don't drive back in a drunken state."

"Since when have we been friends?"

"Tsk tsk." Erma shook her head. Lizzie was understandably angry and defensive. Erma knew that the woman was scared. She would be, too, if she'd always depended on someone else to take care of her. "You and Phil have a fight the other night?"

"You know we did. Everyone knows we did." She glanced at the buffet. "I'm going to get my food."

Erma watched as Lizzie pushed back her chair and flounced toward the food. Could it be possible that last Friday night Lizzie had gone outside to cool off? Had she perhaps stood under the house, out of Kitty's sight, and stepped in when the opportunity presented itself, finishing Phillip off?

Lizzie, in a jealous rage, would have been strong enough to beat the hell out of someone. And having been drinking the whole evening, her thinking would certainly have been impaired. So, the possibility of Lizzie being the killer was not so farfetched. Statistics showed that in most cases someone who knew the victim committed the murder. In this case, everyone at the party knew Phillip, but statistics also said that most often the perpetrator was a spouse or a boyfriend or a girlfriend. Lizzie would definitely be the most logical suspect. But, and here was the clincher, could she, Elizabeth Haynes, find it in herself to wield a weapon repeatedly against Phillip's face until she had smashed it to smithereens?

Anxious to question Lizzie about her whereabouts Friday night, Erma drummed on the table and watched Lizzie's movements.

"Here you are, Madam," the waiter said as he placed a tall glass of iced tea before Erma, along with a long spoon, one at Lizzie's place, and turned toward the buffet.

"No goddamned broccoli, waiter," Erma said. "I hate the sight of the stuff. Pick it out of those mixed vegetables. And plenty of pasta, that beef, and a side plate of salad with Italian dressing. Oh, some of those little cubes of cheese, especially that one with jalapeno in it."

"Yes, Madam," the waiter replied and hurried to the far side of the buffet as if to escape.

"And crackers. Don't forget the crackers." Erma poured sugar into her tea, squeezed two lemon slices, stirred vigorously, and drank half of it.

After Lizzie sat down, Erma noticed that Lizzie's hands shook. Was it nerves or the d.t.'s? She waited for the appropriate moment to ask, but it didn't come. An uncomfortable silence arose between them as the minutes ticked by. Erma said, "Go ahead, eat. I'll join you in a minute."

Lizzie released a deep breath and stabbed at her food. Finally, the waiter returned and gave Erma her plate. Both of them ate in silence for a few minutes, Erma observing

Lizzie like a bug in a bottle, Lizzie, head down, forking food into her mouth.

"Liz, if you don't mind, I'd like to know what you and Phillip fought about last Saturday night." Erma thought she'd phrased the question fairly, non-aggressively, and smiled as she poked a piece of lettuce into her mouth and chewed as she waited for Lizzie's response.

She remembered earlier days when Elizabeth Haynes had been a beautiful woman. Phillip first brought her around the house on a couple of Friday nights, as if for approval. Erma remembered telling Sandra that she hoped Lizzie would bring some happiness into Phillip's life. And she had. But in the last few years, things had soured. Phillip had behaved badly toward Lizzie in front of other people. He didn't always treat her with respect. Erma had wanted to say something, but such wasn't the nature of their relationship.

Lizzie could still be a beautiful, albeit older, woman if she didn't drink and get hysterical. The red highlights in her natural strawberry blond hair shined under the fluorescent lighting. All the makeup in the world couldn't hide the fine lines around her eyes, though. The effect of too much alcohol was evident in the puffiness she tried to hide with thick makeup. She also had black circles under her eyes that Erma could only assume were from sleepless nights and hours of grieving. She felt intensely sorry for her.

"He was meeting that slut," Lizzie said suddenly.

Erma glanced up, saw a look of hatred in Lizzie's eyes, and waited for her next words.

"After I gave him the best years of my life." She cupped a hand over her eyes like a valance. Erma couldn't see her face clearly, but she suspected Lizzie was on the verge of a crying jag.

"Um, this salad is delish. Have you tried yours?"

Lizzie sniffed and blotted her nose with the mauve cloth napkin from her lap. "I'm sorry. I know this must be unbearable for you. You had known Phillip a long time also."

"Listen, Liz," she slid her hand over Lizzie's and held it, "you need to know a few things right off the bat here. One, Phillip was my best friend, but, goddamnit, I didn't always approve of the way he behaved. Two, Kitty has been charged with his murder. Three, Sandra—our firm—has been retained to represent Kitty. And four, Kitty is his biological daughter."

" 'Cuse me?" Lizzie shouted in an ear-bursting timbre.

People at nearby tables stared at them, but there wasn't much Erma could do about it. She whispered, "Goddamnit, Lizzie, keep your voice down. What I'm saying is that Kitty wasn't exactly fixing to split the sheets with the man."

"I don't believe it. Phillip would have told me if he'd had a kid."

"Just like he told you that he had been married once years ago and never got a divorce?"

Lizzie's face screwed up as she grew angrier by the moment. "That's outrageous. How dare you suggest such a thing."

"I'm not suggesting it, goddamnit. It's true. His wife didn't divorce him and, as best I can tell, he didn't divorce her either. That's why he never married you, Lizzie. He wasn't free to get married."

"This whole thing has got me so confused." She swallowed the last of her martini. Her anger had petered out as quickly as it had come.

"I apologize. I thought you had read the papers. They reported that Kitty has been arrested and that Sandra is representing her."

"Never read 'em. Gave it up long ago. Too scary." She stabbed her salad and stuffed a huge forkful into her mouth.

"At least you ought to feel better knowing that the only reason Phillip didn't marry you was because there was an impediment to his doing so."

Lizzie chewed for a few moments and then swallowed. "Yeah. I would if I knew what that meant."

"That he couldn't legally have two wives."

"Erma? Does this mean I can't inherit anything from him?"

"No. It all depends on the will."

"The will." She stared down into her food. "Erma?"

"Yes, Lizzie?"

"When will we get to see what's in the will?" She raised her brimming eyes to Erma's.

"Uh, soon, Lizzie, real soon. Arrangements are being made to have a reading at Phillip's office." She patted Lizzie's hand. "Soon," she said again, not wanting to admit that she was in charge of the estate.

"Erma?"

"I'm still here."

"Why were you asking me what Phillip and I were arguing about? If Kitty killed him, what difference does it make?"

"Uh, Lizzie, goddamnit, I'm trying to figure out just what happened last Friday."

"You don't think she did it, do you?" She nibbled on one of those tiny ears of corn. Erma thought for a minute that Lizzie might pick it up and eat each row like she'd seen Tom Hanks do once in a movie. From the way Lizzie looked at it, Erma wondered whether Lizzie was thinking the same thing.

"Now, Lizzie, have you ever known Sandra to represent a guilty person?"

"I didn't kill him, Erma, if that's what you're after. If you ask me, if it wasn't Kitty, it was that creep, Bubba."

"Oh. Yeah. All fingers point at Bubba. Now why do you

suppose that is, Liz?" Erma made a production out of cutting her beef and putting it into her mouth. She was trying not to be accusatory. She knew she came across harshly sometimes and wanted to keep Lizzie talking.

" 'Cause we don't like Bubba. Besides, I've seen him eyeing Phillip's watch and ring." She glanced from her empty glass to the bar. "I bet he kilt him and stole it."

"Lizzie, how did you know about the watch and ring?"

"Oh—Stuart told me. Don't you think Bubba did it, Erma?"

"It's a real possibility." She put another bite into her mouth. She figured if it had been Bubba, it was after Kitty had knocked Phillip over the side of the balcony. What a perfect opportunity for a robbery. The victim already has an alleged perpetrator to accept the blame. The victim is the sort of person who, with his demanding behavior, practically asks for it. The perpetrator has an opportunity. What better criminal than Bubba? They needed to find that watch and ring in the worst way if they were to win Kitty's case.

"I don't know who did it," Erma said. "That's what defense lawyers do; they try to figure it out. By the way, where did you go after you left Phillip's room?"

"Me? You don't seriously think—"

"I'm just asking where you were, that's all." Erma sipped some iced tea and watched Lizzie's face. She thought Lizzie was hiding something. She probably would never know what it was.

Lizzie tossed her head but didn't do a very good job of looking haughtily angry at being accused. "Went down to one of the spare rooms. Sandy must have told you that, Erma. She came in there and talked to me on Saturday morning."

"Hmmm. That's all you did? You didn't leave the room afterward?"

"Why would I have done that?"

Why indeed, she wanted to say, but kept quiet. Their eyes met. Erma quickly averted hers.

"I got undressed and went to bed," Lizzie said.

"And stayed in that room all night?"

"I don't like your tone of voice, Miss Erma Townley. You know how upset I get. I—I guess probably I drank too much, that's all."

"Okay, Liz. If you say so." Erma shrugged and motioned to the waiter.

Lizzie picked at her food for a moment. "I still say it was Bubba. That watch and ring are worth a fortune. Besides, how long is a man supposed to put up with someone like Phillip?"

Erma looked at her. "So he didn't treat Bubba right, is that what you're saying?"

"Shit, Erma. You have to know how he treated him. A whole lot worse than he treated Raymond, and I'm sure you've heard of that!" She got up to go back to the food bar. "Bubba had every reason to take what he could and get away."

"And so did Raymond. That doesn't make sense."

"Well, Raymond could have just been mad at Phillip wanting to screw Kitty. Don't you see?"

What she saw was Lizzie pointing the finger at everyone but herself. She sat watching while Lizzie filled her plate with more food than she could ever eat and returned to the table.

"What I see, Lizzie, is a household full of people who may have had reasons to kill the man. Maybe not good ones, but reasons, nonetheless."

Lizzie leaned over her food and shoveled it into her mouth. She wasn't a pretty drunk. Erma wondered if Phillip had been thinking of dumping her for that very reason. Or was she a drunk because Phillip was thinking of dumping her? Those were just a couple of things they needed to discover. She and Sandra had less than a week to try to piece it all together.

Chapter Ten

Although the temperature exceeded ninety and the humidity was one hundred percent, Sandra needed a few minutes to get her thoughts together before she talked with Raymond. Pulling into the Sonic Drive-In on Broadway, she drove around the back and parked as close to the rear as possible. Several other vehicles were between her and the street. Putting down her window, she pushed the button and ordered a hamburger, fries, a Coke, and heaved a huge sigh. When she got home that night, she would scrub her skin until she got every ounce of Bubba breath off her.

On her mental list of suspects, Bubba pirouetted on the top. He had the means: any blunt instrument he could put his hands on in the downstairs of Phillip's house. She couldn't prove he had the modus because she didn't know if he had a criminal history which included assaulting people with instruments, but perhaps if she put a bug in Dennis Truman's ear he'd check Bubba's criminal background. And opportunity. Oh boy. He sure as hell had the opportunity, coming on and off Phillip's property in the middle of the night essentially unobserved. At the very least, she would be able to point to Bubba and yell reasonable doubt, reasonable doubt, reasonable doubt.

When her order came, Sandy breathed in the beef and onion smell before tearing into it, taking a huge bite of hamburger and emptying little plastic packets of ketchup all over the fries. She needed to be careful that she didn't drip grease on her clothing. If her mother saw it, she'd never let her forget it.

Phillip Parker and Associates' offices covered two floors of an 1852 building a block south of The Strand in downtown Galveston. The exterior still looked as it must have when it was built. Sandra parked at a meter, paid for two hours, and hurried inside to the air-conditioning. When she reached the restroom, she darted in, rinsed out her mouth and washed her hands to get rid of the hamburger smell. She never regretted eating them, but she didn't want to wear a sign that advertised it.

Carrying her briefcase like a schoolgirl, Sandra approached the front desk and identified herself. Two young, beautiful, very professional-looking women in their twenties stood behind a tall counter. One offered her a drink. The other got on the intercom. There were two of them, so that the front desk was never left unattended. Sandra declined the drink and crossed the thick carpet to sit on a leather chair. She smiled at the one still watching her when she sat down. Most ordinary defense attorneys would never be able to afford two people to staff the front desk. A tiny bit of resentment surfaced, but she swallowed it and waited for Raymond.

"What are you doing here, Sandy?" Raymond whispered when he showed up. He hurried her down a long hallway and past open doors to his office. "Kitty has called three times from the jail. When are you going to get her out? She's scared to death."

Sandra began to answer as they reached his office but when she entered, she saw Erma sitting across from Raymond's desk like she owned the place. Erma wore one of her regular office outfits, a variation of a black suit, to-wit: a long black skirt, black vest, and black and white polka dot blouse.

"Hello, Sandra," Erma said, as though it was the most natural thing in the world to find her in Raymond's office.

"What are you doing here?" Sandra asked. Raymond showed her the chair next to her mother's, but she stood.

"Well, goddamn, it's a free country. Least last I checked."

Sandra said, "You know what I mean. You should be home, resting."

"Fuck that," Erma said.

Raymond looked at his feet.

Sandra sat in the chair next to Erma and dropped her briefcase on the floor. "What is going on here?"

Raymond said, "Miss Townley came in to set up the will reading, that's all."

"Erma," Erma said.

Sandra studied her mother. She knew Erma was up to something. "So if it's all set up, you can go home. Perhaps you could take a nap this afternoon or at least rest for a while."

"Rest for what? For my own goddamn funeral? If it was up to you, I'd stay in bed until I croaked."

"No, I'm just worried about you. Your heart attack was only a couple of weeks ago, you know. You could easily have another one. There's no reason to work so hard when I can do things for you."

Erma sat up straighter, the toes of her shoes brushing the carpet. "I'm feeling fine." She looked at Raymond. "So, Raymond, when you see Stuart, you'll verify that everything is okay the way I've set it up?"

"Yes, ma'am," Raymond said. "Will Kitty be able to come?"

"That'll be up to her attorney, dear boy," Erma said. "What do you say, Miz Salinsky?"

Sandra gritted her teeth and swallowed. She couldn't help

but wonder what else Erma had been up to all morning. If she was meddling in the case without checking with Sandra first, they were going to have a come to Jesus meeting. She said, "I filed a writ of habeas corpus yesterday afternoon."

"A writ?" Raymond asked. "Why was that necessary?"

"No bail. Think back to your law school days, Ray. Criminal law. Criminal procedure. The constitution and the laws of the state of Texas permit the defendant to post bail, remember?" She had the strongest urge to stick her tongue out at her mother who she just knew doubted Sandra's ability to practice criminal law no matter what lip service she paid to her.

"Oh, right." He looked from Sandra to Erma. "So how come Kitty didn't have a bail set?"

" 'Cause Edgar Saul is a son of a bitch," Erma said.

Before Erma could say anything else, Sandra said, "He talked the judge into not setting one. So I had to file a writ and get a hearing, and Thursday was the earliest I could get it."

Raymond bounced out of his chair as though poked in the bottom by a sharp spring. "Thursday! That's two more days. I don't think she can stand it that long."

"She's going to have to. I asked the undersheriff if he'd have someone keep an eye on her—to treat her nice. She should be okay."

"Oh, my poor Kitty."

Erma rolled her eyes. Sandra gave her a warning glance.

"She'll live through it, I promise. It's unpleasant in there, but it's not life threatening. It just smells bad and the company is not what she's used to."

Raymond looked lost. "She'll never forgive me for this."

The hackles rose on the back of Sandra's neck. "What do you mean never forgive you? What has she got to forgive you for?" God, she wished Erma would leave. She just didn't feel that she could be as effective with Erma hanging on her every word.

He stared at Sandra and then at Erma like he just remembered they were there. "I meant that I should do something. To help get her out."

"Goddamnit, Raymond," Erma said, "if you have something to tell me—us, you'd better spit it out. Right now."

Sandra swallowed hard. She and her mother were going to have choice words later.

"No. No. I promised to protect her, to take care of her. Don't tell anyone this, y'all, but we're engaged. We've been keeping it a secret because she said she had some things she had to work out, but I promised to take care of her always and here she's in jail. Don't you see?"

"Yes, Raymond. So what? It's not your fault." Sandra studied him. "Unless you killed Phillip and are letting Kitty take the rap for it."

His face flushed. "No, no, of course not, Sandra. Miss Townley, you believe me, don't you?"

Erma said, "Erma."

Sandra said, "Then quit with the guilt trip. I'm doing everything I can as fast as I can and, trust me, no one," she looked at Erma, "no one, could do it any better. Now, I came over here to see if you could help me build our defense. If you want to do something, that's what we need most."

"Yes, that's what we need most," Erma echoed.

"All right. Whatever I can do, you name it." His nondescript face held just the right amount of solemnity, but Sandra couldn't help feeling a bit of distrust.

"Tell me—us what happened last Friday night at Phillip's beach house after we left," Erma said.

Raymond put his elbows on his desk and leaned forward, his eyes sweeping from one of them to the other. "I see. You're trying to place everyone."

"Quit worrying about what we're doing," Sandra said, the irritation plain in her voice. "As I was leaving, everyone seemed to be going up to their rooms. Correct?"

He nodded. "Bubba had finished cleaning up around the bar and had fixed himself a plate when Phillip and Lizzie got into an argument. Bubba went downstairs. I don't think he liked to see them fight. I've always thought he cared for Lizzie and didn't like Phillip yelling at her."

"So Phillip was yelling at Lizzie."

"You know how he is, I mean, was," Raymond said. "Especially you, Miss Townley. He hollered a lot. It was his way. Full of bluster. He didn't mean anything by it." Raymond cleared his throat and looked away.

"Like he didn't mean anything by pulling you around by your ear?" Sandra asked.

He cleared his throat again. "You heard about that?"

"Yes, I heard about it. It wasn't exactly a secret when he did it at the courthouse. How could you let him humiliate you like that, Ray? God."

"Aw, he didn't mean anything. You had to understand him, Sandy. He was . . . sensitive and high strung."

Sandra was convinced he was about to cry. She could see that he loved the man, though she couldn't understand it. "Tell me what you admired about him so much."

He shook his head. "I wouldn't know where to start. He was like a father to me. You know how he always referred to himself as the Prince of Personal Injury?"

Erma laughed. "Yes. Prince Phillip Parker. What a mouthful. That was a joke that started probably before you were born, Raymond."

Raymond smiled. "Well, he told me that if I'd stick with him, maybe someday I could be the Duke of Damages."

Erma let out a raucous guffaw. "That sounds like Phillip. He could be so full of shit."

"Erma, please," Sandra said. Not that she didn't think it was funny also. Lawyers and their egos. She cringed sometimes when she remembered she was one. Ridiculous how they did battle to enhance their reputations. Some would spend hours thinking up schemes to make themselves better known. They would compete to see who got the best topic and who wrote the longest paper at continuing education courses. Of course, the other lawyers had to suffer because they had to read their papers and would have much preferred something short and succinct. Well, be that as it may, here she was in conversation with the future Duke of Damages and her not even the Duchess of Defense.

"Okay, so Phillip was going to make you his heir apparent?" Sandra asked. "So for that you put up with humiliation and abuse? Didn't it occur to you that it wasn't necessary?"

"He didn't mean anything by it. It was just his way."

"But Raymond I've seen you. You are such a good lawyer."

His Everyman face actually blushed and, staring at the floor, he said, "He taught me everything I know."

"Bullshit," Erma said. "You're a natural. I've even seen you argue. He may have taught you some things, but jurors find you a likable fellow. You have a way with words. Surely you know that?"

Raymond shrugged. "I guess."

Sandra and Erma exchanged looks.

Erma said, "If someone had ever pulled me down the hall by my ear or nose or hair, I'd have kicked their goddamned butt from here to the ferry landing."

He remained silent.

"Was it worth it?" Sandra asked. "What does it take to rile you?"

"I don't know. Phillip never managed to do it, though. I guess my higher goals stopped me from getting angry." He got up and stuck his hands in his pockets and perched on the side of his desk. "I don't know, y'all. Can we go back to what you came here for?"

They were there. He just didn't know it. Sandra said, "Okay, so Phillip and Lizzie were fighting and Bubba went downstairs. What were they fighting about?"

"I'm not sure. Actually, when they both drank, they did a lot of yelling and screaming. I mostly wouldn't pay attention anymore."

"So were you around a lot? I mean, more than Stuart and other lawyers?"

Erma said, "Yes, he was. Phillip liked to have him around."

Raymond nodded, glum as an undertaker.

Sandra realized that Phillip used Raymond as his whipping boy, and the man let him get away with it. "So you were used to it."

He nodded again. His eyes shifted toward the window.

"You went to your room with Kitty," Sandra said.

"Yes. We went straight to bed."

"And to sleep?" Sandra asked.

His face flushed pink. "Yes. After we brushed our teeth and washed our faces."

"Do you fall asleep quickly?" Sandra asked.

"Usually."

"Did you that night?"

He stood up, wandered around his office, and began picking up things and examining them.

"Ray? Do you have something you want to tell us? Or should I tell you what happened?" Sandra said.

He turned to face Sandra. "What do you mean?"

"Did you follow Kitty up to Phillip's room?"

Raymond crossed to Sandra's chair and took her hands in his. "But she didn't kill him, Sandy. I know she didn't."

"How do you know that?"

"I woke up when she slipped out of bed and put her clothes back on. I guess I hadn't fallen into a deep sleep. I didn't say anything to her."

"Why not?"

"I don't know. I haven't said anything to her yet." He held his hands out in a helpless gesture. "I guess I'm just afraid of losing her. She's the best thing that ever happened to me in my whole life."

"Where did you think she was going?"

He stared at her face, his eyes burrowing into her own. "To Stuart."

Sandra swallowed hard and glanced at Erma. Erma licked her lips and looked as though she were enjoying herself. Sandra said, "Huh. And you didn't say anything?"

"No. I should have, I guess, but . . . well, I don't know. I wasn't sure what was going on and I guess, if she didn't want me, I would just let her go."

"A real man," Erma said.

"So did you follow her?"

"Not really. I waited a few minutes and when she didn't come back, I went to Stuart's room and listened at the door but I didn't hear anything."

"That doesn't mean nothing was going on."

"No. So I went down to the kitchen and got a glass of milk."

Sandra gave him a look.

Erma said, "Goddamn."

"I thought it would settle my stomach," he said to Erma.

"Yeah. So then what happened?" Erma said, staring into her lap. Sandra could tell Erma was trying not to laugh at poor Raymond.

"I heard Phillip. I didn't know where his voice came from, but I knew it was him. Finally I went out to the balcony just off to the right of where he was and heard him cussing and calling out foul things. I looked down and saw him lying on the grass. I knew he wasn't hurt too badly by what he said. He yelled up to someone. I heard him call out Kitty's name so then I figured out she had gone to him, not Stuart."

"What did you do then?"

"I went back to my room to see if Kitty had come back."

Sandra said, "You didn't go downstairs and smash Phillip's face in for saying all those vile things to her?"

"No. I didn't do it, Sandy. Miss Townley. I swear."

Erma said, "Erma."

Sandra wasn't so sure, but he obviously wasn't going to confess right then and there. She remembered Kitty saying she had gone back to bed and then Raymond had come in, but she hadn't gotten any sense of how much later. "Why didn't you go downstairs and help Phillip?"

"He didn't look like he needed any help. And, anyway, Kitty is so high-strung. I knew that if Kitty heard him saying those things to her, she would be upset."

"So you went to her instead?" Erma asked.

"That's right. But she pretended to be asleep when I got there."

Sandra bit her knuckle to stop herself from contradicting him. Kitty hadn't said she pretended to be asleep. She said they'd talked. Why was Raymond lying? "Didn't you think that was weird?"

"The whole thing was stranger than anything. I suppose I should have woken her up—said something to her, but I didn't know what was going on. Damn, I could kick myself sometimes for being a coward. I just didn't want to lose her."

"And why would you care if you lost her?" Erma said. "She got up and left your bed, for God's sake, and went to another man who ended up on the ground cussing her out. Just what the hell did you think was going on?"

Sandra said, "Erma—"

"There's no telling."

"Yes, there is," Sandra said. "And surely you're dying of curiosity. Or has Kitty already told you?"

"I didn't ask."

"Raymond. Raymond. Raymond. You never asked her to explain?" Sandra asked.

"No. I figured she'd tell me when she was ready."

Sandra was having a hard time believing that Raymond was the saint he painted himself as. Would she be able to goad him into a confession? "Did she tell you that Phillip made a pass at her?"

He shook his head again. "No. Is that what happened?"

"Did she tell you that Phillip was her father?" Erma asked.

"What? I knew there was something weird about this whole thing."

"Does that make you mad? That her father would make a pass at her?" Sandra asked.

"Did he know he was her father?" Raymond asked.

"No, not then." Sandra watched Raymond. He still seemed only mildly excited. "But he did when he sexually molested her at age five."

"Oh my God." He collapsed into a chair and practically assumed the fetal position.

Erma looked like a cloud about to burst.

"So she hadn't told you?" Sandra asked. He continued to clutch his stomach and bow his head. "Raymond, you honestly didn't know? Kitty didn't tell you when you came back to the room?"

His head wagged from side to side and a low groan escaped his lips.

Sandra had a theory that it was possible that Kitty explained pretty quickly what had transpired and that Raymond was so angry that he went downstairs and finished off Phillip. She wanted to bounce that off Raymond, but waited a few moments for him to pull himself together. As she did, she studied her surroundings.

Phillip's lower echelon lawyers didn't do too poorly. Raymond's office held a top-of-the-line desktop computer and printer, a rack of legal CDs, and evidence that Phillip spent princely sums on Raymond's continuing education.

So Phillip had cared about his associates. That was interesting. And logical, she supposed. No one wanted an attorney on staff who didn't know or keep up with the law. Perhaps Phillip's firm wasn't as much of a sweatshop as she'd imagined. But just because he paid for nice offices and continuing education courses didn't turn that toad into a prince in her book.

"Hey, Raymond. Don't go comatose on me," Sandra said. "You okay, Erma?" Erma still looked puffed up.

Ray lifted his head. His eyes met hers. He wore his pain like a name badge on his shirt pocket. Instantly she felt an iota of remorse. Maybe he really hadn't known. So how was she to be sure without asking him?

"Is that really true?" he asked, straightening up a bit.

She nodded. "That's the killer, Ray. That's her motive. Revenge. That'll be the basis of the state's case, if they figure it all out."

"They're going to say that publicly? That Kitty killed her father because he had sex with her when she was little?"

"No. They don't know that yet. And I hope they won't. They're alleging he abandoned Kitty and her mother. They say she had plans to blackmail him. When he wouldn't pay and was calling the police, she killed him. And to top that off, they're going to say she stole his watch and ring, each of which was worth thousands."

He bit his lip. "Impossible. He was still alive when I saw him."

"His watch and ring were missing the next morning."

"I was with her the rest of the time. She couldn't have done it."

"You'll testify to that then?"

Raymond's look was the angriest and most direct she'd seen out of him yet. "Of course I'll testify. She needs me now more than ever."

Erma muttered, "You know that they'll say you're giving her an alibi because you love her."

"She didn't do it, y'all. I didn't do it either. You can cross us both off the list of people who could have killed Phillip. Even if I'd known what he had done to her, I wouldn't have killed him. I would have pitied him."

"Oh, for chrissakes," Erma said.

"But Miss Townley, he must have been sick and in need of help."

"For the last time, call me Erma before I punch you in the nose."

"Yes, ma'am. But don't you think he needed help if he did that?"

"Sure, kid," Erma said.

Sandra said, "Okay. Okay. Okay. But do you see our dilemma? You can testify, but I can't put Kitty on the witness stand. They might believe you, but I don't think they'd ever believe her."

His head dropped into his hands. “Oh my poor Kitty.”

Sandra stood and pulled at Erma’s sleeve. “Come on. It’s time for us to go.”

Erma picked up her cane and eased herself to her feet. “We’ll be talking more, boy. And we’ll be taking care of Kitty. Don’t you worry about it.”

Sandra rolled her eyes at the ceiling as she stepped outside the door. “Goodbye, Ray. I’ll be in touch.”

As they walked outside to the street, Sandra said, “Just what do you think you were doing in there?”

Erma coughed. “Setting up the reading of the will.”

“After that. After I got there. What the hell were you doing?”

Erma looked up and down the street as if checking to see whether the coast was clear. “Working on our case. What did you think?”

“Our case? Our case? What made it suddenly our case?”

“You asked me for my help, didn’t you?” She started walking toward The Tremont House hotel.

“Mother, I swear. You know I didn’t intend for you to run all over town trying to find evidence.”

Erma got to the corner and stopped. She harrumphed a bit and then headed toward The Strand. Sandra followed her.

“Where are you going?” Sandra asked. “It’s hot as hell out here.”

“To get my car. I left it with the valet at Petronelli Brothers.”

“I don’t even want to know—well, I’m parked back by Phillip’s office.”

“Well, then, I’ll see you at the office.”

Sandra turned back. “No. You go home and rest up. I’m going to track down Lizzie.”

“Goddamnit, Sandra, I ain’t going home. And if you’ll

meet me back at the office, I'll tell you what Lizzie said over lunch."

Sandra felt as bottled up as Erma had looked earlier. She turned on her heel without saying anything else and quickly strode to her car. She'd be damned if she was going to have a shouting match with her mother right there on the street in front of God and everybody. But wait until they got to the office.

Chapter Eleven

Sandra reached the office before Erma. She had a lot of work to do and no time to fight with her mother. Call her a control freak, but she needed to prepare for any contingency. There were about half a dozen messages on other cases, a couple from Stuart, and one from Kitty at the jail. She saved Stuart's for later, knowing that they needed to talk about the evening's arrangements. Kitty, she could do nothing about. An inmate in jail can't receive calls. Sandra would have to go see her as soon as she could. The remainder she took care of right away, so that she could start outlining Kitty's defense.

Sandra was making notes on a legal pad when she heard Erma's car out back. She hadn't really expected Erma to come to the office, since she hadn't shown up right away. She figured Erma had decided to put off a confrontation. Now, Sandra mentally prepared for one. But when she glanced up, the anger left her. Erma's flushed face and shortness of breath, coupled with her holding onto the doorframe, made it clear that any fight would have to be put off.

"What in the hell—" Sandra rushed over to help her mother. "I told you that you should be home in bed." Leaning down, she draped Erma's arm around her own shoulders and helped her to a chair.

"Goddamn, you didn't expect me to stay home for the rest of my life, did you? We've got a defense to prepare." She shook Sandra's hands off as she reached the chair. "I didn't think the heat would get to me this bad, though," Erma muttered.

"Let me get you some water," Sandra said.

"What I need is another shot of bourbon."

"Another?" Sandra found Patricia exiting the restroom. "Quick, get Erma a glass of water," she said. Turning back to her mother, she tugged at Erma's vest. "You need to get out of these clothes. You've probably got heat exhaustion."

Erma shucked her vest and took the water from Patricia when she returned. She swallowed a couple of sips. Sandra produced a cold, wet washcloth and mopped Erma's brow.

"Don't start looking for my will yet," Erma said. "I'm starting to feel better."

"Mother, really, you are too crass sometimes."

Patricia was fanning Erma with Sandra's legal pad. "Miss Townley, how about I get you a stool for your feet?"

Erma frowned at Patricia. "When did you get here?"

"Oh my God," Patricia said.

"Just kidding." She chuckled. "Just kidding, really. Both of you calm down."

Sandra sighed. "I can't believe you."

"I had to come in, Sandra. I work here, remember? I was going nuts at home." She snatched the washcloth out of Sandra's hand and swiped at the back of her neck with it. "Last time I'm wearing a girdle in the summer."

"Sure," Sandra said, rounding her desk again and sitting down.

"Just give me a few minutes to get my breath." She kicked off her shoes. "Patricia, finished working on those estates?"

Patricia gasped. "Well, if you're sure you are going to be okay . . ."

Erma just stared at her. Patricia tucked in her blouse,

straightened her skirt, and took her dignity back with her to her desk in the next room.

Sandra said, "I had just started writing out some possible scenarios. If I can have that legal pad back." When Erma handed it across the desk, Sandra scribbled out the last one before she completely lost her train of thought. She turned her attention back to Erma.

"What'cha got so far?" Erma pushed her hair off her forehead and then scooted her chair up close to the front of Sandra's desk, where she propped up her feet.

"Okay, you ready? Here goes. First, heat of passion. Phillip didn't know Kitty was his daughter. He had the hots for her—" She glanced at Erma to see if that offended her. He was, after all, her long-time friend.

"Go on, goddamnit. Forget about our relationship."

"Fine." Sandra continued. "She rebuffed him. He got angry before she had a chance to explain why. Then she does explain. He gets even madder—not at her. At himself. He feels stupid, but with his ego, he can't admit he was a fool." She tried to gauge Erma's response. She stared at her, no visible sign of distress. "And then he's embarrassed that this beautiful woman is confronting him about something that he did. To him, it was a million light years ago. Another time, another place. He starts to walk out on her before she's fully had her say. She grabs at him. He yells at her. They struggle and he goes over."

"But we both know he was still alive. He bounced off the grass."

"Yeah. So here's the heat of passion defense. He's really pissed now. He's screaming up at her. He's totally lost it. Calls her horrible things like whore, slut, and cunt. She has just as bad a temper as he does. She runs downstairs and tells him to shut his mouth. He keeps up with the diatribe. She finds the handiest thing and clobbers him over and over until he can say no more." Sandra found herself breathing as though she'd run down a flight of stairs.

"Just like that."

"Yep. Manslaughter."

"What did she kill him with, her purse?" Erma asked.

"Yuk, yuk. All right. I don't know what the weapon is yet. She could have picked up something on her way out of the house. Something in the bedroom? The living room? Or there might have been something downstairs."

Erma shook her head. "Don't let's speculate on that. Hank might be able to help us there."

"Okay." Sandra wrote herself a note to check with the medical examiner on what he thought the killer used to break Phillip's face into bits. "Well, how do you like that one?"

"Possible. If she has as hot a temper as he did. If she had been holding in her anger all these years. But I don't think she's the murdering type. Besides, you may not really be able to walk her with that defense. I can't see that poor girl doing any hard time in the big house, can you? Let's keep that in mind though. What's next?"

Sandra rolled her eyes at Erma's euphemism but held her tongue. "Okay, this one is good, but it has its problems. Self-defense. Same scenario, except Kitty runs downstairs to help him because she didn't mean for him to get hurt."

"I like it," Erma said with a grin. "So what happens?"

"So, Phillip is his usual blustering, bullshitting self and is yelling at her and cussing her the same as before. She gets mad and tells him that she's going to tell the world that he's a child molester. He loses it and gets up and begins choking her. At first, she's shocked that he would try to do such a thing, but she recovers her senses. She grabs the nearest object and beats him in the face with it so he'll get off her. He struggles and won't let go until she has killed him."

Erma got up during Sandra's recitation and began to haltingly pace on the Oriental rug that covered the area in front of Sandra's desk. Erma had bought it with a referral fee from Phillip years earlier and had given it to Sandra as an office warming gift when she and Sandra became partners. She wiggled her toes in the pile as she listened to Sandra.

"You've got some obvious problems there, besides still not knowing what the murder weapon is."

"Yeah, I know. Like no finger marks on Kitty's neck where he tried to choke her," Sandra said. "But by the time we get to trial, that would be the state's problem. If we could get an all-male jury, we might be able to sell it. We could dress her in virginal white, have her wear very little makeup, and leave her hair down. By the end of the trial, they'll all think she's their daughter. By the way, she does have some minor bruising on her arms and wrists where he grabbed her. And I happened to have film in my camera when she came to see me."

"That's good, but I don't like it that she doesn't have any strangle marks on her neck."

"I could fix that if you really want me to."

Erma gave Sandra the look she used to reserve for when Sandra, as a child, had committed an offense. Then they both started laughing.

Erma finally said, "Didn't you say something about his having a separated shoulder? Could he get up and strangle her with his shoulder separated or would that be just too much pain?"

"I thought of that. Maybe he was so angry that his adrenaline was pumping and he did it in spite of the pain."

Erma said, "I'll call Doc Shepherd and ask her if that's possible."

"If she says yes, ask her if we could use her as a testifying expert. We could use a doctor in our defense."

Erma cleared her throat. "Let's hope we don't get that far. Doc Shepherd doesn't like to testify."

"Who does?" Sandra made another note. "This one I don't like at all. Kitty is lying from the get go. She and Phillip have an argument and she bashes his face in while she's up in his room and then throws his body over the balcony."

"I've thought of that," Erma said. "Or what if she isn't really Phillip's daughter and she's trying to scam us. What if she murdered him but is trying to get off and then get his money?"

"Oh, so she's going to get some money from his estate?"

"Never you mind, girl." Erma crossed her arms about her chest.

"Okay. So what if Raymond is in on it with her?" Sandra laughed. "What if Kitty met Raymond and he's hooked on her and she persuaded him that this was a great scheme and that's why he's covering for her and saying that he heard Phillip hollering and saw him on the ground?"

Erma chuckled. "I haven't had this much fun in a long time. I hate to tell you, though. Phillip did have a daughter. And her name was Kathryn Parker. And I'm about positive it's her. But don't think I'm not going to check her out, and soon."

"Well, if we're going to make up stories, I wanted it to be a good one."

"I guess she could have bashed his face in and thrown his body over the balcony. But from what you say, the girl is just not the type. Besides, wouldn't the police have found blood on her clothes, the object she used, and possibly spatter somewhere on the balcony?"

"I like that. If the state tries to say that's what she did, we'll use that against them." Sandra leaned back in her chair and pulled out the lowest drawer in her desk, which she used as a footrest. "Here's a more likely scenario: just as Kitty says, she struggles with Phillip and he goes over the balcony. He's injured and hollering. She runs back to bed and hides. Bubba hears him and goes out there. Phillip verbally abuses him and Bubba sees his chance to make a few bucks and finish the old boy off. He beats in Phillip's face, takes his watch and ring, changes clothes, and drives to the East End to The Cantina and stays until closing. Afterwards, he dumps the clothes and drives around the island and doesn't return until the sky starts turning blue. When he gets back, he raises an alarm and pretends that's the first he's known of it."

Erma leaned over Sandra's desk. "You've been out to see Bubba."

Smiling, she said, "Yes. I guess while you were seeing Lizzie. Bubba's not being real friendly. Or cooperative, either. I'm sure he's got that jewelry hidden somewhere, if he hasn't fenced it already."

"There's a ring of truth to that. I'll never be convinced that Kitty killed Phillip. It had to be someone else. Bubba is a real possibility. Lizzie thinks so, too."

"Everyone seems to think so except the police. Well, we've got Raymond to back up Kitty's story. Or almost. There are a few discrepancies. What did Lizzie have to say?"

Erma settled back in her chair. "She and Phillip had a fight. He kicked her out of the bedroom. She went to one of the downstairs bedrooms."

"That's where I found her on Saturday."

"Phillip was going to have a liaison with Kitty, she thought, anyway. I apprised her of their relationship. She wasn't any too happy to hear that Phillip had a daughter."

"Huh. From a financial standpoint, I'm sure."

"Well, she did really love the man. We know that." Erma pulled out a long brown cigarette that looked like a skinny cigar.

"What are you doing? You're not going back to smoking those again, are you? You are so in denial."

"I'm not lighting it, goddamnit." She stuck it in her mouth and proceeded to suck on it.

"You tell Lizzie what was in the will?"

"Sandra, look, no one is going to know what is in the will until I read it. Okay?" Erma shook her head. "I hate to say this, but I like Lizzie as a backup to the Bubba scenario."

"She's turned into an awful drunk."

Erma said, "She could be a mean drunk on occasion."

"You think she was so mad that she killed him? I thought y'all were friends."

"Has nothing to do with being friends."

Sandra mulled that over a minute. "So, what, she didn't go to her room? Or she went to her room and left again. Maybe went outside for a walk. There was a bottle beside the bed. She could have gone to the bar, gotten the bottle, wandered around the premises drinking from the bottle."

"Saw and heard him fall."

"Lizzie could have killed him then."

"She could have heard him hollering and gone down there and finished him off," Erma said.

"I think it was Raymond or Stuart who said something about all their bedrooms being on the other side of the house. They could only hear the commotion if they were not in their rooms, so she would have had to been out of her room."

"Convenient," Erma said. She sniffed at her cigarette. "We'd have to place her out of her room."

"Sounds like no one was in their room when all this took place, except Stuart."

Erma looked at Sandra over her glasses. "Any of them could have come out of his or her room, heard Phillip screaming to high heaven, seen their chance, and gone down and beat the holy shit out of him." Erma's shoulders hunched up around her ears, her eyes seeming to glow as she stared at Sandra like a hawk studying his prey on the ground below.

Sandra knew what her mother was thinking and verbalized it. "I know I have to check out Stuart. You don't have to tell me." She sighed. She didn't want it to be him, but there was always the slightest possibility. "But Kitty had the most motive. He was going to call the police and try to get her arrested for blackmail."

"Where was Stuart?" Erma asked.

"In his room asleep. He was the one who Bubba told when he supposedly found the body. Stuart was the one who covered Phillip with the blanket."

Erma nodded. "What a mess. Well, one good thing about defense work," Erma said, "is that you don't have to prove who did it. You just have to prove reasonable doubt."

"Right," Sandra said. "This has been fun, but I have a more immediate problem. What do you think the chances are that I can get McWheeter to set a nominal bail?"

"Aw, fairly good. Edgar might bust a gut, but McWheeter can be reasonable."

"I think so, too."

"And he likes pretty women."

"I know you're talking about me, not Kitty." Sandra smiled, glad to be on a different subject. "My next step is the examining trial. I'm hoping I can get the J.P. to make a finding of no probable cause. I can't figure out what they have just yet except Kitty's statement, and all she says—all I let her say—is that he was still alive after he went over."

"If that's all they have, they ain't getting the case referred to the grand jury," Erma said.

"That's why I think they'll have to go through with the examining trial. If Edgar thought he could get away with it, he'd have her indicted the day before the examining trial, but he just can't have enough evidence by then."

"You're hoping."

"Yes, I'm definitely hoping. If she didn't do it, he can't have the evidence."

"Has he got the murder weapon?"

"Not that I know of."

"No witnesses?"

Sandra shook her head.

"Where were the cops working extra duty for Phil?"

"Good question." Sandra wrote that down on the page she had started for questions that needed answering. "I remember Dennis, or it was Jorge Gonzales, saying that one man was down at the station on Saturday morning. I'll have to check that out."

"You know what, Sandra?"

"What?"

"Edgar Saul ain't got nuthin'."

Laughing, Sandra said, "You know what? You're right. Besides her statement, all he's got is a theory. He must be losing it. He must have thought he could get her to confess by charging her with capital murder." She clapped her hands together. "Hot damn. Erma, I look forward to kicking Edgar Saul's ass."

Erma smiled a wistful, small smile. "This case is going to be like taking candy from a baby." She checked out the wall clock. "You going to be free to come with me this evening?"

Sandra straightened up. "Six, is it?"

"Yes." Erma cleared her throat. "I wouldn't mind having a little drink first."

Sandra frowned, but didn't say anything. It just wasn't the right time. "It's almost five. Let's take off." Sandra pushed open the doors that separated her office from the secretary's. "Patricia, you coming?"

"Sure. Where're we going?" Patricia switched off her machines and stood up, making an unsuccessful attempt at smoothing the wrinkles out of her skirt. She pushed the edges of her blouse down under her waistband and grabbed her jacket off the hall tree. Mascara smears under her eyes made her look ghoulish. "We're a little early, aren't we?" she whispered, glancing furtively at Erma who stood near the back door.

"Going to get the old lady a couple of stiff ones first."

"Good idea. I could use a belt of scotch myself."

Sandra followed them out and locked the door. They rode in her mother's black Lincoln Town Car. Sandra got in the back where there was more leg room, since her mother had to pull the bench seat all the way forward. Patricia wasn't tall either, so she got to ride in the front.

Erma took them to 21 Postoffice. Because the martini bar was a block from the 1894 Grand Opera House and only a couple of blocks from the courthouse, it was popular with an upper middle class clientele. It had a three-sided bar, dark booths on a platform, and tiny tables under the windows. Late at night it could be a pickup joint, but early in the evening it was full of white-collar professionals getting loaded before going home.

The three of them slid into a booth. Jake, the bartender, waved and sent a cocktail waitress over. There was no anonymity in Galveston. No secrets. If you didn't want it known, you didn't do it. If you wanted to have an affair and you didn't want everyone to know about it the day after the first tryst, you went out of town. Better yet, out of state. Perhaps even out of the country. And you'd best not fly out of Houston Hobby Airport together, because it would be all over Galveston way before you ever got back to town.

Sandra told Becky, the cocktail waitress and a former child support client of hers, "Give us the usual, but make Erma's a double on the rocks and bring Patricia a scotch."

Erma grinned. "You're sending me mixed messages, daughter."

"I know I'm enabling you, but I'm just making this one exception due to the circumstances."

"Oh, quit with the AA talk."

Patricia laughed behind her hand and swallowed largely when her drink arrived.

Sandra usually drank wine spritzers when out on the town. It took a lot to get high. The weaker, the better. Her mother, bourbon on or off the rocks. Sandra had ordered the rocks as a concession to Erma's doctor.

They stayed in that booth Tuesday evening for almost an hour. Erma got as loaded as one of the cargo ships in the harbor. Patricia came in second. Sandra drove when it came time to leave. She had stretched her one drink over the whole hour, not being anxious to be a cellmate of Kitty's.

"People usually don't appear at cremations," Erma said as they walked out to the car. "It's just not done; the manager told me. But I convinced him that we're not people. A little cash makes a big exception."

Sandra let Erma and Patricia off at the front door and went to park the car. When she got inside, she instantly became depressed. The place seemed like something out of a science fiction movie. Patricia's eyes connected with Sandra's over Erma's head. Neither of them said anything. They were there to support Erma. They walked one on each side, like bodyguards. The manager spoke in quiet tones, like at a funeral. Erma said a little prayer. The rest of the time they stood mute. When it was accomplished, the manager gently ushered them to the door.

Sandra dropped Patricia off at her car. She seemed able to drive okay. Her mother, she drove home and fixed some dinner for, and listened to the ramblings of. Later, she helped her to bed. She knew Erma probably wouldn't stay there. Sandra knew Erma would probably wander around her house like a sleepwalker, as she'd been wont to do since Sandra was a small girl. She'd probably be into the booze and cigarettes before dawn.

Locking Erma's door behind her, Sandra shook her head. It was hard to see people get old and lonely. She walked the five blocks from Erma's house to their office. Although it was close to ten p.m., she wasn't afraid. In the past she would have been, but Galveston had changed and was much safer than it used to be. Besides, the mood she was in, a mugger wouldn't have wanted to meet up with her.

Walking around to the back of the office where she had parked under a tree, Sandra found that one of her friends had left a note on the windshield telling her what bar they were headed to since she wasn't in the office. Moments later, she pointed the Volvo toward the West End of the island and her condo. Her friends would have to party without her. She wished for the middle of the day. It had been beautiful and clear since early morning. She wanted to get out and walk for a while. She wanted to hang her legs over the side of the seawall and feel the gulf breeze upon her face and smell the salt and watch the seagulls and the sandcrabs. Well, she couldn't see the sandcrabs in the dark, but she could sure do the other things.

When she got down to the San Luis Hotel complex, Sandra parked and skirted the cars as she hurried across to the beach. Salt air filled her lungs. Pungent seaweed smells, lightly spiced with that of rotting fish, swirled around her. It might have been offensive to some, but to her it was aromatherapy. Her whole life she had drawn strength from the ocean and all its accouterments. If more than a few days passed without her seeing the waves lap over each other, she felt as though she were in a foreign city. She longed to sink her toes into the sand and her teeth into some local seafood. Perhaps she'd get up early the next morning and take a short run down the seawall. She had been backsliding lately. But right now, just for a few minutes, she inhaled, peace settling around her. She sat on the edge of a rock. Emotionally, she felt overflowing. Breathing deeply a few times, Sandra meditated, trying to focus solely on her breath and put everything else out of her mind.

When she got home, the red light on her answering machine flashed. As she shed her clothes, she listened to a message from Stuart, another message from Stuart, another message from Stuart, a message from her daughter, two from clients, and another message from Stuart.

She put on her nightgown, used the bathroom, washed up, brushed her teeth, and huddled down in her bed. After she called her daughter and told her where her grandmother and she had been, she called Stuart and put him off. Then she pulled the covers up to her chin and fell asleep.

In her dreams, Phillip fell off his balcony. His body bounced on the grass like a basketball. Someone dribbled him. Then they hit him. Over and over. Blood spewed everywhere. Sandra couldn't see the face of the person hitting Phillip because blood had splashed into her eyes. She wiped and wiped, but her eyes wouldn't clear. She could only hear

Phillip shouting and see blood splashing like a breaker on the beach. When she awoke early Wednesday morning, she found that she had knocked her water glass off her night table, drenching her books, her purse, and the covers on the side of the bed. And she still hadn't figured out who had killed Phillip.

Chapter Twelve

Thunderstorms had moved over the island during the night and showed no signs of letting up. It was one of those days when Sandra wished she could call in sick and stay inside, but since she worked for herself, she knew she couldn't get away with it.

Pulling on an all-weather coat, the hood covering her head, she ran out to the parking lot. Strong winds made the rain feel like thousands of grains of sand driving into her skin, and it soaked her before she got to her car. It wasn't as bad as a hurricane, but this was no light shower. Rough, brown breakers crashed onto the beach. Flocks of seagulls huddled on the ground like little old people clutching their coats around them. Traffic crept along, but since the island was only thirty-four miles long from tip to tip, it still didn't take more than fifteen minutes to get to work.

It was Wednesday. Phillip's memorial service would be that evening. If the weather didn't clear by then, the turnout could be disappointing.

After stopping at the office to pick up some files, Sandra went to the courthouse. She was headed to Judge Olsen's court, where she had a child custody hearing scheduled, when Edgar Saul accosted her in the hallway.

"Can we talk?" he asked.

Sandra put her briefcase down and waited. "Sure. You ready to drop the charges on all my clients? Each and every one of them is innocent."

"Cut the comedy, Sandra. I just wanted to inform you that I've decided to let you go ahead with that examining trial instead of indicting your client beforehand."

"If you're talking about Kathryn Fulton's examining trial, that's real big of you, Edgar, since I already requested it and the J.P. agreed."

"Don't kid yourself. You know damn good and well that I could put a stop to it simply by getting the grand jury to indict her beforehand. I just decided that I'd give you a chance to see how weak your defense is."

"Oh, right."

"Sandra, a capital murder trial is very expensive." He waved his finger in her face. "This county doesn't need that right now with all the costs of building a new courthouse—"

"Spare me the lecture on how broke this county is. I take it your reasoning is that if I go through with the examining trial, I'll see how weak my case is and I'll negotiate with your office. Why not go ahead and make an offer right now and save us both a lot of time?"

Edgar Saul licked his lips. He reminded her more than ever of that cartoon wolf with the long snout and longer tongue. "Life?"

"Tsk tsk. See you in court, my friend." She picked up her briefcase and walked away. She didn't know what Edgar's game was but suspected that he knew he didn't have enough evidence to indict Kitty, so he was trying to save face.

In a couple of long strides, he caught up with her. "Now don't go off half-cocked, Sandra. We can talk."

"Not if we're talking time." She wasn't interested in negotiating at all, but she wasn't going to tell him that. It was considered bad form in legal circles not to engage in the negotiation process.

"You'll change your tune as soon as you hear what we've got. Why not talk a deal now?"

"Edgar, please." She pushed him away and pulled open the courtroom door. "The only thing we can talk about now is the time and place of the hearing. If you know that, you can save me a trip to the J.P.'s office."

His face grew grave as he whispered, "Monday at nine-thirty. If you want to talk more, call me." He stalked away. Sandra turned to go inside the courtroom and found the bailiff, who was almost seven feet tall, standing in the doorway, glaring like a linebacker. She knew then why Edgar didn't stick around to taunt her. Ducking her head apologetically, she motioned to the other attorney who sat on a bench with his client. As they went into the conference room, she couldn't help but wonder if there had been something else on Edgar's mind.

They were able to stipulate to a few things on the custody case, but the rest of the trial took the remainder of the day. When Sandra finally got to the jail to see Kitty, it was feeding time, which she always equated to that at the zoo. Since Sandra had to attend Phillip's memorial service that evening, there was no other time she could see Kitty. By promising to stay only a few minutes, she persuaded a jailer to let her inside immediately. Normally they didn't let anyone come in during dinner; that was when they counted heads. All inmates were supposed to be in their cells before they ate.

The jail policy of allowing inmates to shower only once a week made being in close proximity to them for any length of time in the small glassed-in cubicle uncomfortable. Kitty wore the same orange county jumpsuit as the other female inmates and tattered slides on her feet. Orange was definitely not her color. Her face appeared sallow and her skin blotchy. No one got makeup. Her hair was pulled back in a ponytail.

All of her jewelry had been inventoried by the jail sergeant and locked in a safe under the control of the property sergeant. She had been stripped of all her worldly adornments, but her natural beauty was still very much apparent even with dark circles ringing her eyes.

The aroma of ammonia was, that evening, mixed with beef and pinto beans. Sandra caught a whiff of Kitty's dinner before she even got inside. A jailer brought Kitty's tray while they talked. Dinner didn't look half-bad. In addition to the beef patty and pinto beans, there was cornbread, tossed salad, and iced tea. Sandra was hungry in spite of the ammonia smell. She'd missed lunch.

Kitty fussed at Sandra as soon as the jailer closed the door. "I'm not used to being treated like this," she said. "I can't seem to stop crying."

Sandra made soothing noises and explained about Edgar Saul and the examining trial.

"All I want to know is when I'm going to get out of here," Kitty said repeatedly.

"Tomorrow's the hearing on the writ of habeas corpus. You'll be able to post bail as soon as the judge sets it."

"Oh, thank God," Kitty whispered. "You don't know what it's like."

"I can only imagine, Kitty. Listen, we have to discuss tomorrow's testimony. I'll ask you basic questions about your name and address, and then we'll go into your background and your attachments on the island. It's important for the judge to realize that you have ties here and won't skip town."

She nodded. "So I should tell him about my condo?"

"Yes. And Raymond. You'll have to tell him that you two are engaged."

"Raymond told you that?"

"Isn't it true? Are you going to eat that patty?"

Kitty pushed the tray at Sandra. "We were going to keep it a secret for a while longer." She shook her head. "It doesn't matter."

"Okay. How much bail do you think you can make?" The alleged ground beef patty had the texture of cardboard but a familiar flavor.

"How much does it cost?"

Sandra swallowed. "For this charge, if a bondsman will make it, fifteen to twenty percent of the bail. So on a hundred thousand bond, fifteen to twenty thousand dollars."

"Shit," Kitty said.

Sandra thought her anger was at least an improvement over feeling sorry for herself. "Don't you have any more money?" Sandra took another big bite of the meat. She held it with two fingers. It wasn't half bad.

Kitty looked at Sandra holding her dinner and back at her face. Her nose wrinkled up. "I just hate to spend it for something I didn't do. I work hard for my money, Sandy. I don't want to give it away to some jerk who is just sitting back getting fat on my misery."

"That describes it to a T. You must have been talking to the other inmates. How about property other than your condo? Could you put up a property bond? Or if you have the whole amount, like a certificate of deposit, you could put that up without using a bondsman. The county would give it back after the case is over. It's just to secure your appearance for trial, to make sure you don't run." She stuffed the rest of the patty into her mouth and reached for Kitty's napkin.

"I don't have that kind of cash. I have some stocks and bonds, but it could take a while to cash them. I don't think I have a hundred thousand anyway."

Sandra dropped the soiled napkin in her lap. "Tell you what, put pen to paper and see what you can figure out. I'll call Raymond and see what he can raise. The trouble is, we won't know until tomorrow how high the judge will set it. What we'll have to do is tell him how much bail you can make. They're supposed to take that into consideration." She finished wiping her hands and stood.

Kitty sighed as she pushed back her chair.

"What else is on your mind?"

"The funeral's tonight, isn't it? My father's funeral."

"Well, the memorial service, yes. He's already been cremated."

She winced. "I sure want to go, Sandy. Is there any way I could go?"

"Damn it, Kitty. I had no idea." She shook her head. "I don't think I'll be able to catch a judge this late."

Kitty stared down into her beans. "That's okay. That was what I've been calling you for, but if it's too late, it's just too late." She got up. "You want the rest of my food? I'm not hungry now. Would you call the deputy?"

Talk about guilt. Sandra pocketed the corn bread and hurried out to the lobby to call the criminal courts. Every last one of them was closed. On the way to her car, though, she crossed paths with Judge Olsen, the family district court judge who'd heard the custody trial earlier. The judge was in a discussion with two attorneys. Sandra approached and waited until a break came in the conversation, then she not too subtly persuaded the judge, begged the judge, to let Kitty go to Phillip's memorial service. As it turned out, Judge Olsen was planning to go. She accompanied Sandra back inside the courthouse, where they found a prosecutor. The arrangements were made inside a quarter of an hour.

Minutes later, Sandra was back at the jail face-to-face with Kitty. "How fast can you get dressed if a deputy takes you home to change for the services?"

"I knew you'd manage it," Kitty said and threw herself at Sandra.

Sandra was glad to be able to assuage her guilt. Still, she continued to be surprised that Kitty wanted to attend, after what Phillip had done to her. Kitty's personality and motives were apparently a lot more complicated than Sandra had previously given her credit for.

"How did you do it?" Kitty asked, looking tearful again.

"You let me worry about that, honey," she answered. "I'll take care of everything and bill you later. You have anything here in the jail that you need to take with you?"

"Just my purse. It's got my house keys in it. Uh, I'm going to have to come back, aren't I?" She sounded melancholy, but rather accepting of her plight.

"Yes. Right afterward. But we still have the hearing tomorrow. I'm sure we can get a bond set. Don't let your hopes down." Sandra opened the door and approached the desk sergeant. "Did you get word to release Miss Fulton for the evening, Sergeant Hunt?"

He nodded. His job included keeping an eye on the video cameras directed over each entrance as well as answering the phone and allowing admittance to the jail. Sandra liked to watch him work. When his arms moved, they were like that of an octopus under water, flowing around his torso, hovering over the phones and control panels, pushing buttons.

"We'll just need her purse from the property room. She needs her keys."

"Hang on, Miss Salinsky," he said as he took a call. While he was on the telephone, he buzzed a police officer and a prisoner through the sallyport and another deputy through the bars leading to the stairs to the second floor.

When he hung up, Sandra said, "The D.A. was supposed to arrange for Deputy Flores to accompany Miss Fulton home to change and to her father's memorial services. Have you heard from Flores yet?"

He smiled and pressed the buzzer that unlocked the first door to the outside world. "She's coming through now." Sandra watched while Flores shoved the door closed and turned toward the second door, the one made up of thick, paint-chipped iron bars. The huge lock clanked as it unlatched.

Flores was a stocky woman with black hair pinned back in a French twist, hazel eyes, and olive skin. Her short-sleeved tan uniform fit snugly. "Hi, Sandy," she said. "That her?" She pointed at Kitty, who stood outside the interview room.

"Yes, this is Kathryn Fulton." She beckoned to Kitty to join them in front of the cage. "Kitty, this is Deputy Mary Flores. She's a regular deputy sheriff, but she's off duty and we're paying her to accompany you to your place and to the services. Okay?"

Nodding, Kitty asked, "Do I have to go in handcuffs?"

"No, ma'am," Mary said, her chewing gum popping. "But if you try to escape, I'll have to shoot you." She slapped the leather holster that rode on her hip and grinned.

Kitty grimaced and bit her lower lip. The scene would have been funny if Mary hadn't been completely serious. "Well, let's get going before we're late." Sandra turned to the desk sergeant. "Hunt, we'll just need Miss Fulton's purse now, if you don't mind."

He held up a plastic bag with Kitty's purse sealed inside and pushed it through the small opening, together with a release for Kitty to sign. A few minutes later, they arrived at Kitty's house. Kitty quickly showered and changed. They got to Memorial Methodist Church with five minutes to spare. Sandra double-parked along the curb. Deputy Flores parked behind her. A large crowd of people overflowed into the street. They pushed their way through, Flores leading.

Inside, more people milled around the pews and lined the walls. Kitty, Deputy Flores, and Sandra took turns signing the guest book, and Sandra pulled Kitty through the crowd toward the front of the church. Deputy Flores stood at the rear.

It had been relatively quiet when they entered, but Sandra heard voices rise row by row as they walked by, like waves crashing over the breaker line. When they got to the front, Kitty paused and glanced at each side of the aisle. To their left sat Erma, Patricia, Stuart, and Raymond. To their right sat Lizzie with a box of Kleenex in her lap. She wept into a handful of tissues. Next to Lizzie were two of Phillip's other associates, who looked like they wanted to make their escape.

Kitty approached Lizzie and whispered something into her ear. Lizzie's head jerked up like she'd been shot. She rose off the seat as though elevated by a magician. "Murderer! How dare you appear here, you little murdering bitch!" Like a cat, she sprang onto Kitty.

"No! No!" Kitty hollered. "It wasn't me. I didn't kill him. It was—"

Raymond cut her off. At the sight of Lizzie attacking Kitty, Raymond had bounded off the bench and jumped into the fray. He wrapped an arm around Kitty's ribcage and jerked her toward him. Deputy Flores appeared and restrained Lizzie long enough for Raymond to pull Kitty over to Erma and deposit her in between them. Erma wrapped her arms around Kitty protectively, shielding her from view.

Deputy Flores gave Lizzie a talking to and pushed her over so she could sit down next to her on the end of the pew. Sandra squeezed herself across the aisle next to Stuart. The services began as though nothing had occurred. Sandra leaned forward and met Erma's eyes. She wondered whether Erma was thinking the same thing she was. My, my, my, Raymond must have had a reason to be so quick on his feet.

Chapter Thirteen

During the service, Kitty stayed on one side of the aisle. Lizzie stayed on the other. The moment the service ended, Deputy Flores beckoned to Kitty and hurried her down the aisle. Erma hadn't had time to talk to Kitty during the eulogy. She'd barely had time to stand up before Flores whisked Kitty into the waiting sheriff's car. She'd hoped that Sandra would ask Kitty what Kitty had started to say before Raymond dragged her away from Lizzie, but Sandra seemed as surprised as she to find that Kitty was gone.

Erma had been happy to see the large number of people who turned out for the memorial service. She'd never been sure how well-liked he'd been. Since she didn't get out or mingle with the rest of the bar much, she had no way of knowing. And not many people stopped by the office to see her, to visit with her like they had in the old days. Gone were the drinking bouts, the poker parties, and what Sandra called her "Salon." Almost all of the lawyers who came to the office now were there to see Sandra. Erma would be given the cursory hello and the time of day. What the hell, she thought, time moved on. At least she and Phillip used to have their monthly dinners to keep in touch.

So she'd been surprised to see such a large membership of the bench and bar at Phillip's services. She also recognized people from local charitable organizations, civic groups, and the Galveston Chamber of Commerce. A lot of oldsters, retired directors, managers, and board members sitting with their younger counterparts. Phillip would have been pleased. The old fart.

The first speaker was the minister of Memorial Methodist Church. She spoke as though Phillip not only had been a long-term member, but active, being more than generous with his time and money. Subsequent to her speech, the minister introduced Alex Bailey.

At ninety years of age, Mr. Bailey was the oldest person in the Galveston County Bar Association. Erma smiled when she saw him hobble to the front of the room. He had been a great help to her when she'd set up her own law practice. Two other lawyers assisted Mr. Bailey to the podium and took care of his walker until he was through. Mr. Bailey didn't practice law anymore, but still made his rounds to see what was going on. He enjoyed courthouse gossip. Mr. Bailey surveyed the faces before him and said, "You all may not believe it, but there was a time when Phillip Parker knew nothing about the practical aspects of law. Yes, he was book educated, but that was it." He smiled, a gold cap briefly flashing. "I went up to him one day after seeing him founder in a hearing and asked if he wanted my help. The result? You've seen it over the years. He grew into a fine, gentleman lawyer."

Mr. Bailey cleared his throat. "I can see from your faces that you are not impressed. A simple story of a lawyer making good. But let me finish. Later, Phillip Parker represented friends of mine for a lower percentage than the normal thirty-three percent. I can see by your faces, again, that you are thinking that wasn't such a generous act." He laughed, a quiet, gentle rumble. "But I found out later, quite by accident, that the remainder of his fee Mr. Phillip Parker had been donating to the charity my auntie founded in 1932, the children's home."

Erma glanced aside and saw Sandra leaning over to get her attention, her eyebrows raised. She was glad that Sandra was hearing things from others. Perhaps she'd be a little more sympathetic. Erma wiped away the tears that had sneaked down her cheeks. Rummaging around in her handbag, she found a shredded tissue and mopped her face. She'd wanted to be a part of the eulogy but had passed on the opportunity. There was no way that she was going to make a goddamned fool of herself in front of hundreds of people. She had helped put it together, made sure that the people who spoke represented all that was good about her friend, that was enough. Erma felt eons older than she had even at the cremation. A void had opened in her life. Her friend of many years. Her confidant. Gone. Her life would go on, but she would have to work hard not to let the quality of it go down. It would be so easy to give in to the loss. Who would fill the vacancy?

Raymond approached the podium sheepishly. His full eyes met Erma's. Pulling his hands out of his pockets, Raymond read from a piece of paper. He'd told Erma that he could not do it unless he could read. He'd known he couldn't hold himself together. Raymond's tribute was short, telling of Phillip the teacher, who had taken him under his wing and had been in the process of instilling everything he knew about the law, as Mr. Bailey had before him. Erma hoped that she wouldn't have to reconcile Raymond's actions with Kitty with those words of eulogy. She didn't want to, but she could bear it if Raymond was implicated in Phillip's murder.

As they filed out of the church, Erma spotted Bubba at the back. He had cleaned up for the occasion. His spit-shined black loafers were worn down at the heels. His gray polyester pants and striped shirt didn't match. His tie was incorrectly knotted, his jacket needed pressing, but at least he'd made the effort. He turned away when she got close to him, but Erma hollered his name and hurried after him and grabbed him by the elbow as he started down the sidewalk. When he whirled to face her, he tucked a handkerchief into his back pocket. Since it didn't get dark in the summer until past nine, the temperature was still well over eighty. But Bubba had not been outside long enough to be wiping sweat from his brow.

He jerked his arm away. "What do you want, Missus Townley?" he asked, a heavy bouquet of gin assaulting her nose.

Steadying herself with her cane, Erma backed away a step and looked up into his face. "There are some things I'd like to discuss with you, Bubba."

"I said everything I have to say to Miss Sandra and the police. You want to talk to me, you call my lawyer." He sneered as he started away again.

"Okay. Who is your goddamned lawyer, smart-ass?" Erma followed him, but at a distance, hoping he wasn't trying to lure her around a corner and beat the shit out of her.

"Let you know when I get one." His laughter echoed as he ambled down the street.

Erma watched him for a few moments before she got an idea and hollered after him. "Hey, you're in the will, you know."

That stopped him quicker than airbrakes on a Mack truck. He reversed direction and came at her. "The boss's will? How come you to know what's in it?"

Erma stood solidly affixed to the ground. "I represent the estate, you dolt. Who'd you think it would be?"

"And you've seen the will?"

"Seen it, hell. I drew it. I wrote it up, Bubba. Of course I know what's in it. If you'll meet with me, I'll go over the terms of it with you."

"You mean what I got in it?"

"Yes, what you got."

"When?"

There he had her. She hadn't even discussed this with Sandra, and it might not be so ethical, but they needed to act on her idea. No time to waste looking for Sandra to ask her what she thought. Erma looked every which way and didn't see Sandra. Didn't know whether Sandra would go along with her scheme or not. But this was no time to half-step. Sandra had to be in court the following morning for the hearing on the writ of habeas corpus, but as far as Erma knew, Sandra was free the remainder of the day. She smiled up at Bubba. "What say after lunch tomorrow? One o'clock? Our office?" She dug around in her purse for her card case and handed him a business card.

"So you want me to come to your office tomorrow, is that it?" Bubba looked skeptical, but he plucked the card from her hand.

"Yeah, and one last thing I want to know. You want yours in cash or will a check do?"

A grin spread across Bubba's face, revealing teeth that would be every dentist's dream, provided the owner had a lot of insurance. "Either one, Missus Townley. I ain't a greedy man." He made a mock bow, grunted under his breath, and turned back in his original direction.

Satisfied that she had him on the hook, Erma edged back toward the church in search of Sandra. She needed to convince her that she had a workable plan. A few of the people she pushed past stopped to express their condolences. Erma, nodding as she went, headed home when she couldn't find Sandra anywhere. What she needed was a stiff bourbon and a good night's rest. Tomorrow was another day. And tomorrow she'd need her energy to deal with Bubba.

* * * * *

The temperature in the courtroom the following morning would have been enjoyable for a polar bear. As for Sandra, she was extremely uncomfortable. It made thinking on her feet more difficult. The constant complaints from attorneys over the years had caused the judge not only to swear up and down that he had no control over the thermostat as he huddled behind the bench in his robe, but he'd had a sign printed and hung on the wall behind his head that said: DIRECT ALL COMPLAINTS TO COUNTY COMMISSIONERS. Each morning before court began, he instructed the bailiff to open the windows, but the room never got warm.

Kitty wore slides and an orange jumpsuit again. Leg irons lay on the floor beside her feet, yawning open like they were hungry for an ankle.

Judge McWheeter's schedule called for him to handle the felony jail docket that morning. That meant that the deputies had to bring chains of defendants over from the jail. Sandra looked through the narrow window in the side door. From the looks of things, Kitty appeared to be the only female. She sat alone on a bench, the male defendants lined up on several rows in the front of the courtroom.

Edgar Saul sat at the table closest to the jury box. There was an unwritten rule that the prosecution always got that table. Since there was nothing in writing anywhere, sometimes it was a bone of contention between attorneys, but Sandra didn't care to make an issue of it in a non-jury hearing. Kitty was staring at Edgar when Sandra saw her. Fear and something akin to loathing painted Kitty's face. Her expression quickly changed when she spotted Sandra tiptoeing in. Several prisoners and lawyers stood before the judge.

Nodding to Edgar, Sandra slipped past to the holding area

where she could sit beside Kitty. She listened to the proceedings underway with one ear while whispering to Kitty. "Remember what we talked about last night?" Sandra tried to keep her voice down. The judge was good enough to let lawyers speak to their clients in the courtroom. Generally, lawyers didn't abuse the privilege, except for a few jerks, but they didn't do it more than once.

"Yes, ma'am," Kitty replied.

"How was life at the jail last night?"

"Same as always. Awful. It's loud and you can't sleep. The people are so nasty."

"That's the understatement of the century. What did you think of the memorial services?" Sandra watched the courtroom proceedings. Edgar Saul watched them and drummed his fingers on his case file. Usually Edgar was very controlled. Something serious must be preying on his mind. A reporter strolled up and hissed Edgar's name. Edgar rolled his chair to the bar and leaned back. The reporter whispered in Edgar's ear.

Kitty answered her question, but all Sandra thought of was that she had just missed her chance at getting some good pretrial publicity. If the judge ruled against them and if the tide of public sentiment appeared to be against Kitty, Sandra would file for a change of venue to get the case moved to another location. In order to do that, there would have to be some good, prejudicial publicity. Edgar Saul was not stupid enough to make any remarks that would cause the case to get transferred out of town unless he was goaded into doing so. Another time, Sandra could probably aggravate him enough, but in a whispering conversation in a courtroom, never. She watched as the reporter listened to Edgar and nodded. What a missed opportunity for her.

A deputy took away the men who had been standing before the judge. Another deputy replaced him. The judge announced a five-minute recess and left the bench.

The tables in the district courts sat perpendicular to the bench, parallel to each other. Edgar sat on the far side of his table, the jury box behind him. Sandra put Kitty on the far side of their table, her back to Edgar, but facing her. Sandra sat on the opposite side of the room from Edgar but with the same advantage of being able to survey the whole courtroom. After spreading the contents of her briefcase and Kitty's file in front of her, Sandra got a pen and a legal pad. She glanced at the reporter. He winked at her. She nodded at him. The judge returned.

"State of Texas versus Kathryn Fulton. Writ of habeas corpus," Judge McWheeter said.

The three of them stood. The reporter slid into a chair behind the first row.

"State's ready," Edgar said.

"Relatrix is ready." Kitty looked at her. Sandra whispered, "That's what you're called in a writ hearing."

Kitty nodded and stared at the judge. Sandra thought Kitty looked rather angelic.

"Did you want to give some evidence, Miz Salinsky?"

"Yes, Your Honor. The state has recommended no bond. We wish to show the court that the Relatrix is not a flight risk and also to show the amount of money that she can afford to post."

"Any objection, Mr. Saul?"

"Your Honor, the great state of Texas is objecting to any bond being set for this woman. We are most likely going to indict her for capital murder in the death of her father." Edgar spoke in a monotone, as if they charged people with capital murder every day and it was routine to deny them bond.

"I see," said the judge. "Is there an examining trial set, or have you already presented the case to the grand jury?"

"The examining trial is set for next Monday, Your Honor," Sandra said. "In Justice of the Peace Court One. Judge, I need Miss Fulton out of jail to help me prepare for the examining trial. It's only four days. We're ready to show that she is engaged to a local attorney, that she has a residence here, that she can afford to post a satisfactory bond, and next Monday, we'll be asking that she not be referred to the grand jury because there is not enough evidence to indict."

The judge held up his hand. "I'm not interested in what you think is going to happen next Monday. What do you have to say, Mr. Saul?"

"With a charge like capital murder hanging over their head, anyone would be liable to run, Judge. We, the people of the great state of Texas, request you to deny any bond."

The judge frowned at Edgar. "Raise your right hand, ma'am," he said to Kitty. "Do you solemnly swear or affirm to tell the truth, the whole truth, and nothing but the truth, so help you God?"

"Yes, sir," Kitty said.

"Take the witness stand," the judge said. "You two sit down."

When Kitty sat in the witness chair, she turned to face the judge like Sandra had instructed her. She folded her hands on the counter in front of her and smiled demurely.

"Proceed, Miz Salinsky."

"State your name for the record."

"Kathryn Fulton," she said, still looking at the judge. "But everyone calls me Kitty."

Sandra said, "Would you mind if I called you Kitty during this hearing?"

"No, ma'am," she said, her eyes on the judge's face.

The judge rocked back in his chair and smiled at Kitty.

Sandra heard, rather than saw, Edgar throw his pen onto his legal pad. She knew that he knew they'd won. It was only a formality before the judge set a bond. The question was, how high? Sandra continued with her examination for a few minutes before turning Kitty over to Edgar. At the conclusion of the testimony, the judge said, "Bond set at an even one hundred thousand dollars, cash or property. I'll be in chambers." He pushed back in his chair and was gone.

Kitty's face became red as Sandra hurried up to the witness stand. "A hundred thousand dollars, Sandra?"

Edgar picked up his things and slammed out of the courtroom without a backward glance.

Sandra said, "Step down." She motioned for Kitty to come around the stand. "Be glad it isn't cash-only."

"Why so high? I don't understand." The deputy stood tapping his watch.

Sandra gave Kitty a little squeeze and said, "Don't worry about it. I'll be over this afternoon after lunch and we'll figure out something. I promise you'll be out tonight."

The deputy took Kitty by the arm, led her over to the bench, and picked up the leg irons. He didn't shackle her. Sandra mouthed, "Thanks," and nodded as the deputy led Kitty away. Now all Sandra had to do was figure out a way to make that bond before her client got upset enough to fire her.

Chapter Fourteen

Sandra hurried back to the office to catch a bite to eat and see whether Erma had arrived. They'd missed each other after the memorial service. Patricia sat at the kitchen counter. A liver and cheese sandwich on white bread with real mayo sat in front of her. Sandra had no stomach for liver, too much fat and cholesterol. Besides, she thought it tasted like creamed bile and knew why they called it liver worst. Yellow cheese also never crossed her lips. She didn't want her insides dyed. And she couldn't see any redeeming social value to white bread, particularly couldn't see bleaching her digestive system with it. Lastly, she certainly never used anything but fat-free, cholesterol-free mayo.

Sandra stepped into Erma's office to tell her about the bond hearing and caught Erma hiding a glass of bourbon behind a stack of files. Sandra could smell it the minute she walked in the door. It always reminded her of college, when everyone had at one time or another drunk too much and thrown up in the dorm. Sandra didn't say anything, although Erma wasn't supposed to be drinking at all, much less before lunch. If she could just get Erma through the next few weeks, Sandra thought her mother would recover nicely. She'd worry about Erma's drinking when Erma was through mourning. Shaking her head, she went back to the kitchen, pulled open the refrigerator, and rooted around for something to eat.

"How'd the hearing go?" Erma asked.

There was some wilted zucchini, a few leftover slices of onion, a potato, broccoli, and lowfat, low-cholesterol mozzarella cheese. Enough to make a meal. "Hundred thou, cash or property." Sandra pulled out the wok and set about making lunch. "Pissed off Edgar."

"I'll bet. That old S.O.B. Can Kitty raise that much?"

"I don't know, Erma. Get a couple of plates out."

"I'm not eating that. I'll have the leftover tuna," she said. "I need to talk to you about something."

Erma got a plate for Sandra. She took the bowl of leftover tuna salad out of the refrigerator and some crackers and walked around to the other side of the bar, where she hiked herself up onto a barstool next to Patricia.

Patricia quietly munched away. They had long ago declared a truce over discussing any of the weird things that each of them ate. Sandra smiled at Patricia. Her blouse pulled loose at the waistband and hair mussed, mayo smeared next to her mouth, Patricia was a sight. Sandra also knew Patricia was covering for her mother. It made Patricia very nervous, so she usually kept a low profile. Sandra shook her head but didn't say anything as she watched Erma use crackers to shovel tuna into her mouth. At least the old lady was eating.

"So what is more important than getting our client out of jail?"

"Bubba's coming over here in a few minutes," Erma blurted. "I made him an appointment with me so you could search his apartment while I kept him here. I told him that he was in the will."

"Tell me you're lying. You want me to go search his apartment? That's burglary of a habitation." Sandra stirred the vegetables in the wok.

Erma smiled. Tuna fish clung to her front teeth. "Not if

you don't get caught." She pulled a paper towel off the roll and wiped her face. "The more I think about it, Sandra, the more I'm sure he stole that watch and ring off Phillip's body. If you can find it and turn it over to Edgar Saul, not only might the state lower the charges against Kitty, but they might drop them altogether if they think Bubba did it." Erma's eyes beamed like she'd just won a major prize on "The Price Is Right."

"Yes, and I could go to jail on a first-degree felony."

"Um, I'm not sure it's burglary if you have a key given to you by the executrix of the estate. You could always say you were inspecting the premises for me prior to his vacating."

"You have a key to Bubba's apartment?"

"Of course, my dear. I have keys to everything, including Phillip's safe deposit box."

Sandra grimaced. "I'm not in the habit of breaking the law."

"Goddamnit, quit acting so high and mighty. Just go search the place."

Sandra scraped the vegetables onto a plate and shredded some mozzarella cheese over them. A quiver of excitement flushed through her, but she didn't want Erma to know it. She took a bite of her food and sprinkled more salt on it. "I don't know, Erma."

"Look, all you have to do is drive out there and search. I'll keep him here. No one else will be there, I can assure you. What could happen?"

"Is this how you used to practice criminal defense law?"

"Sandra—"

"But to tell him he's in the will—"

"Well . . . I'll give him a little something. He'd never know the difference. Say a thousand or two?"

"You would give him two thousand dollars?"

"Me? Well, I suppose we could take it out of Kitty's fee."

"Yes," Sandra said. "Your half."

"Ha ha. I'm sure that if you find the watch and ring, Kitty will be more than glad to give us a couple more dollars. So you'll do it?"

"So Bubba's really not getting anything under the will?"

"The reading of the will is tomorrow, Friday, at ten-thirty in the morning. You know that."

"Shit, Erma. I'll do it, but you have to keep him here long enough for me to get out there and really conduct a search. I'm not going if I only get a few minutes. And if I get caught, you're going down with me."

"Oh, I'm sure everything will be all right," Erma said.

Patricia's eyes had grown wide during the conversation. As soon as she could stuff the rest of her sandwich down her throat, she slipped off the barstool and left the room.

"Okay. I don't care if you give him any money or not, but stall him here long enough that he doesn't come back and catch me. I'd hate to see what Bubba would do to me. The idea of his even touching me. Yuck." Sandra glanced at her watch. She had just enough time to finish eating and get away from the office before Bubba got there, not enough time to play any more games with Erma.

After a few minutes of silence, Erma said, "I didn't mean to lie to the man, Sandra. I just needed some excuse to get him away from the apartment. It's not like you have all the time in the world before the examining trial."

Sandra frowned. "I don't like being used in your schemes."

"No. Only your own."

"I would just like to win this case with a good defense," Sandra said.

"Yeah, wouldn't we all, Sandra, but it doesn't always work out that way."

"Just make sure that I have a good fifteen minutes search time. If I can get there before he gets here, that'll take about twenty minutes, then at least fifteen minutes to search." She pushed her plate away. She couldn't eat any more. "Just keep him here thirty to forty-five minutes. Jesus, I hope you can do that." Sandra jumped up and dumped her plate in the sink. "I've got to get out of here now." She was angry, but she'd have to worry about that later. She quickly used the restroom, yelled goodbye, and removed the apron.

As Sandra reached her car, Erma stuck her head out the back door. "By the way, don't forget the key."

Sandra caught the key ring and saluted as she slid into the car. Erma saluted her back, but it wasn't the Girl Scout salute.

As Sandra pulled out of the alley, she saw Bubba parallel parking Phillip's BMW. She knew, if anything, it would be a close shave for her to get down the island and complete the search before he returned. She silently prayed for Erma to come through for her.

To save time, Sandra skipped Seawall Boulevard, which at any given time in the summer is not much quicker than crawling because of the tourist traffic. Instead, she headed for Stewart Road, named after Maco Stewart, a county commissioner back in the 1950s. He had been big into beach development—hence, Stewart Beach and Stewart Park. She followed Stewart Road until she had to cut over to the entrance to the subdivision.

Patricia came into the back of the office where Erma was cleaning up the kitchen. "There's a man at the door. I haven't unlocked from lunch yet. Want me to let him in?"

Erma stood in her stockinged feet and wore an old embroidered apron over her black dress. "It's probably Bubba. Let's let him wait a few minutes. Sandra hasn't been gone more than a moment."

Patricia turned away. "I don't want to know what's going on. Just holler when you want me to let him in."

Erma chuckled. She knew Patricia relished the goings-on in the office but felt insecure. "Okay. Keep an eye on him." She dried off the last plate and put it away. She wiped the counters and the stove and removed the apron. The doorbell rang incessantly. Stopping in the restroom on the way to her desk, Erma peed and washed her hands. Checking her face, she rubbed at the shiny spot on her nose and applied a very red lipstick. She fluffed her hair and picked some lint from the apron off her dress. The doorbell had stopped before she was out.

Patricia called, "He's leaving, Missus Townley. What do you want me to do?"

Erma jerked open the door. "Run after him! Quick! We can't let him get away." She heard Patricia's footsteps on the wood floor and the key turn in the lock. Patricia hollered. Erma, still only in stockinged feet, hobbled down the hall toward the front door, careful not to slip. It was ten after one. When she got to the stained-glass front door, which stood open, she could see Patricia standing in the parking lane on Broadway and waving her arms. From the top of the porch, Erma could see the rear end of the BMW driving through the break in the esplanade.

"Goddamnit!" Erma said. There was no way he wouldn't catch Sandra if he went straight back home. If traffic hadn't been coming from the other direction, she would have told Patricia to run across the street. "Did he see you?"

"I don't know." Patricia breathed hard as she climbed the five steps up to the porch where Erma stood. "Can you still see the car?"

"Yes. Wait." She trotted to the end of the porch. "Patricia, look, he's coming back! All right! He must have seen you. Good girl."

Patricia smiled. "Thanks, Missus T." She tucked in her blouse and straightened her skirt. "I need a drink of water."

"I'm going to my office. Let him in as soon as he comes up the stairs." Erma hurried inside to her desk and put on her shoes. When Bubba got there, she stood as if nothing out of the ordinary had happened. "Hello, Bubba. Come in."

"I thought you was closed." He stood in the doorway and stared at her.

Erma rounded her desk and showed him to a chair. "No. I apologize. I was in the ladies' room."

"I musta rung the doorbell fifty times." Bubba sat down in one of Erma's leather chairs. He wore a T-shirt, shorts, and thongs. He removed his sunglasses and frowned at Erma.

"Again. I'm sorry. We have lunch in the back sometimes and can't hear the bell. Anyway, you're here now. Was it a nice drive from down the island?"

"Yeah, it was all right. Lots of tourists."

Erma nodded. "That's to be expected in the summer. Did you take the seawall?"

"Yeah. I guess it would be faster if I didn't, but I ain't in no hurry. You know what I mean?"

Erma thought she did. He was still on Phillip's payroll until she told him different. Besides, she could imagine him trying to use Phillip's BMW to pick up girls on the beach. It might work if he wasn't the one inside the car. "Yes. That's something we'll need to talk about, Bubba. How do you see your future now that Mr. Parker is dead? I mean, do you have any plans?"

His eyes darted from left to right quickly, like he was watching a Ping-Pong match. "What do you mean?"

Erma pulled her chair closer to her desk and sat taller. "You understand that you can't stay out at the beach house forever, don't you?"

Bubba hit the back of the chair as if he'd been struck. "Oh." He looked for a moment like he might cry. "What's going to happen to the house, Missus Townley? Maybe whoever gets it will let me stay on. I mean, I guess Mr. Parker didn't by any chance give me the house in his will?"

The heirs and legatees of estates never ceased to amaze Erma. Bubba certainly was no exception. Greedy was the best way to describe them. She'd have laughed at the ridiculousness of his question if it hadn't been so pathetic. Shaking her head, she said, "No. He did not leave you the house."

"So that's what I'm here for, right? For what he left me? And now you're telling me I have to get out? Am I understanding you right?"

"More or less."

"But I'm getting something."

"Yes. The official reading of the will is tomorrow. Then I'll file it for probate."

"I thought you said you was going to give me what I got today?"

Erma cleared her throat. "Well, if I gave you that impression, I apologize again. Oh, I am doing a lot of apologizing to you, aren't I, Bubba? By the way, would you like a cup of coffee or something else to drink?"

Bubba glanced all around him. He looked over his shoulder across the hall through the open doorway to Sandra's office. "Where's Miss Sandra today?"

Erma shrugged. "Probably at the courthouse. Is that a yes? You want coffee?"

"I don't want nothing except what's coming to me, you hear?"

Erma could feel his impatience growing. She needed to keep him there as long as possible but was running out of ideas. "I understand, Bubba. I did review the will before you came in this afternoon. Mr. Parker has left you a sum of money which I, as executrix of the estate, will be authorized to pay to you."

"So what's stopping you, Miss Townley? Let me have it."

"Yes. Well. There are some conditions attached, Bubba."

"Is something going on here? Are you trying to trick me or something? Why don't you just give me my money and I'm outta here?"

Erma lectured him about his impatient behavior and then said, "I'm authorized to give you an advance today."

"An advance? Not all of it?"

"No. There's the reading of the will, as I mentioned."

"Okay, so I'm supposed to go there?"

"Would you be available to go there tomorrow at Mr. Parker's office?"

"If I have to. How much can you let me have today?"

"Well, Bubba, it's not exactly kosher, but I can advance you the sum of five hundred dollars out of my own account. How would that work for you this afternoon?"

"I don't know what you mean by kosher, but I'll take it." He stood. "Right now, Missus Townley. And no, I don't want nothing to drink or eat. Just give me my money. We can talk about everything else tomorrow at the will reading."

Erma looked up at the man. In spite of her decades of dealing with the worst sorts of people, he did seem a bit menacing. She glanced at the clock above the bookcase behind him. Sandra had better hurry. "Let me just get my checkbook," she said. Pulling open the bottom desk drawer, Erma got out a binder of business checks. She made a production of cleaning her glasses before writing out the check.

"Come on. Come on," Bubba said.

"My, you are in a hurry," Erma said and smiled. Carefully making the notation on the check stub, Erma looked up at him before writing out the check. "You understand that this amount will be deducted from the final sum that you are left in the will?"

"Of which you still haven't told me."

"Yes, well, I haven't told anyone the contents. Tomorrow is soon enough, don't you think?"

Bubba snorted. "Just get on with it."

"And so I should make this out to you in your formal, birth name?"

Bubba shrugged. "Make it out any way you want. I'm taking it to a bank to cash with my driver's license right away."

Glad to hear that, Erma couldn't think of any way of stalling longer. She wrote out the check as slowly as she thought she could get away with, tore it out, and handed it to Bubba. "You may take it to my bank for cashing if you like. It's printed on the front."

"Don't you worry. I'll find a bank. I'll see you at Mr. Parker's office bright and early tomorrow morning, Missus Townley. I'm outta here."

As soon as the front door slammed shut, Patricia came into Erma's office. "Think I should call and warn her?"

"Yes. I think he suspects something. Tell her to get the hell out as fast as she can."

Patricia picked up Erma's phone and punched in Sandra's cell number. It rang and rang. "Voice mail, Erma."

"Hang up and try again."

Patricia hit end and talk. After several rings, voice mail came on again. And again. And again.

Chapter Fifteen

Parking in the driveway at Phillip's house, Sandra hopped out and hurried to Bubba's apartment. The door was locked, but after a few tries, she found the correct key on the ring and threw open the door.

She'd never been in Bubba's apartment, a large one bedroom. Clearly Phillip had provided the furnishings, which ranged from a black leather sofa and solid wood coffee table to an iron queen-sized bed. The place resembled a pigsty and smelled like the inside of a septic tank.

Dishes overflowed the sink. Several grocery bags of garbage sagged near the front door. Mold was growing on the outside of the refrigerator. Empty, smashed beer cans and cigarette butts decorated the tabletops. In the bedroom, layers of filthy clothing covered the chair and floor. The sink and tub hadn't been scrubbed in a month. The toilet needed flushing in the worst way.

Sandra searched the chest of drawers and the dresser first, fervently wishing she could open a window or put a clothespin on her nose. Nauseated, she knew if she had more time she could vomit her guts out.

Although Bubba had plenty of space to store his meager belongings, most stood empty. It didn't take long to find nothing in his drawers, except for a loaded .45 semi-automatic, some new pajamas still in their plastic wrapper, several unmatched socks, and a red, cowboy-type handkerchief.

His closet was next. Sandra ran her hand along the top of the shelf and found a brittle roach body and dust. The pockets of the few articles of clothing on hangers gave up nothing but some matchbooks. The hems of the jackets and cuffs of the pants contained nothing. Same with the drapery hems. Nothing dropped out of his shoes when she held them upside down and shook. In a way, she was relieved.

Next, she searched the pockets of garments that carpeted the floor. Afterward, she searched the medicine cabinet. She tried to leave everything the way she found it so as not to arouse suspicion. It was difficult. She had an inclination to neaten up the place, the opposite of what usually happened when someone ransacked a joint.

Finally, Sandra shook some men's magazines, but nothing fell out except the earmarked centerfolds. She seconded her mother's inclination that Bubba had stolen the watch and ring and felt sure they were in his apartment someplace. Glancing at her watch, she saw that her fifteen minutes had expired.

Standing in the middle of the apartment, Sandra could see nowhere obvious. She had searched the normal places like the ice trays, looked for canned goods with fake bottoms, and even taken a screwdriver to the switch plates to see if there was a hiding place behind them. Nothing.

A folded slip of paper sat under a beer can on the coffee table. She pulled it out, not expecting to find anything and didn't think she had. It was only a name. Jerry Fulshear. And a time. Noon. Both printed in blue ink, the lettering neat, like a teacher's. It didn't ring a bell with her, but she wrote it down and put the paper back under the can. Continuing her search in the kitchen, Sandra came across a blank note pad next to the phone. The paper was the same size as the piece under the can. Perhaps that was significant.

She knew she had to get out. She felt it in the pit of her stomach. She had stayed too long and risked getting caught. She couldn't imagine what Bubba would do if he found her in his apartment. He wouldn't call the police, that was for sure. What he would probably do was beat the holy crap out of her. He knew she wouldn't call the police. She'd have to confess that she had burglarized his apartment. There was also the possibility that Bubba would kill her. She didn't want to end up like Phillip, with her face smashed off.

Sandra had gone outside and was locking the front door when she heard her cell phone. The ringing was not loud. She wondered how long it had been going on. She finished locking the door and ran to answer it.

Patricia screamed, "Get out of there, now!"

"Patricia?"

"Now!" she hollered. "Back that son of a bitch up and get out while you can. Mr. Carruthers is on his way!"

Sandra's shaking hands found her keys and managed to insert the ignition key into the right hole and twist it. Slamming the car into reverse, she backed into the yard, over Phillip's beautiful Bermuda grass, leaving tread marks for the yardman and Bubba to fret over. Patricia was still screaming into the phone, which Sandra held between her ear and the crook of her shoulder. Sandra could hear her, but there was no way at that time that she could have answered her.

Patricia said, "He was furious when Erma told him that there would be no reading of the will until tomorrow. She tried to get him to sit down and have a cup of coffee, but he kept demanding to know what Mr. Parker left him."

Sandra threw the gear shift lever into first, gunned the engine, spun the tires, and tore back up the oyster shell driveway until the tires hit the pavement. She didn't dare go back the way she'd come. If Bubba was on his way out, they'd pass each other. There was no way she wanted a confrontation with him either on foot or in a vehicle when she was alone, down the island where it was desolate, where no one could help her if she needed it. She might have agreed to burglarize his house, but she wasn't completely crazy.

Patricia said, "I've never seen someone so mad that your mother couldn't calm them down with that sugar and spice way of hers. She started getting her back up. She told Mr. Carruthers that all the years she had known him, she had never seen him behave like that and what was his problem. I hope you're getting out of there, Sandy. Sandy? Are you listening?"

Sandra turned right. In her rearview mirror, she could see the dust from the shells she had run over, and a faint view of the front end of a car. A trickle of perspiration ran down her forehead. She pressed the accelerator to the floor. Whether it was Bubba behind her or not, she was getting the hell out of there. It looked like the front end of a BMW. Never was she so thankful that she had splurged and bought that five-speed turbocharged Volvo S60 than at that moment. As she peered behind her, she saw that the vision of the car had disappeared, but she didn't slow down. She wasn't sure what was going on, but she kept driving until her hands quit shaking and her knees quit knocking.

Sometime or another, the phone had tumbled from her shoulder into her lap and Sandra hadn't noticed. Picking it up, she listened. Silence. She hit end, dropped it back into her lap, and continued driving toward the end of the island. No way was she going back by the turnoff to Phillip's house. She paid the dollar toll on the San Luis Pass Bridge and kept going toward Freeport. It was the long way around, but she drove it. Through Surfside without getting a ticket, which is a feat unto itself, around on the farm-to-market roads, she arrived at Highway 6 on the way back to the island some hours later after she had stopped for gas and to pee—not necessarily in that order.

Finally, she reached the office. Patricia yelled at her for not calling her back. Her mother was also quite put out. More aptly described as madder than hell. They thought that Bubba must have caught her and beaten her to a pulp. Erma had been heavily into the liquor cabinet. Sandra could tell.

After she calmed her two mothers down, Sandra described the apartment to them. Erma was not a happy executrix. "Tomorrow afternoon, that son of a bitch will be out of there," she said. "And a cleaning crew will be in on Monday. So did you find the jewelry?"

Shaking her head, Sandra said, "I can't think where he could have hidden them. I searched as well or better than an evidence cop. The only thing I found and I don't know who it is, is this." She pulled the crumpled piece of paper out of her pocket and handed it to Erma.

Erma studied it. "What's it say?"

"Jerry Fulshear. Put your glasses on," Sandra said.

"The fence?" Pulling her glasses up by the chain that hung around her neck, Erma held them in front of the piece of paper. "Jerry Fulshear. Noon. What do you know about that? I thought Fulshear was history."

"So he's a fence?" Sandra asked.

"Was, back in the old days," Erma said. "Was a client of mine. Must be seventy years old by now. Represented him in, let's see, the sixties or seventies—Patricia, look in that old card file." Erma smiled at Sandra, quite pleased with herself, while they waited for Patricia to return.

Sandra smiled back. So Bubba had met with, or was going to meet with, a fence. My, my, my.

Patricia returned with a five-by-seven card. "You first represented him in 1964, receiving stolen property."

Erma said, "I knew it. Let me see that."

Patricia handed the card to her. Sandra could see it from where she sat, and it was covered with entries. He'd been an active client. That meant that Erma had known him well.

Erma turned the card over and looked at it. "Last time was in 1989. Looky here, the son of a bitch still owes me two thousand dollars. I wondered what ever happened to him. Humph."

"Looks like we're going to have to find out," Sandra answered. "And soon."

"Now that you're back, I'm out of here," Patricia said. "You two may not have a life outside of this office, but I sure do."

Sandra wanted to say, "Sure," but didn't. She and Erma both wished Patricia goodnight and remained silent until she'd gathered up her purse and jacket and fled out the back door, locking it behind her.

"In the meantime," Erma said, breaking the silence, "what do you propose to do about Kitty's bail?"

"She can't make the cash," Sandra said and shrugged. Erma had obviously been at the bottle for the few hours she had been driving around two counties. "Why don't you let me take you home and put you to bed? Tomorrow will be an eventful day for you."

"And you don't think I can handle it?" Erma asked, her words slurred.

"Well, no—"

"I want to hear what you intend to do about Kitty."

Sandra rolled her eyes. "What's this about?"

Erma smiled. She looked like the Walt Disney version of Dopey of the seven dwarfs. "I already did it, that's why."

"You already did what?" Sandra was worried that Erma was going to wobble right off that barstool in the kitchen, but she kept right on sitting on the opposite side so she could see Erma. Sandra hated talking to people next to her. It was one of her pet peeves. How could anyone communicate with anyone when they couldn't look him or her in the eye?

"While you were out gallivanting all over the island, I was busy making Kitty's bail."

"I thought you were talking to Bubba."

"After Bubba."

"I thought you were busy being worried about me. I could have had the snot kicked out of me. You didn't go over to the jail drunk, did you? God, what would that do to our reputation?"

"You must think I'm crazy, Sandra," Erma said.

"You have your moments. Now what are you talking about?"

"I called the sheriff. I told him I'd make the bail. As we speak, Raymond has taken her home, poor girl."

"No shit? You really made her bond?" Sandra was truly surprised. "Sheriff Johnson took your word for it?"

"No, silly. That would be illegal. Had property posted for years. Used to make bonds all the time when you were little. Just used that. Besides, she's good for it. After Bubba left, and after Patricia got you on the phone, I went over there and got her out. I called Raymond to take her home. Then I came back here and had a few drinks. Ha ha ha."

"Yeah. You trust Raymond?"

Erma grasped the edge of the bar and reached toward the cabinet where Sandra had put the bourbon bottle when she had returned from Bubba's. Erma had a bad habit of finishing off opened bottles. She and Sandra had discussed that propensity, but Erma didn't care. She used to like vodka and rum as much as bourbon, but not anymore. Bourbon made her feel the best so bourbon was what she drank most of the time. "Much as I trust anyone else. Seems like a good boy." She stretched her arm out but couldn't reach. She'd have to get up or ask for help. Sandra doubted that Erma would do the latter.

"Goddamnit, Sandy, what'd you do that for?"

"I'm really confused here, Mom. Just a short few days ago you thought Kitty was a cold-blooded killer and today you make her bail. Am I getting mixed messages, or what?"

"That poor girl couldn't hurt a fly."

"That leaves Bubba, Lizzie, Stuart, and Raymond."

Erma nodded. "And the cop. You going to give me that bourbon or not?"

"I think we can safely rule out the cop who was there for security. Remember what the doctor said? Are you supposed to drink so much?"

"Fuck the doctor. And we can't rule out the cop until we know something about him. Didn't you tell me that Lieutenant Truman sent that cop to the station as soon as the lieutenant arrived on the scene and figured out that Phillip was dead?"

"My, my, my. Such language for a woman of your age and delicate sensibilities. Don't you remember the reading of the will is tomorrow? You want to look and feel your best, don't you?"

Erma held onto the counter and tried to pull herself and her barstool in the direction of the cabinet. Sandra tried to figure out why Erma didn't just get down off the stool and climb up on the next one. Probably not thinking clearly—alcohol fuzz.

"You didn't answer me," Erma said. "Did he or didn't he send the cop to the station?"

"He did. And do you or don't you?" Sandra didn't wait for Erma's answer. "What say I get you one last drink and then we go to dinner and then we both go home so that we can be fresh for the reading of the will tomorrow? I know you know what is in the will, but I don't. I'm quite excited about seeing what the old boy did with his money."

"What the shit," Erma said. "If it'll get me out of this delicate position, I'll humor you." Her knuckles had turned white from holding on to balance herself.

Sandra got up and went to the other side of the counter. Erma's stool stood on two legs. It wouldn't take much to send it and Erma crashing to the floor. Sandra steadied the stool onto all four legs so that Erma could rest her weight back on it. She retrieved the bottle and poured two fingers into Erma's empty glass. Recapping it, Sandra placed the bottle in the cabinet next to the refrigerator on the top shelf, out of Erma's reach whether she was on a barstool or standing on the floor.

"I'm glad you have such faith in Kitty now, Erma," she said. "You were hesitant before, I know, but I'm happy you've had this change of heart."

Erma shrugged, downed the bourbon, and slid off the barstool. "Let's go eat."

Chapter Sixteen

The following morning, Sandra phoned Kitty to arrange to pick her up. At dinner the night before, Erma told how she'd verified that Kitty was who she claimed to be and would need to be present at the reading.

Erma amused Sandra by observing all the formalities, like in the movies. Usually in real life whoever found the will read it and took it to a lawyer's office to see what to do with it. After it was probated, the executor had certain rules to follow under the lawyer's supervision.

Sandra recognized Raymond's voice when he answered Kitty's phone. "Hey, this is Sandra. What are you doing there?"

"I came to take her to the office."

"I'll accept that," she said. "I was calling for the same reason. I'll meet y'all there in fifteen minutes, at a quarter after."

As Sandra drove down the boulevard, gray clouds moved in from the Gulf. Choppy, olive drab waves splashed on the sand. A few surfers paddled in designated areas. Several kids wheeled around on rollerblades and pedaled fringed surreys dangerously close to the seawall. Wall-to-wall cars lined the parking zones. People lay on beach towels and sat in chairs in the middle of the sidewalk.

At Phillip's law office, it was standing room only. Lizzie sat in a leather armchair. She wore a green pantsuit and layers of gold chains. Her neatly coifed hair looked like it wouldn't move even in gale-force winds. To see her was to believe that she was a wealthy woman, perhaps worth half a mil or more. Sandra imagined Lizzie hoped she'd receive enough money for it to be true.

Bubba stood by himself to one side of the others. Sandra avoided his gaze. She didn't know whether he knew she, or anyone, had been to his place but didn't want to invite conversation.

Raymond hovered over Kitty. He wore his normal nondescript blue pinstriped suit, pinstriped shirt, plain blue-and-gray tie, and black loafers. Sandra wondered whether Raymond had a closet of identical clothes. It also occurred to her that maybe, after the events of the last week, he'd break out and become more of his own man.

Kitty, however, looked stunning all in white, from the toes of her spiked-heel sandals to her pearl jewelry. Her carefully made-up face hid everything except the black circles that looked like they had been brushed on under her eyes.

Stuart stepped through one of the side doors into the reception area where they waited. He wore a double-breasted tan silk suit, snakeskin boots, mauve shirt, and matching tie and handkerchief. Sandra thought he looked distinguished and handsome, though from the smoky color of his eyes, she had the feeling that he was angry with her. He nodded in her direction.

"About time you got here," Erma said in a loud voice. All eyes turned to Erma, and from Erma to Sandra. She stood between the reception area and the hallway that led to individual law offices.

"Were you speaking to me, ma'am?" Sandra asked.

As hot as it was in the summertime in Galveston, her foolish mother had worn a long-sleeved, two-piece black wool suit and a gray long-sleeved blouse. Sandra recognized the outfit because she had helped Erma pick it out to wear to the funeral of a revered judge three years earlier. Erma had worn it to every funeral since, except for Phillip's memorial service. Sandra figured that with the characteristically hot weather, Erma would have thought better of it. She wondered if it was a sign that her mother's thinking was muddled and, if so, whether she should do something about it. She'd been giving her a lot of leeway lately. Maybe that wasn't the best course of action.

Even in Phillip's air-conditioned office, perspiration dampened Erma's hair. She looked extremely uncomfortable. Sandra could just imagine that Erma was dying for a drink and anxious to get it all over and done with.

Erma gave Sandra a hard look and said, "Y'all come on back to the conference room," and led the way just like she belonged there. They followed. In addition to the aforementioned individuals, two distinguished-looking gentlemen in business suits accompanied them.

The girth of the conference room, which Sandra had seen before but which never failed to impress her, exceeded that of the county law library. There were rows upon rows of shelves filled with law books of every kind, by several different legal publishing companies. In the center of the whole thing stood a huge black marble table surrounded by black leather Queen Anne chairs. Erma seated herself at one end. The rest of them sat in no particular order. After everyone quieted down, Erma began.

"Good morning. As y'all know, I am the executrix of Phillip Parker's last will and testament. I have invited each of you to be present not necessarily because you are a beneficiary under the will, but because you are somehow connected to Phillip or someone who is a beneficiary. Phillip Parker gave me specific instructions on how he wanted his estate handled. I don't think it is necessary for me to go into that here; that is mostly for the heir or heirs to know." She paused and breathed deeply.

Lizzie glanced around the table. Her smile looked forced. "Could we just get on with it . . . please?"

Raymond sat beside Kitty. His hand covered hers. Stuart sat next to Sandra, on her right. Erma sat on Sandra's left. Sandra could not see Stuart's face without turning, though she could feel the pressure of his hand on her arm. Bubba was across from Sandra. The two gentlemen Sandra didn't know were next to one another, a vacant chair between them and Bubba. Sandra wondered whether it was because they were uncomfortable and out of place or because of Bubba's usual aroma. The table separated them by enough distance that she couldn't smell anything.

"Okay," Erma said, "does anyone have any questions?"

When no one replied, Erma placed her glasses on the end of her nose and picked up a thick document in one of their firm's blue-backs.

"Last Will and Testament of Phillip I. Parker. Paragraph one—"

Lizzie broke in. "Erma, really, could you dispense with the formalities and just get to the part where he says who gets what?"

"That's not customary, Elizabeth," Erma said.

The lawyers in the group who had ever handled a probate case knew differently, but hadn't the nerve to contradict her. Besides, as far as Sandra knew, none of the lawyers in the group were going to get a nickel, so none of them cared. She was just there as Kitty's attorney. Raymond was there as Kitty's intended. Stuart was there because he had been Phillip's partner. Sandra didn't know whether the two men down the way were lawyers or what, so she wasn't including them in her thoughts. She also wasn't going to piss off Erma, so she kept quiet and let Lizzie act like a greedy little bitch.

Lizzie looked pleadingly around the room, but found no supporters. She sighed, crossed her arms, and scooted back in her chair.

Erma continued reading each of the first three paragraphs, which were filled with Phillip's intentions and acknowledgments. She glanced at Lizzie. "I was married to Mary Edwards Parker in Tennessee. To the best of my knowledge and belief, I am still married at the time of this writing."

"What?" Lizzie shrieked. "So it's true."

Erma stopped. Lizzie had jumped up from her chair, run over to Erma, and grabbed the will before anyone had time to stop her. Lizzie read for a moment and screamed, "That son of a bitch. It's really true." Stuart had rounded the table and stood ready to restrain her. Erma waited a few moments. The rest of them were silent. Lizzie traced the words with her finger. She reached the bottom of the page and threw the will down on the table in front of Erma. "That sorry son of a bitch," she said again and sat back down.

Sandra doodled on a legal pad. Would Phillip have married Lizzie if he had known his wife had died? Had he really been planning on dumping Lizzie and finding someone younger? She glanced back at Erma, who had reached the part where he acknowledged his only child, Kathryn Parker, a female born to him and his wife in Tennessee.

Finally, Erma turned a page and began with the bequests. "Mr. Morgan, listen up." It was the first time that Erma had paid any attention to either of the men near the back of the room. "I give, devise, and bequeath to the Children's Home of Galveston County the sum of one million dollars, to be invested and the interest to be used to set up a program for homeless adolescents."

Morgan laughed aloud and turned to the gentleman next to him. They shook hands. "That's wonderful, Missus Townley. The answer to our prayers." He got up and hurried to the end of the table where he vigorously massaged Erma's hand. "Thank you. Thank you."

"You're welcome, Mr. Morgan. But remember, I didn't give it to you. Phillip Parker did. Now you go sit down and we'll talk about the distribution later."

"Yes, ma'am," he said. He nodded at each of them and, chuckling, walked back to his chair.

Erma ran the back of her hand across her mouth as if to wipe her smile away. "All right. Mr. Franklin, your turn." She paused. "I give, devise, and bequeath the sum of one million dollars to the Gulf Coast Coalition Against Child Abuse in hopes that young men such as I once was can be rehabilitated through education, counseling, and treatment programs."

Kitty uttered a cry. Tears filled her eyes. Mr. Franklin clasped his hands together and bowed his head as if in prayer. When he opened them, Sandra could see that he was tearful also. Lizzie's jaw flexed as she gritted her teeth. Bubba crossed his arms, his elbows resting on the table.

Mr. Franklin, after a few moments, turned and shook Mr. Morgan's hand and then, like Mr. Morgan, got up and went down to Erma and pumped her hand. She grinned like someone who had just won the lottery and told him to go sit down.

It occurred to Sandra then that Erma had known for years that Phillip had abused his one and only daughter. No wonder Kitty's revelation had not shocked her. Sandra wished that she could keep a secret like that. The only secrets she could keep were her clients'. But perhaps that was how Erma viewed it, rather than that of a friend. Whichever it was, Sandra was pretty astonished to learn that Erma had known and accepted the man as one of her dearest friends. She'd have to mull that over.

"To the following charities, a lump sum of ten thousand dollars each," Erma continued after Mr. Franklin took his seat. She read off a list of fifteen of the best-known organizations in Galveston County.

"Now we come to you, Lizzie," Erma said.

Lizzie took a deep breath and didn't seem one bit embarrassed to cross the fingers of each hand and hold them up. Closing her eyes, she said, "All right, go ahead."

Erma shook her head slowly, pityingly, Sandra thought. "To my friend and companion, Elizabeth Haynes, I give a lump sum of one hundred thousand dollars and the Mercedes Benz she has been driving for the last two years."

The room grew utterly still. Lizzie's eyes flew open. "Is that it?" she demanded as her fist slammed down on the table.

"I'm afraid so," Erma said.

"I don't believe it," Lizzie screamed. "Give me that thing." She grabbed for the will again.

Erma held on tight and pushed back her chair. "Stop that or I'll have you removed from the room."

"It can't be true." Tears streamed down Lizzie's face, black mascara running down her cheeks in vertical stripes. "After all we've been to each other. I gave him my youth."

Erma said, "If you don't believe me, you can examine the will after it's filed for probate."

Lizzie bounded out her chair and started screaming. "It can't be true! It can't be true!" She turned to Kitty. "You little bitch! You don't have to remove me, Erma, I'm leaving." Grabbing her purse, Lizzie ran out of the room.

Stuart hurried after Lizzie and closed the door behind him. Kitty, who had already had a good cry after she heard the bequest to the child abuse people, started weeping again. The whole scene had grown tiresome.

"Tsk, tsk." Erma shook her head as if to say she'd expected as much. She glanced at the will and the faces of the remaining people.

"The rest and remainder of my estate, I do hereby give, devise, and bequeath to my daughter, Kathryn Parker, to keep or dispose of as she sees fit." Erma put down the document and stared at Kitty.

Kitty released a long sigh. "I don't think I want it," she said.

"Oh, don't be silly, girl," Erma said. "It's a huge amount of money. Of course you shall have it. We'll not discuss that idiotic idea any further."

"What about me?" Bubba asked.

"What?" Erma appeared to have forgotten he was there. "Oh, you. Of course. There's a recent codicil. That means an addition or change, Bubba. It's a generic gift to whoever took care of the house. Mr. Parker left you the car—that would be the BMW—and a gift of five thousand dollars."

"All right!" Bubba said. "When do I get it? The money, Missus Townley. When do I get it?"

"Well, if you're in that big a hurry, as soon as you vacate the house and I can inspect it, I'll get your money to you. Will that do?"

"All right!" he said again. "Can I come and get it on Monday?"

"That'll be just fine. I'll pay you your last wages at the same time, and you'll bring me your keys. Not that the keys matter much; I'm sure Miss Kitty will be changing the locks."

Bubba, nodding to some kind of rhythm heard only in his

head, got up from his chair and shook Erma's hand like he'd seen the others do, one hand covering the other. "Can I go now?"

"You're excused," Erma said. "In fact, you all may be excused now. I have a few things I'd like to discuss with Miss Fulton. I'll contact you again when I'm prepared for the distribution."

It took all of two minutes for the room to clear. Sandra asked Kitty to wait outside for a few minutes. She wanted a word with her mother before the two of them got into a lengthy discussion about the estate. Sandra just had one thing on her mind and she needed to ask Erma. She closed the door behind them, and then went back to the table after checking the stacks to be sure they were alone.

"Just tell me one thing," Sandra said. "Is there any way at all that anyone could have known the contents of Phillip's will? Anyone at all?"

"Absolutely not," Erma said. "Unless he told them himself."

If there was no question in her mother's mind, then there was none in Sandra's. Kitty's ignorance of her inheritance was her best protection against a motive for murder. It was just too bad that there was no way Lizzie could have known about hers. Judging by Lizzie's behavior, the comparatively small bequest would have been all the motive she would have needed to bump Phillip off out of anger, if nothing else. And Sandra doubted that Phillip would have told her.

Stuart waylaid Sandra as she started to leave Parker and Associates. Stuart's office, the second largest after Phillip's, was long and half-again as wide. Navy and green plaid drapes covered the windows. Navy deep pile carpet, dark green leather sofas and chairs, and mahogany tables gave it a masculine Scotch/Irish flavor.

Stuart closed the door behind her and took her into his arms. When they came up for air, Stuart rubbed at the smudged lipstick around her lips and led her to a chair. Sitting beside her, he said, "I've missed you."

"Me, too," she said and squeezed his hand. "How'd you like what happened in there? Lizzie sure didn't take it very well. Did you follow her out to her car?"

"She stood screaming and raving in the middle of the sidewalk. You should have seen her. I thought she would bust a gusset."

"Huh. I'm not surprised. I'm not sure what's going on with her. She seems to be drinking more than ever. Can't she go to work, Stu? I thought she had a job years ago."

"She was a legal secretary. In fact, she was Phil's legal secretary. At least until they became involved."

"Boy, what a cliché. And what a nice way of putting it, too. Well, I guess she'll have to go back to work. What a joke on her. Really, Phillip could have left her a little more than a hundred thousand dollars and a car." She wondered why Phillip hadn't made better arrangements for Lizzie.

"He did give her a lot of expensive jewelry."

"Yeah. I guess she could sell that and the car, if she has to. There are a lot of decent cheaper cars out there."

"Phillip was a strange duck," Stuart said with a quirky smile.

"Understatement of the century. Imagine him turning out to be a real prince, giving all that money to charity and to his daughter after what he did."

"Yes, imagine. Well, now that that's over, you think we can have a little more time together?"

"I can't right now, I've got a shitload of work on my desk." She stroked his cheek. "But did you have something particular in mind?"

"Tonight? Dinner at DiBella's?"

Sandra smiled. He certainly knew the way to her heart. She got up and headed for the door. "Pick me up at six."

She headed back to her office to map out her cross-examination of the state's witnesses for Kitty's examining trial. She also had two appointments that afternoon. One was to prepare for a divorce trial on Wednesday of the following week. Her client was the husband who was distraught because his wife played bingo seven nights a week. She wrote checks for every bingo session but never deposited any of her winnings. Consequently, they had run into financial problems.

The other was a first meeting with a juvenile she'd been appointed to represent on a home invasion case. Lucky her. She hoped he didn't want a jury trial. The sentiment in the country was decidedly against him. But she was jumping the gun. She wasn't sure the state could tie him to the shooting yet. She needed to file a discovery motion and have a hearing in the next few weeks before the boy's first trial setting.

On Fridays, Sandra liked to clean off her desk. She would answer the mail, sign or correct orders, and process other legal paperwork.

A bit after five, she kicked back for a few minutes rest and then touched up her makeup and perfume. By six-fifteen, Stuart and she and a bottle of white wine nestled in a corner booth. DiBella's, a small neighborhood restaurant hidden in the middle of the island, had crowded rooms, a short bar, and the best pasta for miles around. Erma might have to have her bourbon, but Sandra had to have a fix of baked artichoke with a garlicky breadcrumb jacket or marinated blue crab claws floating in garlic butter every once in a while. It had been several days since she'd had a good meal, meaningful conversation with a man, or hot sex. Stuart took care of each one that night.

About seven-thirty the next morning, Stuart rolled off her arm, where he'd been lying for a good half-hour, which enabled her to get out of bed. Sandra preferred his sleeping at her place rather than the reverse. It didn't take as much effort on her part to get herself together the morning after. He would sleep in. She would get up and get the day started quietly.

That particular Saturday, after she showered, put on a sundress, and ate breakfast, she set about trying to figure out who had killed Phillip Parker. With her cup of tea and a notebook, she sat at the table and jotted down some notes.

Was it Lizzie? Had she somehow found out that the S.O.B. intended to use her up and throw her away without taking care of her? Perhaps he had told her in an argument? Or would that have been a better reason to keep him alive? Suppose she had thought that Kitty was going up to Phillip's room to have an affair and that he might dump her for Kitty. And suppose she had known that his will only left her the car and the hundred thousand dollars cash. And suppose she'd known that for a long time but was kissing-up to him to keep him from dumping her because it was more beneficial to her to keep him alive. And suppose that on Friday a week ago, she figured that Phillip would change his will if he got a new girlfriend and then she, Lizzie, would get nothing after all the years with him and her loss of looks. That would be motive enough for any woman.

Then there was Bubba. Suppose Bubba had been cheating on the food and/or liquor bills. Suppose Phillip had found out that Bubba had been padding the bills and Bubba knew that Phillip knew. And suppose that when Phillip landed on the ground, they had a nasty argument and Phillip threatened to fire, or did fire, Bubba, and Bubba smashed his face in and took the jewelry to make it look like a robbery.

Or could it have been a robbery by a stranger? There could have been some sleaze-bag drifter hanging out down the island who heard the music, laughter, and general party atmosphere. He could have wandered by to see if he could mooch some food or a couple of drinks. He could have found Phillip downstairs. Phillip, pissing and moaning, and the slime-ball saw his chance to steal the watch and ring to make some quick bucks. Okay, but where were the cops who were working security? If all of them had gone home except one, where was he? Wouldn't he have barred the creeps from coming in?

Sandra needed to find out. She phoned the Galveston Police Department and got Truman on the line. "Hi, Dennis, this is Sandra Salinsky."

"Don't you sleep? It's Saturday morning."

"Yes, well I was wondering whether you could tell me something about that police officer who was still working when Phillip was killed?"

"You need to get a life, Sandra. All you do is work."

"My life's still asleep, thank you very much."

Dennis grunted. "So what do you want to know?"

"About the cop who was working security at Phillip's house. Where was he?"

Dennis cleared his throat. "You mean at the time of the murder?"

"Yes, that's exactly what I mean. Wasn't he there?"

"Yes, he was there. But he didn't see or hear anything, or so he says."

"He wasn't there, then. At least you don't think so?"

"Let me say this, Sandra. The department's investigating it, all right? As soon as we make some findings, you'll be the first to know."

"What's his name?"

"Robert Earl Bradshaw. But you can't talk to him."

"Why the hell not?" She hated it when someone told her she couldn't do something.

"He's on a leave of absence. Went out of town for a few weeks."

"Oh, sure. Where does he live?"

"Texas City, but I swear he's gone till the first of next month."

Sandra nodded at the phone. Was there something suspicious about that or was it just her? "Okay, Dennis. Thanks a lot."

"You're welcome. By the way, you might be interested to know that Erma already called yesterday with the same questions."

"Oh Holy Mother," Sandra said. "Thanks anyway." She hung up and dialed Erma's number. It wasn't surprising when she got no answer. She could only hope that Erma hadn't gone looking for Bradshaw. Perhaps she was at the grocery store or napping. That sounded ridiculous even to Sandra, but, determined to find Bradshaw before the weekend ended, she got out the telephone book. There were just three Bradshaws in Texas City and LaMarque, two contiguous towns on the other side of the causeway bridge.

There was no listing for Robert Earl, Bobby, or Robert. Usually cops have unlisted numbers, but she phoned the numbers anyway, hoping for a relative who would give her his whereabouts. The first person cursed her. The other two simply said there was no such person at that number. She made a note to try the one who cursed her, but she would have to go out there since he'd hung up in her face.

Back to her list, the next person with a possible motive was Raymond. She outlined her suspicions. Raymond, who gossip said Phillip had publicly humiliated. Raymond, who spoke of Phillip as he would a father. Raymond, who was a

Kitty devotee. Could he have killed Phillip after Kitty knocked him off the balcony?

1. If he suspected that Phillip intended to harm Kitty?

2. If he suspected that Phillip intended to steal Kitty from him?

After some contemplation, she could not rule out Raymond.

Lastly, there was Stuart. She couldn't ignore the fact that Stuart had been on the premises when Phillip had died. Her stomach turned over at the prospect of Stuart's being involved in the sordid mess, but still, something could have been going on between them that she didn't know about. She couldn't think of a possible motive, and so far, no one had indicated that Stuart was anyplace other than where he was supposed to be when the murder had taken place. Nevertheless, she added Stuart's name to the list. She was staring down at it when his arms encircled her from behind. She felt a whiskery chin nudge the back of her neck. Closing her notebook, she wondered whether and what he had read over her shoulder.

Turning in her chair, she returned Stuart's hug. He smelled of sleep and morning breath. "How about a shower while I fix you some breakfast?"

Stuart pulled her up and pressed himself against her. "How about a shower together?"

She laughed. "I can't believe you have any energy left. Besides, I already had my shower and my breakfast. You go ahead." She pushed him toward the bathroom. "Food'll be ready when you come out."

He frowned, but playfully, not angrily. She thought she knew him well enough to know that after what had gone on between them during the night, he wouldn't have the get-up-and-go for more anyway. He headed for the shower and she for the kitchen. Flipping on the radio, Sandra tuned to some oldies but goodies while she toasted a couple of bagels, brewed some coffee, and poured orange juice. Stuart could have eggs all the time when he was cooking, but at her house he had to eat what she ate. He had yet to complain; besides, he had slept so late that lunchtime wasn't that far off.

He still wasn't out by the time she set a place for him at the table, so she took a glass of orange juice and the metro section of the Houston newspaper she'd gotten from the condo lobby and went out onto the balcony. A calm breeze blew warm air in from the Gulf. It had rained during the night and the sidewalks below glistened in the sun. Whitecaps topped muddy brown waves as they washed over pink granite boulders.

She contemplated what the day held for her. While it was tempting to lounge around all day with Stuart, she had been spending so much time on Kitty's defense that she needed to catch up on other things. She had cleaned the easy stuff off her desk the day before but had a lot of other things that required attention. She also needed to begin working on Kitty's trial notebook. Her notebooks had a section for each part of the trial and at least a page assigned to each witness, whether her witness or the state's.

The glass door rumbled behind her. Stuart had put his food on a tray. "Pretty day," he said, placing the tray on the table. His feet were bare. He had dressed in tan walking shorts and a tan-and-green striped polo shirt. He looked squeaky clean.

"Um, getting hot though." She hid behind the newspaper for the next few minutes.

"Thanks for making breakfast."

"You're welcome." She could smell the coffee. The aroma was pleasant, even though she didn't often drink the stuff.

"May I have some of the paper when you're through?"

"Sure. There's some good Harris County Courthouse smut today." She turned to the last page of the metro section, finished reading, and handed it to him.

They sat in silence for a while as Stuart ate and read. It was pleasant, which is why she bought the condo in the first place. She heard one of the neighbors come out on her balcony. Leaning forward so she could see around the separating wall, she waved at her. Cars whizzed by below. People jogged and bladed past. A man stood on the seawall and threw bread up to the seagulls circling overhead. She only hoped the birds didn't reward him with a surprise package.

Stuart startled her by breaking the silence. "What were you working on when I got up?"

Shrugging, Sandra said, "Nothing much. Kitty's defense."

"Was that my name I saw on that sheet of paper?"

Her breath didn't come easily as she contemplated how to respond. She looked into his eyes, smiled, and pushed her apprehensiveness aside. "I made a list of everyone who was present when Phillip died."

Stuart nodded. "A suspect list. Do you consider me a suspect, Sandy?"

"Look, Stu . . . you know that I have to develop other possibilities if I'm going to get Kitty off. I don't have to prove that she's innocent; I just have to poke holes in the state's case. Raise reasonable doubt."

"Objection, non-responsive."

"Well, what kind of question is that to ask?" She could hear her own voice echoing in her ears. It seemed loud and strident. She wondered whether her neighbor could hear them. Whispering, Sandra said, "Would I be sleeping with you if I thought you were a murderer?"

Stuart grinned. "All right, then. It just startled me to think you thought I'd killed Phillip." His eyes rested on hers. "But that does mean you're going to raise my name in Kitty's defense, doesn't it?"

"There's no getting around it. Could we change the subject, please? It's only going to make us fight and I don't want that."

"I told you not to take this case," he said, folding the paper into a small rectangle and throwing it down on his tray. "You can still get out of representing her if you withdraw now." He reached for the door handle.

"I don't know what's gotten into you, Stuart."

His face loomed over hers. She could see by his flared nostrils how angry he was. "You're going to point out each of us who was at Phillip's house that night and give the judge or jury a reason why Kitty couldn't have killed Phillip. How the hell do you think that's going to make me look to the legal community? And what about Raymond? He's a budding lawyer. This could ruin him." He jerked the glass door open and stepped inside.

She followed. "If it wasn't me, it'd be someone else. Hell, Stuart, with Kitty's money, she could afford to hire someone with a big name that would attract a lot more publicity. You should be grateful that I took the case. If a big name had it, it would probably be splashed all over the front pages of America. They'd be milking this for all it's worth. You know how it works."

He rinsed his dishes and put them in the dishwasher. His jaw muscles flexed. Sandra thought he would have looked very handsome but for the way he snorted like an angry bull. She stood in the doorway and waited for him to make further comment. Stuart dried his hands and headed for the bedroom. She followed.

"I'm going down to the office," he said.

"We're not going to spend the day together?"

"Not if I'm going to the office." He refused to look at her as he bundled up his clothes from the day before.

"Okay. I have some work to do anyway." She began to make the bed. He stood on the other side. "Want to have dinner tomorrow night?"

He stared across the breach at her. "What about tonight?"

"My daughter's coming."

"When are you going to let me meet her?"

"We just had one argument. Let's not have another."

Stuart grabbed his gym bag off the floor and stuffed his clothes into it. "Okay, Sandra. But I'm getting tired of only being permitted into part of your life. We've been dating for what, a year? When are you going to take our relationship seriously?"

Dropping the sheet, she went around the bed and slipped her arms around his neck, hugging him. "I don't know, Stu. I just don't know. I know I've said this before, but please don't rush me."

They stood there for a few minutes, neither of them speaking. He finally pushed her away. "All right. We'll discuss this later. I've got to get going right now." He pulled on his deck shoes and picked up his bag.

He kissed her cheek at the door, unbolted it, and was gone. Sandra stood there wondering how she would feel if her name was spoken aloud in a courtroom in connection with a murder. She wouldn't much like it either. There but for the grace of God.

Chapter Seventeen

Erma had gotten out of bed and immediately decided: a. that it was a nice day for a drive across the causeway, and b. that Sandra wasn't entitled to have all the fun. After breakfast, she donned lightweight rayon pants and a blouse and headed for Texas City. Bumper-to-bumper traffic moved onto the island, whereas only light traffic flowed to the mainland. She'd lived in the area so long that half the time she drove as if on automatic pilot. Today was no exception.

A large number of the residents of Texas City were union oil and chemical plant employees whose wages allowed them to live a middle- to upper-middle-class lifestyle. That wasn't to say that there weren't still poverty-ridden pockets in the shadows of the plants, but most people lived a fair, if not good, life.

The Bradshaw house stood in one of the older residential neighborhoods but still middle-class with mostly one-story, single family, frame homes. An elderly man mowed the lawn next door; a couple of kids rode their bikes in the street; sprinklers left puddles on walkways and in the gutters.

Erma parked in a dry spot and walked up the sidewalk to the front door. The smell of freshly cut grass permeated the air. The neighbor studied her and her car. She had seen a Neighborhood Watch sign posted on the subdivision entrance and stared right back. Leaning on the doorbell, Erma felt relieved when someone opened the door so that she could quit staring at the neighbor.

A woman about Erma's age stood behind a screen, her face devoid of makeup. Wisps of gray hair curled about her face. Deep frown lines framed her mouth. The apron tied around her waist partially obscured her T-shirt and polyester pants. They looked each other over for a few moments. Erma realized that she could have been the frumpy one behind the screen except for an accident of birth. Instead, she was the frumpy one on the front porch.

"May I help you?" The woman did not open the screen door.

"I'm looking for Robert Earl Bradshaw, the Galveston police officer."

"He doesn't live here." The woman stepped back as if to close the door in Erma's face.

"But you know him."

"Who says I do?"

"Missus Bradshaw, I don't mean him any harm, or you either."

"You the woman that called this morning? The lawyer?" She said it in a monotone, simply stating a fact.

"No, ma'am. I'm her mother. She's representing Phillip Parker's daughter and needs to talk to him before Monday morning." Erma smiled. "Just trying to help my daughter out here. You know how it is. My name's Erma. What's yours?"

"Glenda." She glanced over her shoulder and then said in a lower tone of voice, "He doesn't know anything. He done told me so himself."

It was difficult for Erma to hear over the lawnmower. "Is he here? May I speak with him?" She dropped her voice like a co-conspirator. "I just want to ask him a couple of questions."

"I'm his mother, you know," she said proudly.

"I figured as much. Missus Bradshaw, no one is pointing the finger at Robert Earl. We just need to know where he was when Mr. Parker was killed. No one thinks Robert Earl did it, or anything like that. We're just trying to eliminate people. A good cop like him is sure to have known everyone's whereabouts." Erma could hear the television in the background. She wondered if Robert Earl stood just on the other side of the door or whether Glenda was worried about someone else overhearing the conversation.

"He's taken a leave of absence," she replied. "Was going on vacation, he said."

"When will he return?" The sun overhead burned the back of her neck. She wiped the perspiration away and looked at the woman's face behind the screen.

"Glenda," a deep voice called from the living room, "who is it?"

Mrs. Bradshaw tossed a glance over her shoulder once more before saying, "I've really got to go. Wish I could help you."

A burly man, with hair as white as his undershirt, came up behind Mrs. Bradshaw. "You selling something?"

Erma glanced at Mrs. Bradshaw's face and noted the grim set of her mouth. "Yes, sir. Hard way for an old lady like me to make a living, but yes, sir, I am." She leaned harder on her cane and made eye contact with the man. He looked like a mean old bulldog. "Swimming pools. Now that summer is here, my company has placed all our pools and pool supplies on sale. You can have a pool designed for your own backyard at a fraction of the cost it would have been last spring. Your wife here was hesitating—"

"We don't abide no door-to-door selling in this neighborhood," he said as he shut the door in her face. His voice was muffled, but as Erma turned back to her car, she could hear him say to his wife, “How many times have I got to tell you just to tell ’em no as soon as they start up with their spiel?”

The lawn-mowing neighbor had worked his way to the other side of his yard but kept Erma in his sights. As she pulled away from the curb, she saluted him. He nodded and pushed his mower forward.

While on the mainland, Erma took a chance that someone would be at the morgue, which was in the middle between Texas City and LaMarque, behind the hospital.

A small building compared to the hospital, the morgue seemed to suffice for the little county of two hundred fifty thousand people, except that it lacked specimen storage. There had been a big write-up in the local newspaper a few years earlier that had caused the medical examiner some embarrassment. Because of lack of space, he had stored specimens outside under a tarp. Not new ones, yet specimens that he had some reason to keep.

Erma parked beside the only car in the lot. She hoped whoever was there would know something new about Phillip’s murder. She found the sallyport door unlocked. A private transport ambulance sat in the port area next to the entry door, so someone must be there to take delivery of a body.

Leaning hard on the metal rail, Erma climbed the stairs and went inside. On the right stood a refrigerator room. Down the hall was the examining room, where the bodies were laid out on stainless steel tables at stations. Each station held a microphone and a table. There were sinks and hoses and a tile floor. Almost everything was stainless. When they were through with the autopsy and stored the body or sent it to the funeral home, they hosed down the whole room. Drains in the floor caught the water and any excess blood or fluid.

Erma had learned more than she ever wanted to know about the practices of a medical examiner when she was a new criminal defense attorney. She used to frequent the morgue and give the doctors and technicians the third-degree so she'd understand how everything worked. She'd never been the squeamish type, though she'd seen more than a few young district attorneys throw up after looking at a body.

Through a small square of glass in the door, she saw the assistant to the medical examiner stooped over the body of a gray-haired female. Lawrence, one of Dr. Michaels' assistants, was a very tall, skinny fellow with a shaved head and wire-rimmed glasses, thirtyish. Erma banged on the door and waited for him to let her in. A toilet flushed down the hall and a young man drying his hands on a paper towel came out and walked in her direction. He reached her as Lawrence opened the door.

After giving her the once over and apparently deciding she was of no interest to him, he said, "See you, Larry," waved, and went toward the sallyport door.

"Erma," Larry said. "What in the world are you doing here? I thought you retired." He started to reach for her hand. She could see he thought better of it when he glanced at his rubber-gloved ones.

"I don't know where in the hell you got that idea, but it's not true," Erma said.

"You want to come in? I'm getting a patient ready for Dr. Michaels." He held the door open and she edged her way past him.

"I was in Texas City on some business and thought I'd drop by. Save Sandra the trip." She followed him over to the wide table, where he began to undress the deceased. The dead woman looked eighty, if a day. Erma wondered why there had been an autopsy requested, but that was none of her business.

Larry laughed. "Yeah, like you're out shopping in the mall and you decide, 'Hey, I don't have anything better to do, so why don't I go over and see what's doing at the morgue.' " He finished unbuttoning the decedent's flannel nightgown and pulled it gently over her head, easing the sleeves over her arms and laying them back gingerly on the table as if she could feel his touch. When it was off, he covered her breasts with a hand towel.

"All right, goddamnit, it wasn't exactly like that. I didn't know who I would catch here, so I thought I'd take a chance."

"Let me guess, the Phillip Parker case."

"I'm that transparent?"

"Would you mind turning your back for a moment?"

Erma faced away from the body until he told her she could turn back. He had removed the dead woman's panties and covered her pubic area with a dry washcloth.

"Did you assist Michaels with him?"

"Yeah, as a matter of fact, I did. Michaels was as careful as I've ever seen him with a patient." He gazed into her eyes and shrugged. "I wondered whether he knew him or just realized how important the case would be to the D.A. . . ." He hesitated. "Maybe both."

"What was your first impression, Lawrence? I mean, as you prepared the body?"

"Well, since it was a homicide, it was treated differently from what I've done here today. You know that." He glanced at her as he carefully folded up the old lady's clothes and put them in a plastic bag. "Anyhow, I think whoever did it was awfully pissed at him. Boy, did they do a job on his face."

"I heard about that. Did y'all figure out what was used?"

"A brick. There were tiny pieces of red brick embedded in some of his facial bones."

"You mean like an ordinary brick one builds a house with?"

"Yes. Nothing exotic about it."

Erma nodded. There were bricks all over the place at Phillip's house. The yardman made fancy patterns with them around the flowerbeds and trees. Some were stacked under the house. A convenient weapon. She wondered whether the cops had checked anyone's hands for abrasions on the day Phillip's body had been discovered. "Anything else that caught your eye?"

"His clothing. The pocket of his dressing gown hung almost by a thread. He wasn't wearing any underwear."

That seemed consistent with what Sandra'd said about Kitty's story that he was making a play for her. "So all he had on was a dressing gown?"

"A pair of very expensive bedroom slippers with his initials monogrammed across the top."

It would be like Phillip to have a monogram even on clothes no one would ever see.

"He had a suntan line on his left wrist where he would have worn a watch and also one on one of his fingers, but I can't remember which finger. I guess Sandra or you could ask Dr. Michaels during your cross-examination."

"So you know."

He laughed again. "Of course we know, Erma. Why else would you be asking me questions? Doesn't bother me. We're not doing anything wrong discussing our findings. Dr. Michaels hasn't ordered me not to talk to anyone about it. As a matter of fact, I remember him saying that he wouldn't be surprised if Sandra dropped by sometime soon."

"Our client didn't kill him."

"I don't care if she did."

She smiled at him. "I'd forgotten where your interests lay. Just fascinated by the bodies—"

"And the stories they reveal," he finished.

"Is there anything else that you can tell me about Phillip's story?"

He sighed and looked off into space for a moment. "Some scratches on his arms. Around his wrists. Some wood fragments in his hands. Splinters. A bit of skin under his nails. Matches his daughter's, I hear. You already know about the fractures, right?"

"Yep. I'm just looking for something that would give even the least indication as to what sex the killer was."

He shook his head. "I can't tell you that. An enraged woman could have done the same damage to that face as a man, particularly if she repeatedly smashed it."

"Well, I appreciate you taking the time to talk to me, Lawrence." Erma slowly made her way to the exit. "I'll see myself out." He stayed with his patient. "Hey, when Dr. Michaels gets here, tell him hello. Unfortunately, I won't be in court on Monday. It'll be Sandra."

"Will do. Turn the lock in the outside door handle when you leave, all right?"

After checking the lock on the door, Erma left and went directly to her car. As she headed back to Galveston, she mulled over the information he'd given her. There just had to be something that would point the finger at someone.

From the top of the Causeway Bridge, the island appeared to float. The water sparkled as if embossed with sequins. Tall sailboats, their sails billowing in the gulf breeze, cruised on the bay. A tugboat pushed a loaded barge under the bridge. Small motorboats sped through the green water, leaving trails of white froth behind them like bushy tails. It was a day to idle on the beach, fish in the bay, or ski behind a boat, and here she was delving into a murder.

Chapter Eighteen

Since Stuart wasn't interested in spending the day together, Sandra drove down to the office. Saturdays were quiet enough that she could get a lot done. She took down the messages from the answering service. There was nothing that couldn't wait. Pouring herself a glass of iced tea, she settled behind her desk. First on the list, organizing her examining trial notebook. There was a section for witnesses, one for demonstrative evidence, one for her questions of each witness, an outline of her argument if the judge allowed one, and a section for unusual objections and case law to support them. When through, Sandra felt quite pleased with herself.

Making a list of probable state's witnesses, she came up with Bubba, Stuart, Raymond, Dr. Michaels, Lieutenant Truman, and Lizzie. The state couldn't make Kitty testify against herself. Sandra wasn't sure yet whether she would put her on the stand. If she did, she waived her Fifth Amendment right. Anything she said could be used against her not only at the examining trial, but also at the grand jury hearing, if there was one, and later at trial. If Kitty screwed up and said the wrong thing on Monday, they'd be stuck with it for life. Kitty wasn't ready. Sandra wasn't sure if Kitty ever would be. Sandra didn't want her breaking down and sobbing out nonsensical things.

What, if any, demonstrative evidence would Edgar offer? He really didn't have to offer anything. All the state had to do was raise the question of probable cause. Was there probable cause that Kitty had murdered Phillip? Was there enough for the justice of the peace to send Kitty's case to the grand jury? Sandra needed to talk to Dr. Michaels, to see if he'd identified the murder weapon.

She picked up the phone to call Michaels when her cell began ringing. Hanging up, Sandra answered her cell, expecting it to be Stuart, perhaps to apologize.

"It was a brick."

"Erma?" Sandra recognized her mother's voice. "What was a brick?"

"The murder weapon. There were tiny little pieces in his skin and bone."

"And how would you know that?" Sandra asked, pretty sure that she already knew the answer.

"Goddamnit, I can't just sit here and do nothing."

"So you're home now, not running all over the county doing my job?"

"Okay. Yes, I went to that cop's house. Well, his parents' home, really. His mother was pitiful. His father is a bully. But I didn't get to see him."

"Mother, really."

"And while I was over on the mainland, I thought I might as well drop by the morgue."

"I'm sure you did." Sandra smiled in spite of herself. No use getting angry; it was already done.

"Are we going to have another fight?"

Sandra said, "No. I already had one today, thank you very much."

"Stuart?"

"Yes. He doesn't think it's right that I make implications about him and Raymond in the courtroom, to raise reasonable doubt by pointing the finger at them."

"Tough shit," Erma said. "That's how the game works."

"He thinks I should get off the case."

"Oh, sure. Doesn't he realize any other defense lawyer would do the same?"

"They're not me."

"I'm sure you didn't even consider his suggestion."

"You're right. So the M.E. said a brick, huh?"

"Yep, but it was Lawrence. He said no way they could tell if it was a woman or a man who hit him."

"Too bad. Anything else helpful?" Sandra asked.

"Well, it didn't sound like they had the actual brick. You think Edgar has the brick?"

"One brick's the same as another. I guess he could have a brick and show that the brick used was one of Phillip's bricks."

"Not much help for Edgar," Erma said. "Do you know whether Dennis Truman or the uniforms looked for abrasions on anyone's hands?"

"No. I heard them talking about searching for clothing with blood on it, but no one has mentioned that either."

"Shit. They would have told us if they'd found anything," Erma said.

"You mean they should have told us. If they'd found something that day, they'd have arrested whose ever property it was on the spot."

"Well, if Kitty gets indicted, you can file your Brady motion. I wouldn't waste my time worrying about it now."

"So nothing we can use anywhere?" Sandra asked.

"Not really. And since they seem to be keeping the cop under wraps, I wasn't much help to you there either, so it's good you're not getting all pissed off about it."

Sandra laughed. "You were a help. You saved me going out this afternoon and doing what you already did this morning."

"What have you been doing?" Erma asked.

"Well, since Stuart went away mad this morning, I came down here and put together my examining trial notebook. It looks good, if I do say so myself."

"Fine. Well, I'll see you later. I'm going to go lie down."

"Oh, yeah, sure you are."

"Goodbye," Erma said.

Sandra hung up the phone and laughed aloud. It probably was best to let the old lady have an active role in the case. She was going to take one whether Sandra liked it or not.

Okay, so Edgar wouldn't have the actual brick. Even if he did, she didn't think that fingerprints could be gotten off a brick. She didn't really think that someone bashing in someone else's face would damage the brick enough so that it would be distinguishable from any other brick. It would, however, probably have a lot of blood and other repulsive tissue on it. If the perp were smart, he or she would have disposed of the brick. Thrown it in the bayou.

What else could he have? The dressing gown and the slippers. Not much that would make a difference.

Sandra made lists of questions that she would ask each person. Those at the party, she would ask about their whereabouts and the last time they saw Phillip. Would each of them corroborate the other's story?

And what could Edgar ask Dennis Truman that would lead to probable cause? She couldn't think of a thing.

Edgar wouldn't ask Lieutenant Truman to poke holes in the other witnesses' stories. That would be up to her. She would cross-examine each one on the information she and Erma had gotten out of them. Although ordinarily this wasn't the time to raise reasonable doubt, it seemed the only way to point out to the judge that there was not enough evidence to prove probable cause. She would argue that the D.A. could bring the charges against Kitty just as soon as he did have enough evidence. Therefore, the state lost nothing by the judge not making a finding on Monday. What were the odds of that happening?

Her thoughts wandered to Stuart. She could understand his being upset at having his name mentioned at the examining trial, but she wished he'd try to see her side of the issue. At least she would try to be somewhat kindly about it. Another criminal defense attorney probably wouldn't. She hoped it wouldn't be detrimental to their relationship, but she couldn't let him dictate how she practiced law. She couldn't go easy on him. This wasn't a Spencer Tracy/Katherine Hepburn movie. This was real life. And she was obligated to do whatever it took to defend her client within the bounds of the law.

Her mobile phone rang again.

"Mom, what are you doing?"

"Hello, honey. Working on the Parker case. What are you doing?"

"Calling you." Melinda giggled. Fourteen-year-olds still did that occasionally.

"All right, you. Is your suitcase packed? Are you ready for me to pick you up later?"

"Mommy," it was her little-girl voice. "Susie is having a slumber party. It's her birthday."

"Oh." Sandra tried not to sound disappointed. "So you'd like to go?"

"Do you care?"

"Well, of course I care. But I understand. I'll call Grandma and tell her not to fix dinner."

"Thanks, Mommy."

"You're welcome. How's everything going? What have you been up to lately?"

"They made me an assistant camp counselor the last half of the summer at camp. That means I'll get to go for free. I just have to look out for the little kids. Isn't that cool?"

"So you'll be a big shot at Camp Chillingham. What about Amy and Jennifer?"

"Jen is an assistant counselor, too. Amy didn't want to do it, but she'll be there when we are."

"So I guess you'll be too busy for your old mom."

"Mommy . . . if you'd let me come live with you—"

"We're not going to discuss that right now. You know how I feel about kids moving back and forth between their parents' homes every few years."

"I know, but I've lived with Daddy for ten years and I'd just like to spend my last four with you."

"I'll think about it. You have a good time at Susie's tonight. What did you get her?"

"A CD. You wouldn't recognize the group."

Sandra sighed. "You're probably right. Do you think your dad would let you come next weekend instead?"

"I'll ask him. I love you, Mommy."

Sandra had difficulty swallowing. "Love you, too. Call me later in the week and let me know what he says."

"Okay. Bye." Melinda hung up.

After the call, Sandra couldn't concentrate on the examining trial. She went down to The Strand for a late lunch and then spent the remainder of the afternoon clearing her desk of other odds and ends.

She had a divorce and custody case between a biracial couple coming up. She needed to research appellate opinions to see what restrictions the higher courts had made. Her opponent was likely to attempt to play the race card. Sandra wanted to be ready for him. She also had a juvenile transfer hearing on the following Friday. The D.A. wanted to try the kid as an adult for robbery. There was a lot of work ahead of her that week.

Late Saturday afternoon, Sandra phoned Stuart at his office. One of the associates said that Stuart hadn't been in all day. It wasn't as if he'd been expecting to hear from her, since she'd told him she'd be with Melinda. She just thought he would be there, since he'd said he would. Seemed like over the last few months he was there on Saturdays less and less. She wondered where he was during those times and what he was doing.

Sandra got no answer at his home or on his mobile either. Her curiosity was really aroused. Okay, her interest was piqued. Perhaps she even felt a bit jealous. Her ambiguous feelings would have to be taken out, laid on the table, and examined soon. She knew what he wanted. She just didn't know what she wanted. Except she had hoped they could meet for dinner that evening and put things right. At least put them the way they had been the day before.

Since she couldn't locate Stuart, she decided to go for a run. Her shoulders ached. She needed a stress reliever. Her body needed some attention. She would try him back on Sunday afternoon for Sunday night. Surely he would have cooled off by then.

A bit later, as Sandra ran east on the seawall, the wind gusted between the condominiums and whipped her hair to the south, then seemed to make a U-turn and fly back across the waves' whitecaps and blow it the other way. The sun slid down behind her. The tourists and the locals continued to perform their nightly rituals: bicycling, jogging, blading, walking, and bouncing in the waves. That night she was one of them.

Perspiration clustered on her forehead like polyps. Her ragged breathing evidenced that she'd let her daily routine lapse. She couldn't blame Stuart or her work. She had gotten lazy; that was all there was to it. She had done some swimming, but swimming laps did not substitute for jogging miles.

A pain in her side caused her to slow to a walk as she turned back toward her condo. It would take a lot of work to get back up to snuff, but she would be back pounding the pavement the next morning and would continue day after day until she could go the distance.

Upon arriving back at her apartment, Sandra guzzled several glasses of water, slung her clothes into a pile in the bathroom, and checked the answering machine. The light blinked three times. Hitting the play button, she perched on a barstool. The first one was a high-pitched muffled voice, unintelligible. Then she heard a mumble in a low, obviously disguised voice, "Forget defending Parker's kid if you know what's good for you." There was a metallic tapping or clicking in the background while the person spoke. It sounded vaguely familiar. Other than the one sentence, they said nothing else and hung up. The third caller was apparently the same as the second but spoke in a high voice, "You get her off and you're dead meat." The tapping noise had grown fainter. Sandra would have laughed at how ridiculous the calls were if they'd been directed at someone else. She popped out the tape and threw it into a drawer, replacing it with a fresh one.

As Sandra climbed into the shower and soaped up, she remembered some of the nasty phone calls she'd gotten when working as an assistant district attorney. At first it was scary, but no one ever followed through on them, so she quit worrying. She knew that defense lawyers often received hate mail and threats if they were defending a high-profile defendant. Rarely did it lead to anything. The most dangerous cases lately seemed to be family law, not criminal. The outraged citizen might threaten, but it was just a way to release frustration. In family law cases, the irate husband vented by killing his wife or her lawyer or shooting up a courthouse. In criminal law, it would take a really stupid client to threaten his own lawyer, much less harm her. Not that most of them weren't stupid or crazy. They just needed their attorney to be around to defend them.

She put on silk pajamas, a light robe, fixed a sandwich and some iced tea, and went out on the balcony where she could watch the traffic and the surf. Lingering on the balcony and watching the young people down below, she grew melancholy. Girls with their long hair flowing behind them as they sat next to their boyfriends in their convertibles. Couples walking hand-in-hand or bicycling or sitting on the edge of the seawall, staring out to sea. There she was, alone on a Saturday night. Her youth gone. No significant other. Nothing to look forward to. Lord, she was starting to sound like Lizzie. Hearing a distant ringing, Sandra realized it was her condo telephone and felt almost grateful for the distraction.

She had no idea how many rings she'd missed. "Hello," she hollered unintentionally as she grabbed it.

"Where the hell have you been?" Erma yelled back.

"Oh, hi, Mother. Out and about. The Strand, jogging. Sorry I didn't pick up sooner. I was on the balcony. Are you okay? What are you hollering for?"

"Because you are. I've got news for you, if you want to come over."

That was the last thing on her mind. Television, chocolate ice cream, a beer, and sleep were the first four. Going over to her mother's didn't even come in fifth. "I'm already dressed for bed: got my makeup off, my pajamas on, and everything. Can it wait till tomorrow?"

"Yes, it can wait. What did you do this evening?"

"I told you."

"No. This evening. Did you go out to dinner?"

Sandra suddenly remembered their previous plans. "Oh, hell, Erma. I'm sorry. I completely forgot to call you and tell you that Mel decided to spend the night with a friend. I apologize. Kitty's defense has atrophied my brain. I hope you didn't go to any trouble about dinner." The line was silent for a moment. "You did, didn't you?"

"That's all right," she said in a muffled voice.

That didn't sound like her mother. Before Phillip died, she'd have been cussing her a blue streak. Now she sounded like some little old blue-hair feeling sorry for herself.

"What did you fix?"

"It doesn't matter, Sandra . . . but if you must know, vegetable lasagna, salad, garlic bread, iced tea, and spumoni for dessert."

"No soup?"

"Screw you."

"That's more like it. You sound like I feel."

"Not worth a shit, you mean?"

"Yeah. I was just feeling sorry for myself, too, wondering what kind of spatter I'd make if I jumped off the balcony."

"Aren't there azalea bushes along that walkway down there? They'd mess up any real good stain. You'd probably land on your head and make a gray-and-red blob."

"Guess I'll wait until I have a better location. Listen, Erma, forgive me for forgetting you. I'll make it up as soon as this case is over, I promise."

"You little shit, you'll make it up to me by coming over for lunch tomorrow. I saved everything and I can damn well warm it up. Pick up your brat on the way over."

It was a good thing Erma couldn't see her. Sandra rolled

her eyes and prayed that something would happen before tomorrow noon. Nothing sounded worse than day-old salad and reheated lasagna. The top layer of noodles would have nothing on cardboard. "Yes, ma'am," Sandra replied as if responding to her drill sergeant.

"I'm not accepting any excuses from either of you two girls. Besides, I want to hear all your plans for the examining trial. Be here at noon and don't be late." She hung up before Sandra could reply.

Sandra hit the switch hook and punched in Stuart's number. She got his answering machine. She hung up and dialed his mobile phone. Voice mail. Later, as she dug out the last few scoops of the chocolate fudge ice cream, she wondered if Stuart was paying her back for being so inattentive to him the last few weeks. Or he could be playing hard to get. Worse yet, there could be another woman. They had never agreed not to date others. Worst case scenario, he could be working. Taking her bowl and the beer over to the sofa, Sandra flipped channels in search of the perfect classic movie as she mused over her relationship with Stuart.

She awoke on the sofa, later, her hand dangling in the bowl on the floor, slobber oozing down the side of her cheek, and a crick in her neck, so she turned off the TV and went to bed.

Shortly after seven on Sunday, Sandra awoke again, this time to the ringing of the telephone. Rolling over, she dragged it into the bed with her. "Hello."

A voice so high pitched and phony that a shooting pain spiked her left eye as each word was spoken said, "You *comprende* my message last night, bitch?"

Now that pissed her off. Not his/her calling her a bitch, but the pain in her head. She hadn't done anything to deserve that kind of suffering. It was the same feeling she used to get when she would drink a twelve-pack of Schlitz malt liquor when she had been married to her first husband. "Fuck you, asshole," she muttered before she let the receiver slip back into place.

Snuggling under the sheet and comforter, Sandra tried to relax her neck and the back of her head in hopes that the pain he/she'd inflicted on her wasn't the precursor of a bad headache. She hadn't had one in a long time and just couldn't get one now. No time. She had to be able to function, to think on her feet. The examining trial was the following day. Even if she was prepared already, she couldn't spend Monday recovering from the weak, sick feeling with which they always left her.

The phone rang again. She felt her shoulders stiffen. Two little balls were forming in the back of her neck at the beginning of her hairline. Picking up the receiver, she said, "What is it?"

"Listen, bitch. You hang up on me again and I'm coming over there and beat the ever-lovin' shit out of you." This time, the lower voice. He was doing her a favor and didn't even know it. Okay, she'd play along.

"You and whose commando team, jerk-off?"

"You better listen good. You're going to call your client right now and tell her to get another lawyer, you hear? 'Cause if you don't, your mama's going to feel some pain."

There was something familiar in the cadence of his voice. The background tapping that she'd heard the night before was missing, but the tone, his choice of words—it would come to her. She needed to keep him on the line.

"Who is this? Is this Edgar Saul? Are you so afraid that I'll make a fool of you that you're trying to scare me off the case? Come on, Edgar. You ought to know me better than that."

"No, this ain't no goddamned Edgar Saul. Now you just shut up and listen."

There was a clicking on the line. Call waiting. How was

that for timing? "Hey, I've got someone on the other line. Do you mind?" Without waiting for a response, she tapped the switch hook. "Hello?"

"Sandra?" It was Stuart.

"Stu. I've got this weirdo on the other line. Can I call you back? I don't want to lose him. I'm trying to figure out who he is."

"What do you mean a weirdo? What's he saying?"

"You know, the usual. Let me call you back, okay? Where are you?"

"At seven-ten in the morning? At home. Where else would I be?"

"You don't have to be so terse. Call you back in a minute." She hit the switch hook. "You still there, fella?"

"Listen, Salinsky, you got twenty-four hours to do what I said or else."

"Okay, so this isn't Edgar. Is it one of the other assistants? You guys—" She laughed.

"No. Now shut the fuck up and hear what I got to say. I'm getting mad."

To which she failed to respond with other than a cursory, "Uh-huh."

"You get off the case and stay off or else."

"Why don't you come over right now and we'll have this thing out, okay? I don't have time for this. I've got an examining trial to prepare for."

"Listen, lady—"

"Kiss my ass, jerk-off." She hung up. By then she had to pee big time, so she did that, and then she dialed Erma's number. Sandra knew Erma would still be asleep, but just to be on the safe side she wanted her to know that she was the brunt of some threats again.

"Who the hell is this?"

"Mom. Good morning. It's your favorite daughter. Did you sleep well?"

"What now? Just what the hell could make you call in the middle of the night again?"

"It's after seven, and I know it's probably a false alarm, but you should know some asshole is calling me and using your name in vain."

"Goddamnit. What's this one going to do to me?"

"Inflict some pain. That's about as specific as he's gotten so far."

"Guess I'll get my .45 out of the drawer."

"The twelve-gauge still next to the door?"

"Yup. So can I go back to sleep now?"

"Yes, Mother dear."

"See you at lunch. No, I didn't forget."

Stuart must have been sitting on top of the phone. He picked it up on the first ring. "Yes."

"It's me. I got tired of the jerk. So what's going on?"

"Been missing you. Wondering if we could get together later today. Brunch at the Saltwater Grill?"

He knew the Saltwater Grill was one of her favorites. Brunch there turned her into a piglet. "Can't. Got to go to Erma's with the kid." She wanted very badly to mention that she'd been unable to track him down the evening before, but she didn't. It might be sending him mixed signals.

"Oh. Well, call me when you get back."

She hung up. The phone rang again immediately.

"You're pissing me off, bitch," the high-pitched voice hollered.

The muscles in her neck felt like they'd been wrung out like an old washrag. "Hold on," she said, "if you're going to keep calling like this, I've got to have something hot to drink." Sandra put the phone down and walked to the kitchen, rinsed out the kettle, filled it with fresh water, and banged it onto the stove. After turning on the burner, she pulled a cup from the cabinet, a spoon from the drawer, dropped a teabag into the cup, and then picked up the kitchen phone. "You still there?"

"Goddamn you for a bitch!" he/she shrieked into the phone.

"I'm going to stop playing with you, if you can't be any more pleasant than that."

The phone went dead in her ear. She figured that was it for him/her. She was correct. She didn't hear from the mysterious caller the rest of the morning.

Chapter Nineteen

After she took a late morning dip in the pool, Sandra phoned her "brat" and got her brat's father, Jack Cartwright. He was an accountant, a really nice man, and boring as hell. She made arrangements to pick up Melinda for lunch.

Jack and Connie lived in a two-story brick house on the south side of Offat's Bayou, about two miles from Sandra's condo. The subdivision had been developed in the late 1950s to early 1960s as people moved from the crowded East End of the island, before the big move at saving historical homes.

Jack seemed fine until she went into his house. When she knocked on the door, he asked her in, which was not all that unusual, even though it always made her a little uncomfortable to see furniture that she had bought inside a house that used to be hers, albeit decorated differently. As a rule, though, they got along fine. All hard feelings were in the distant past.

Jack wore a blue polo shirt and a pair of khaki pants. His feet were bare. "Mel's not home yet. Connie's gone to pick her up. They'll be back in a few minutes." He was developing a bit of a paunch, but, she had to admit, looked fit and healthy.

Sandra stood inside the foyer and glanced at herself in the mirror, wondering what Jack saw when he looked at her. "Okay. I guess I'm a little early."

"No. No. Come on in." He beckoned at her to follow him.

When they got to the den, a football game blared on TV. Some things never changed. "I wanted to talk to you about the child support, anyway. Now's as good a time as any."

Her stomach lurched. Here it comes, she thought. He was going to hit her up for a big raise. She could just feel it. She had no one but herself to blame. "Yes, what about it?"

"Connie and I've been talking. You know that extra two-fifty you've been sending?"

She could see it coming. They wanted the extra to be court-ordered, in case she got pissed or something and quit paying it. "Yes, Jack, the two-fifty—"

"Well, we've been thinking about it, and we think you should be putting it in the bank for Melinda's college education."

She let out a deep breath and smiled. "I have a college fund set up for her, Jack. Erma and I both do. We put something in every month," she said, feeling a little irritated that he would think that she didn't care enough about her kid to have a college savings account.

"Good, but Sandra, we don't need that extra thousand a month. That's an awful lot of money. You already send more than enough. You could do something else with it."

"She could have some of it for her allowance."

"No. She gets an allowance. If she wants any more than we already give her, and she does, I'm sure, then she needs to earn it herself. She could get a job during the school year on weekends, even at fourteen."

Sandra studied his face to see if she could detect an ulterior motive. She never heard of anyone turning down money. He seemed sincere enough. "Well, I agree with you there. So is there anything she wants to do that y'all don't want to pay for? I mean lessons or go on a trip or something like that?"

"Tell you what, why don't you put that two-fifty a week into a car account? By the time her sixteenth birthday rolls around, you could get her a pretty decent car."

"First of all, I was going to buy her a car anyway. Secondly, since she's only fourteen, that's going to be one hell of a first car."

"Well, whatever. We can talk about it some more later. I just wanted you to know that we appreciate the extra money, but we don't need it."

"Okay, Jack. Whatever you say."

"You know what you could do though, Sandra."

Okay, here it comes, she thought. She folded her arms across her chest and waited for the bottom line.

"Sandra." He looked into her eyes and wetted his lips.

She knew it must be something serious. "Yes, Jack."

"I'm not trying to offend you, really I'm not, but you could try to spend a little more time with Mel."

Sandra could almost see the smoke issue out of her own nose. "That's what I'm trying to do today, Jack. So I tell you what," she pointed her finger at his chest, "when she gets home, you tell her that her mother will come get her as soon as she gives her a call." She turned to leave.

He tugged on her arm. "Don't get mad."

"Just tell her, Jack," she said, pulling away from him and making her exit.

"Well, at least wait in the car," he called.

She did as he requested, mostly because she didn't want to drive home and back again. Okay, so she was lazy. She sat in the heat and fumed. She knew she needed improvement as a mother; she didn't need to be told by her ex-husband. She wanted to be a better mother. She thought about being a better mother. She missed so much about not being a full-time mother. The trouble was that she really didn't know how to go about improving her mothering. Her only role model had been her own mother.

At a quarter to twelve, Mel and Connie drove up. Mel jumped out of the car almost before it stopped. "Hi, Mom." Melinda threw her stuff into the passenger side of the Volvo, climbed in after it, and hugged Sandra. Her hair up in a ponytail, she looked more like ten than fourteen. She wore sandals, walking shorts, and a yellow camp T-shirt.

"Hi, Mel honey," Sandra said as she hugged her back. She vowed to start being a more attentive mother immediately.

"Are we going to Grandma's?"

"Over the river and through the woods," Sandra sang.

"What was that?" Melinda asked and laughed.

"The generation gap." Sandra drove down Sixty-first Street to Broadway and headed toward Erma's. "So how was the party last night?"

"Oh, pretty good."

"What'd y'all do? Stay up all night?"

She snapped her chewing gum. "Yeah, but Susie's mother let us sleep until ten."

Sandra nodded. She should know more stuff to talk about.

"How is Grandma taking Mr. Parker's death?"

Sandra glanced at her. That was a really thoughtful thing for Mel to ask. Jack and Connie had done a good job with her. "Pretty hard."

"Um, did she cry a lot?" Melinda glanced at her sideways.

"Not around me, but I'm sure she did."

"Did you?"

"Nah. But I felt sadder than I thought I would." That was true. Surprised even herself.

"I cried, Mom. I didn't know him very well, but he's one of the first people I've known who has died."

"Oh, Melinda. I didn't think about that. I guess that's true."

"Yeah. Makes me feel old. Like, you know when you're a kid, it doesn't really register when people die. I mean, you mostly don't know anybody real well who dies. You know what I mean?"

"Some kids' grandparents die when they are little."

"Well, mine didn't, so for me I guess it was different. Anyway, I felt sad. He was always nice to me."

"Who, Phillip Parker?"

"Yeah. When he was at Grandma's."

Sandra felt sick inside for a moment at the thought that perhaps he had touched Melinda in some sexual way. She glanced at her, weighing whether or not to ask her. Wouldn't Melinda have brought it up? Wouldn't she have told her? Maybe she didn't feel comfortable enough with her to tell her, since she didn't live with her. Oh, God, she was a worse mother than she thought. She looked at Melinda again. "Mel, honey, were you ever alone with Mr. Parker?"

"What do you mean by alone?"

"I mean, when you were at Grandma's and she wasn't around, did Grandma ever leave you alone with him even for a few minutes?"

Melinda pulled a long string of chewing gum out of her mouth and put it back again. "What are you getting at, Mom?"

"Well, did she?"

"Leave me alone with Mr. Parker? What for?" Her forehead wrinkled up.

"Maybe just to run to the store for something?"

"Mother, what's going on? I don't like how you sound."

"Okay. Okay." Sandra asked it straight out. "Did Mr. Parker ever, when you were little or even later when you were bigger, did Mr. Parker ever, ever touch you in a sexual way?"

"Ugh, Mom, no way. Yuck. What's that about?"

Sandra felt immense relief. "Don't tell Grandma I asked you."

"Did he touch you like that when you were little, Mom?"

"Me?" Sandra laughed. "Nah. If he had, you never would have even met him."

"Is that why somebody killed him? That is so gross. Was it because he did something to somebody or their kid?"

"You know, Mel, you're really too young to know about stuff like that."

"You brought it up."

"Yeah. I just thought of it all of a sudden. But I don't like the idea of your being exposed to stuff like that."

"When you were little, you were around Grandma's clients. Weren't some of them pretty bad criminals?"

Sandra laughed. "Most of them. I just didn't know it."

"So . . ."

"Times are different these days. People are different."

"Right, Mom. Kids grow up sooner now."

She had a point there. But Sandra didn't want her kid to grow up sooner. She parked in the shade under a large oak tree. "We'll talk about this later." Sandra got out of the car and saw Melinda give her an odd little glance out of the side of her eye as she opened her door.

Melinda ran up to the front door and pushed the doorbell several times. Sandra could see how much she'd sprouted when Erma let them in and Mel bent over to hug her grandmother. Erma wore her ballet slippers, a long black cotton dress, and the scent of garlic and tomatoes.

When lunch was on the table, Melinda turned to Erma and said, "You know, Grandma, I want to go live with Mom, but she won't let me. Do you think I could come live with you?"

Erma gave Sandra a look. "What the hell is that about?"

Mel didn't give her a chance to say anything. "I've spent the last ten years with Daddy and his side of the family and now I think I should spend my high school years with Mom and her side of the family. Don't you think I'm right, Grandma?"

"Mel, where would I put you?" Sandra asked. "I live in a two-bedroom condo that is more like a one-bedroom and den."

"We could live someplace else."

"So you want me to move?"

"Well, goddamn, Sandra, she is your kid."

Sandra pointed her fork at Erma. "You stay out of this."

"Yes, Sandra, I am your kid."

"Don't you dare call me Sandra, young lady. Would you tell me why all of a sudden—"

"I just think it's time, that's all," Melinda said.

"Is there something going on with your Dad?"

"You mean like what you asked me in the car?"

"No, not that." Sandra glanced at Erma to see how she reacted to that, but apparently it went over her head. "Anything. Are y'all not getting along?"

"No, Mom. It's not that."

"What about Connie? Or your brother?" Connie and Jack had a son four years younger than Mel.

"No, Mom. I love Connie and Richard. I just want to come live with you, that's all."

Sandra heaved a big sigh and rubbed her eyes.

"Well, I think it's a good idea," Erma said.

Sandra gave Erma another look. Maybe if Erma had been a better mother, Sandra never would have sent Mel to live with her father. Sandra knew that wasn't a fair statement, but she felt confused. She thought she had done the right thing.

She knew Jack would get remarried and Mel would have a full-time mother. Sandra worked long, impossible hours like her own mother had and didn't want her kid brought up by housekeepers or around her clients like she had been. Melinda wore such a plaintive look on her sweet face that it was hard to say no, but Sandra wasn't ready to make that kind of commitment. What if they got a new place to live, Melinda moved in, and then it didn't work out? Wouldn't that be worse than just saying no in the first place?

"We could take a vote," Mel said.

Sandra swallowed some iced tea and looked each of them in the eye in turn. "No, we are not going to take a vote. This isn't a democracy. It's my life. Our lives."

"Mom."

"I'm not saying no. I'm saying I'll think about it over the summer. Okay?" She pointed at Erma again. "You don't interfere. I'll think about it."

"That means no; I know you." Mel crossed her arms over her chest.

"No it doesn't, it means I'll think about it. End of discussion. I've got a lot of other things going on just now. Let me get past them, and I'll give it a lot of serious thought."

When Sandra let her daughter out at her father's house, Melinda wasn't nearly as animated as she'd been a few hours earlier. She kissed Sandra on the cheek before she got out and said, "Think real hard, Mom. Real hard." And slammed the door really hard.

Chapter Twenty

"Call your first witness," Justice of the Peace Perez told Edgar Saul the following morning.

"Thank you, Your Honor. The state calls Dr. Henry Michaels, the medical examiner." Edgar stood next to his chair, stiff as a Nazi soldier at attention.

Sandra had always thought that Edgar walked like there was a cucumber up his rear and stood rigidly because it pained him to bend over. He observed all the formalities of the court and then some. Pissed off a lot of them who liked to skip formalities in their rush from court to court. Of course, Edgar didn't hurry anywhere. Always prepared—ever the Boy Scout, early for court, if anything, and never had a schedule conflict. Sandra didn't know how he managed all that, but it was well known that most of the judges considered him Mister Perfect.

The good doctor had waited outside in the hall. Most of the witnesses had been inside the courtroom at the beginning. The judge swore all of them in at once. Edgar and she invoked "The Rule." The judge instructed them not to discuss the case amongst themselves and sent them into the hall. Unlike TV, at least in a Texas courtroom, witnesses did not generally remain inside.

When Dr. Michaels entered, he scanned the people in the gallery as if searching for his audience. Winking at Sandra when he reached the front of the courtroom, he turned to the judge, nodded and grinned, and stepped into the witness box.

"Be sure and speak into that microphone, Hank," the judge said, and bent his head over and wrote something down.

Edgar Saul still stood at counsel table, which they shared: he at the west end, she at the east. Kitty sat on the far side of her, shielding herself from Edgar.

Mister Perfect ducked his head as though bowing. "May I proceed, Your Honor?"

"Sure, sure," Judge Perez said. "Go ahead."

Edgar sat, finally. "Dr. Michaels, please state your name for the record."

"Dr. Henry Michaels." He leaned back in the chair and scrutinized the gallery again. Sandra wondered whether he was looking for someone in particular.

"And, sir, would you tell the court how you are employed?"

"Chief Medical Examiner for Galveston County, State of Texas."

Sandra found that humorous. He was not only the chief medical examiner; he was the only medical examiner. A couple of guys helped him, but he was the only doctor who worked in that capacity.

"And how long have you been so employed, sir?"

"Your Honor," Sandra interrupted as she got to her feet. "The defense will stipulate that Dr. Michaels is, has been, and probably will be the medical examiner for Galveston County for many years. We will also stipulate to his qualifications. Can we please just get on with it?"

Edgar had stood as well. "The state will accept those stipulations from defense counsel, Your Honor."

"Fine, let the record so reflect," the judge said.

They proceeded to hear from Dr. Michaels all about his arrival at the Parker house, his initial examination of the body, his subsequent complete autopsy later at the morgue, and his conclusions. His testimony wasn't necessarily harmful to Kitty, so Sandra had no reason to object to it or cross-examine him.

"Call your next witness, Mr. Saul," Judge Perez said.

Already a note of impatience had crept into Judge Perez's voice. He probably wanted to get to his law office. In Texas, an attorney-justice of the peace could practice law in addition to serving as J.P., so long as it wasn't criminal law. Sandra thought all J.P.s should be lawyers, but the legislature didn't agree with her. The non-lawyer J.P.s had a strong lobby.

Edgar had gotten to his feet again. "Thank you, Your Honor. The state calls Elizabeth Haynes."

The constable, who had been waiting at the back door, swung it open and went out into the hall. They could hear him call Lizzie's name. Lizzie hadn't been there when the rest of the witnesses had been sworn, but Sandra figured that Edgar had probably told her not to come for at least half an hour after they were scheduled to begin.

A couple of minutes later, the constable reappeared and came down the aisle to the bench. "Judge, there ain't no lady out there that answers to that name."

Judge Perez said, "Approach the bench, you two."

Edgar shrugged. They both walked around the table to the bench. It was lower than the ones in district court and they were able to rest their arms on it and lean forward to hear what the judge whispered.

"This is off the record," he said to his court reporter. To them he whispered, "I don't want to wait around for your witnesses, Edgar." He pointed his fountain pen in Edgar's face. "I told both of you, and you both know it's my policy that you have every witness ready to testify when you call them. Now if you can't turn this woman up, you're just out of luck."

Edgar shook his head. "Judge, I instructed her to be here at nine just like the rest of them. I apologize to the court. I'll call another witness if you'll give me a moment to arrange for her to be located."

"All right, then. Sixty seconds and then I want that next witness in . . . this . . . courtroom." His eyes glinted. Maybe he was not so enamored with old Edgar after all.

Edgar said, "Thank you for your indulgence, Your Honor. May I speak to my assistant?"

The judge nodded. Edgar's demeanor made Sandra feel like heaving on him as she followed him to the table. He went to the bar and murmured to a young female. Sandra assumed she was a lawyer, since she sat on a chair in front of the bar. Since Sandra had worked with Edgar, she knew that though he didn't mind having someone second-chair him, he didn't like anyone sitting right at his elbow.

"What's going on?" Kitty whispered. She had kept her own counsel up to that point.

Glancing at the judge, Sandra cupped her hand over her mouth, "Lizzie hasn't shown up and the judge is pissed."

Kitty nodded. "She's late all the time, but you'd think she'd be here to see me fry."

Sandra laughed. "You're not going to fry, Kitty. At least not today."

Kitty bit her lip, but when Sandra smiled and squeezed her arm, she relaxed. Sandra felt like her mother.

Edgar stood beside his chair when he was through talking. The young assistant had quietly departed while Sandra's back was turned. Edgar said, "The State calls Leslie Carruthers."

"Who's that?" Kitty asked.

"Bubba," Sandra whispered.

The constable went out into the hall again but this time returned with Bubba in tow. Bubba shuffled up the aisle and slung himself into the witness box.

"State your name," Edgar said.

"Bubba Carruthers."

"It's Leslie Carruthers, is it not?"

"Yeah, but they call me Bubba 'cause I ain't ever liked Leslie." He glared at Edgar. He didn't seem to like Edgar any more than he did Leslie.

"So Mr. Carruthers, you were Mr. Parker's aide, is that correct?"

"Caretaker of his house."

"Okay. And your duties were what, exactly?"

"Taking care of Mr. Parker's house. His beach house where he was murdered by her." He pointed to Kitty.

Sandra jumped to her feet. "Objection." It caught her so off-guard that she had no grounds ready. "Assuming facts not in evidence," she blurted, not sure of what else to say.

"Sustained," Judge Perez said. "Mr. Carruthers, you must answer only what is asked of you and nothing more."

He nodded. "Okay, Judge."

"On the day of the decedent's death, Mr. Carruthers, you were present, were you not?"

"Yeah."

"What were you doing?"

"You know what I was doing. I told you the other day."

Edgar cleared his throat. "Yes, but now you have to tell the judge."

"I was putting out food and drinks and cleaning up after the party."

"Did you serve the police officers who were working security?"

"Yeah. I made plates for all four of 'em. I took 'em cans of Dr. Pepper, too. What of it?"

"Uh, nothing, Mr. Carruthers. Now tell the judge what happened after the party."

"Well, Mr. Phillip, he said I could finish cleaning up in the morning. They were all going to bed. So, I went to The Cantina."

"So who was there when you departed?"

"When I left? Miss Lizzie and Mr. Phillip. Mr. Raymond and her," he said and nodded in our direction. "And Mr. Stuart and Miss Sandra."

He was wrong, but Sandra would have to wait until it was her turn before she could correct him. She noted that on her legal pad.

"And, Mr. Carruthers, who was there when you returned?"

"I don't know." His voice had grown loud. "They was all asleep. It weren't until I got up the next morning that I saw that Mr. Phillip was dead on the concrete floor under the house."

"And Mr. Carruthers, did Mr. Phillip Parker have on his Rolex watch and diamond pinkie ring when you returned from The Cantina?" Edgar turned to her and grinned.

"I don't know, 'cause I didn't see him. But when I got up the next morning, he sure didn't."

"But he did have them on the last time you saw him alive."

Sandra jumped up. "Objection, leading."

"Yeah," Bubba said, "he did."

Sandra glared at Bubba. "Your Honor, please instruct the witness not to answer when an attorney stands up to make an objection. Request the answer be stricken from the record." Sandra only made that last request as a formality. She'd always thought it was kind of stupid to ask something be stricken from the record when everyone had already heard it, especially in a bench trial. Like the judge would forget he ever heard it.

Judge Perez frowned. "Mr. Carruthers, you've got to stop talking as soon as the lawyer stands to make an objection." Turning his attention back to them, he said, "Let the answer be stricken from the record. And Mr. Saul, don't lead."

Edgar stood. "Just trying to expedite matters, Your Honor." He sat back down. "Mr. Carruthers, what was Mr. Parker wearing the last time you saw him?"

Bubba frowned. "Well, he was headed upstairs to change his clothes, but he had on his watch and ring and also a gold chain with a piece of eight on it. He was unbuttoning his shirt and Miss Lizzie, she was coming up the stairs behind him."

"Thank you." Edgar stood again. "Pass the witness."

The judge nodded in Sandra's direction. She half stood at her chair. "Thank you, Your Honor. Mr. Carruthers, we're acquainted, aren't we?"

Bubba folded his arms across his chest. "I know you, Miss Sandra." He stared over her head.

"In here, I'm Miss Salinsky," she stated. "Mr. Carruthers, isn't it true that the watch and ring were on Mr. Parker when you came back from The Cantina?"

"I don't know what you're talking about. I didn't even see him then."

"Mr. Parker was not lying on the concrete, but was mostly on the grass, isn't that true?"

He shrugged. "Half on. Half off. It don't make no difference. He was still dead."

"He was dead when you came back from The Cantina, wasn't he?"

"Was he?"

"He was lying as I've described, in a velour bathrobe, mostly on the grass, his face smashed in, and his ring and watch still on his body, isn't that true, Mr. Carruthers?"

"You don't know, you wasn't there, Miss Salinsky."

"But you were. You came back earlier than you told the police, didn't you? And you found Mr. Parker dead, didn't you?"

"Objection. Compound question, Your Honor." Edgar was buttoning the second button on his jacket as if he thought he would be on his feet for a while in argument.

"Rephrase, Judge," she said.

The judge said, "All right."

"Mister Carruthers, you returned from the bar earlier than you told the police, right?"

"Who told you that?"

The judge said, "Just answer the question, sir, and we'll all get out of here a little earlier."

"Remember you're under oath," she said as Bubba's eyes met hers. Sandra suddenly knew the meaning of that old saying, "if looks could kill."

"So, what of it?"

"You found Phillip Parker dead at that time, right?"

"Yeah? So what's the diff if I found him dead then or later?" Bubba turned to the judge. "Judge, who cares when I found him? I didn't kill him. I didn't have nothing to do with his dying. I swear."

"But you did with the missing ring and watch, right, Mr. Carruthers?" Sandra asked.

Bubba's face had grown the same color as the ashes in Erma's fireplace. He stared at her, his mouth open like a dead fish's.

When he didn't answer, Sandra said, "In fact, when you found Phillip Parker dead, you removed his diamond pinkie ring and his Rolex watch and immediately called a fence, isn't that true?"

"You're a liar. A damn liar," Bubba said.

"Shall I bring Mr. Fulshear into the courtroom to verify that you called him on the night in question?"

"But I didn't take the stuff to him."

The courtroom grew as quiet as the morgue.

Bubba's gaze went from her, to Edgar Saul, to the judge. "I want a lawyer, Judge. I want a lawyer."

Judge Perez unclenched his jaw and said, "Constable, take this man into custody."

Bubba stood and looked ready to run, but the constable had taken long strides down the aisle, his huge cell keys jangling at his side, his hand on his sidearm. "Hold it right there, Mister."

Bubba's hands went up into the air and he froze.

"We'll take a fifteen-minute recess," Judge Perez said as he stepped off the bench, his black robe billowing behind him. Sandra could still see him as he reached his small chambers and grabbed the telephone off the hook before kicking the door closed.

Bubba's earlier glare at her had nothing on Edgar's now that Sandra met his eyes. She knew he knew that the arrest of Bubba for the theft of the watch and ring weakened the state's case against Kitty considerably. The most they could get her for now would be manslaughter, a second-degree felony, as opposed to capital murder. Under the facts as Kitty had related them, even if Kitty had caused Phillip's death, Sandra didn't think she'd get more than criminally negligent homicide. A state jail felony, the term of years was nominal compared to the other two charges.

"Sandra," Kitty pulled on her sleeve like a child on its mother's. "That was good for our side, huh?"

Sandra leaned over, her eyes not leaving Edgar's. "Very good, kid. At the very least they're going to have to reduce the charges."

Kitty breathed out a gust of air. "That's wonderful."

"We're not through yet." Sandra bent over the other way. "You want to talk, Mr. Saul?" She tried, but she couldn't keep the cockiness out of her voice.

Edgar couldn't keep the edge out of his. "You ain't heard nothin' yet." But she could tell he was a mite irritated with her.

"I thought you guys had an obligation to seek the truth," Sandra said as she pushed back her chair. She took Kitty by the arm and led her down the aisle and outside to the public restroom. Heads turned as they walked out. Stuart and Raymond approached them, but she waved them away. Sandra didn't want the press or anyone else to say they violated "The Rule" and talked about the case with potential witnesses.

They took care of their business. Sandra brushed off a female reporter who thought she had them cornered in the ladies' room. No sooner were they seated back in the courtroom when the judge returned and again told Edgar to call his next witness.

Edgar stood once more. "At this time, Your Honor, the state calls Officer Robert Earl Bradshaw." He peered over his shoulder at Sandra as if to gauge her reaction.

So Bradshaw was out of town, huh? The next time she saw Dennis Truman, she was going to kick his butt.

The constable held the door open while a vaguely familiar young man who had the brawn of a farmhand came striding through. He spoke to the constable and nodded to the other cops in the gallery as he went past. Sandra was unable to catch his eye as he waltzed down the aisle or after he sat on the witness stand. Edgar Saul had probably instructed the young man to deliberately hide from her. That would be not unlike Edgar.

"State your name for the record," Edgar said.

"Robert Earl Bradshaw." He swiped at his blond crew cut while keeping his eyes steadily on Edgar.

"And your occupation, sir."

Any fool could see from his uniform that he was an officer of the Galveston Police Department, but the written record wouldn't show that unless someone verbalized it. Sandra sat mute while Edgar led the officer through that and some other formalities. It wasn't long before she found out what the big secret was.

"Were you working extra duty on the night of Phillip Parker's death?" Edgar leaned forward in his chair. His little head protruded so that he reminded her of a baby bird in the nest, a featherless head wobbling on a long naked neck, chirping through a large yellow beak.

"Yes, sir. It was my job to guard the entrance to make sure no one came in off the street."

"Had you been in Mr. Parker's employ on a prior occasion?"

"Yes, sir. Any time I could work for Mr. Parker, I wouldn't pass it up. He usually fed us and paid us well."

"Us?"

"Sometimes for the larger events, there were three or four off-duty police officers."

"And the night in question, how many were there?"

"Originally?" He tapped his chin. "Four."

"Where were the other three when he was killed?"

"I don't know. I mean, sir, they had went home early." He sat taller in the chair. "I was the only police officer remaining 'cause there was only a couple of folks left."

"Okay, now, Officer Bradshaw, on the night of this particular party, did Mr. Parker feed you?"

"Well, yes, sir. We had plates of roast beef and crab claws and red sauce, stuff like that."

"Who brought the food out to you?"

"Normally it was Bubba."

"Was it Bubba that night?"

"Yes, sir. At least early in the evening. Bubba brought us plates of food and some Dr Peppers."

"Did someone else bring you food later in the evening?"

Bradshaw fidgeted in his chair. "Miss Lizzie, sir, she brought us some cake."

Sandra remembered that cake. She had thought it rather gauche for Phillip to celebrate his asbestosis case victory with a specially-made cake in the shape of a lung. But then Phillip had been nothing if not confident in his cases.

"Anyone else?"

"Well, sir, not exactly."

"What do you mean not exactly?"

For the first time Bradshaw looked in their direction. "That young lady over there, sir," he said, pointing at Kitty.

"She brought you food?"

"No sir, drink."

"Another Dr Pepper?"

Sandra knew damn good and well that it hadn't been a Dr. Pepper, or Edgar wouldn't be making such a production out of Bradshaw's testimony.

"No, sir. Bourbon and Coke."

"Bourbon and Coke," Edgar Saul repeated loudly, in case the judge and anyone else in Galveston hadn't heard.

"Yes, sir, but it was more than that."

"Why, what do you mean, sir? Was it strong?"

"Yes, sir. Real strong. What I mean to say, Mr. Saul, is that I believe that Miss Fulton slipped me a Mickey, 'cause it knocked me out."

Chapter Twenty-One

Sandra heard the door in the back of the courtroom open and turned to see Edgar's female assistant racing up the aisle like a woman on a mission. She whizzed through the gate and applied her brakes as Edgar stood and addressed the court.

"May I have a moment, Judge Perez?"

The judge nodded, leaned his chair back like a recliner, and closed his eyes. Sandra could practically hear him praying that their hearing would soon draw to a close.

Edgar and the young attorney conferred for a moment. "Your Honor, may we approach the bench?" Edgar's voice sounded quite a bit louder than it had been in his direct examinations. When they got up there, he said quietly, "The police have found a body at Elizabeth Haynes' house, Your Honor. Shot to death. May we have a recess until tomorrow morning?"

"It's not Lizzie," Sandra said. Cold fingers caressed her heart. She was not Lizzie's greatest fan but did kind of consider them friends. Not Lizzie, she told herself.

Edgar's tightly pressed lips turned white. He shook his head. "They don't know. Does she have any people around here that can make the identification?"

Judge Perez cleared his throat. "Y'all come back here the same time tomorrow," he whispered. He banged loudly on the wooden pounding block. "Court's adjourned till nine a.m. tomorrow morning." He dropped his voice. "Keep me posted, you two," he said as he turned in his chair and stepped down.

It's funny what one hears in times of high stress. Sandra heard a high-pitched buzz from Judge Perez yanking the zipper down on his robe. She watched his back as he trod into chambers, floating as if in slow motion. Her eyes came to rest on Edgar.

"No. Lizzie has no people as far as I know," she said.

"No next of kin?" He stopped throwing things into his briefcase and glanced at her.

"Phillip Parker was the closest thing."

"Well, who's going to identify the body?" He seemed irritated.

"Is it a woman's?"

"Definitely," the little assistant said.

"Reddish-blond hair?"

"Now that, I don't know." She turned to Edgar. "Mr. Saul, they want you at the house . . . uh, now, the lieutenant said."

"Lieutenant Truman?" Sandra asked.

"Yes, ma'am," she answered. Sandra let that pass. She already knew she was old enough to be the young attorney's mother.

"Go with me, Sandra," Edgar said. From his tone, Edgar was making a request rather than a demand, which was his usual course of behavior.

The thought repulsed her. It must have been apparent on her face.

"You could ID the body."

"If it's her, you mean. The only other person I can think of, off the top of my head, is my mother and I don't think Erma is up to this." Sandra was thinking aloud. "It'll be bad enough if it is Lizzie and I have to break it to Mother."

Shaking her head, Sandra felt nauseated at the thought. She could only hope that her tough-talking old bird of a mother wouldn't break down.

Becoming aware of her surroundings again, Sandra realized that the witness still sat on the witness stand, the constable still stood at the door in the back of the courtroom, and Kitty still waited at counsel table and watched them. Everyone else had cleared out.

While Edgar spoke to Officer Bradshaw, Sandra explained to Kitty what had transpired, got her briefcase packed up, and led Kitty into the hall, delivering her to Raymond's waiting arms. "Where's Stu?" she asked Raymond.

"Went back to the office. I'm supposed to beep him when I'm called to testify, so he can come back over here."

She nodded and started to return to the courtroom. Kitty caught at her sleeve.

"No one will think I did it, will they, Sandy?"

Sandra turned back to her. "Now what made you ask that?"

Kitty stared at the floor. "I'd rather not say at this time."

As Sandra gazed at the top of Kitty's head, she saw a red haze. She grabbed Kitty's shoulder, wrenching her out of Raymond's grasp, and slammed her up against the wall. "Now, goddamn you, you tell me what made you ask that. No tears. No hysteria. I want a straight answer from you and I want it now." Her stomach churned as her eyes penetrated Kitty's frightened baby blue ones. She wanted to hit Kitty. She wondered, albeit briefly, what the State Bar of Texas did to lawyers who punched out their clients.

Raymond pulled at her arm. "Sandy, please. You're hurting her."

"I'm going to hurt her a lot more if she doesn't tell me right now just what the hell she is talking about." Sandra had the strength of ten men at that moment. Raymond couldn't budge her. She glared at the young woman whom she had pinned against the courthouse wall. As angry as she was, she wanted a quick answer, before Edgar came through those double doors.

"Sandy, it's not my fault. Really, it's not. It's just that the other night I found out that somebody stole my gun."

"Je—sus Christ! And this was something you didn't think you ought to tell me?" Kitty's perfume smelled sweet and flowery. Sitting next to her in the courtroom, it was tolerable, but now that their faces were only a few inches apart, it was too strong mixed with the smell of the Dentine gum Sandra had made Kitty spit out before entering the courtroom. Sandra dropped her arms and took a couple of steps back. "Okay. And what kind of gun is it that you are missing?" She didn't bother asking why she owned one, being a model. It wouldn't have made any difference. Besides, this was Texas. She wouldn't go so far as to say everyone owned a gun, but many did.

Rubbing her arms, Kitty gave her a petulant glance. "It was a little one. Fit in my purse." She held her two forefingers several inches apart. " 'Bout that big. Silver."

"No. I meant what caliber? What size bullets?" Sandra had a thing about guns. She didn't think that people who couldn't spell the word should own one.

Raymond interrupted them. "It was a .25. I gave it to her for protection." He brushed past her and took Kitty's hand. "Why didn't you tell me?"

Officer Bradshaw pushed through the courtroom doors behind them. Edgar followed, lugging his huge leather briefcase. "We'll discuss this later," she said. "Keep your mouths shut, both of you."

Edgar said something to his assistant. She took off down

the hall. Turning to Sandra, he said, "Ready to go to Miss Haynes' house?"

Sandra watched his eyes as they traveled to Kitty and Raymond. She knew Edgar well enough to know the thoughts that were behind them. She'd have to face that later. Just now, they all needed to be certain that it was Lizzie who lay dead. "Be in touch with you later," she said to them with her darkest look. She didn't apologize for her roughness. It might just be the beginning of some tough times between them.

Edgar and Sandra walked across the parking lot to the garage. She could feel the heat from the asphalt through the bottoms of her shoes. By the time they reached his Jeep on the far side, her clothes were damp with perspiration. She peeled off her jacket before she got inside. The interior of the Cherokee was much cooler because of the covered parking than it would have been had he chosen a space in the lot outside the courthouse. Once he turned on the air-conditioning, they had relief from the heat in a matter of minutes.

They didn't speak much. Just because they rode together didn't mean they weren't adversaries. Sandra was doing him a favor; that was all. And she had her own motives besides the protection of her mother. She wanted to see the premises. Would there be something to help her figure out what was going on? Why Lizzie was killed? Who might have had a motive? And was it related to Phillip's murder? A small hope that it wasn't lurked in the recesses of her mind.

The idea of Lizzie being dead invaded her emotions like sap oozing from a tree: slow, but unstoppable. She'd been trying not to let herself feel anything from the moment she'd heard those words. Now she began to feel overwhelmed. Staring at the plethora of hotels, motels, and restaurants that flew by as Edgar drove down the seawall toward the West End of the island, Sandra's breath seemed harder to draw. Her eyes burned. She swallowed many times over rather than attempt to respond to Edgar's efforts at conversation. She'd just talked to the woman a few days ago.

Two marked city police cars blocked the driveway. A white unmarked sedan at the curb indicated that Dennis Truman had arrived. An ambulance stood at the end of the sidewalk. Edgar parked across the street. They walked over to Lizzie's house. Sandra had been inside several times. It was in an area they used to call "down the island" when she was growing up. What had been grazing land for dairy cattle was now a subdivision that had sprung up a number of years earlier. The houses were mostly two stories, ultra-modern, squeezed on too-small lots. They were like miniature mansions. Lizzie's even had a circular staircase, but it came right down within a few feet of the front door. Galveston Island had its geographical limitations, but some designs were downright ridiculous.

Dennis met them at the door. "The doc is in there now."

"Is it . . . is it her?" she asked.

Dennis glanced at Edgar and then at Sandra. "I'm pretty sure. You here to make an official ID?"

Sandra nodded. Dennis stepped aside to let them enter. Everything seemed in its place. "Forced entry?"

"No. We already checked all the doors and windows. Nothing unusual. Seems like she musta known the perpetrator."

Sandra grimaced. She didn't want to hear that. She wanted to hear that the back door had been busted open. That the place was trashed. That she came home and got it from a burglar.

Edgar walked toward the rear of the house. The bedrooms were in the back. Lizzie had a large master bedroom with a king-sized bed, an enormous oval-shaped sunken tub, and a wall of closets. Of the other two bedrooms, one was set up as a guest room and the third was utilized for extra closet space and storage.

"Not there," Dennis called out.

Edgar stopped. "Then where?"

"The kitchen."

"The kitchen," Edgar repeated.

Dennis shrugged. "She was fixing dinner from the looks of things."

Sandra walked toward the kitchen, afraid of what she would see but wanting to get it over with. "How did she get it?" she asked over her shoulder.

"Two to the back of the head."

"Ugh." She stopped. "With a large caliber or small caliber?" If it were very large, two shots to the back of the head wouldn't leave much of her face and head. On the other hand, knowing that Kitty's alleged "missing" gun was a .25 made her hope it wasn't a small caliber.

"Pretty small, Sandra. Don't know how small, but there's no exit wound." He walked a few steps behind her. "Let me see if the doc is about to wrap it up."

Dennis and Edgar went into the kitchen. Sandra backed against the wall and waited. She needed time to steel herself for what she would see. She could hear them talking softly.

Dennis said, "Can you give us a rough estimate of when she died, Doc?"

The M.E., whose deep smoker's voice she'd just heard that morning, said, "It wasn't today . . . more than likely yesterday evening."

"Yeah," Edgar said, "she's stiffer than—"

"Let's get Sandra in here," Dennis interrupted. "We can talk about this later." He poked his head around the corner and called her name. Edgar came and she could feel his hand on her elbow. Generally, she wasn't reticent around bodies. Generally, she didn't have to see two people she knew lying dead within ten days of each other. It was cool in Lizzie's house, but the air-conditioning recycling the air had caused the aroma of blood to hang above their heads like smoke in a bingo hall.

Dennis helped Dr. Michaels and Lawrence turn Lizzie over. Her body was as rigid as a bed frame. An outline on the floor showed how she had fallen. The stench of death assaulted their nostrils anew. Lawrence picked up a large, expensive-looking camera and flash and shot photographs from several angles.

The long, flowered sundress Lizzie wore was twisted around her ankles. Bare feet protruded from under light-colored fabric. Her skin looked unreal, like wax, except the side of her face, which had been down, was purple, like a huge birthmark. Smears of dried blood glued reddish-blond tendrils of hair to her face. A broken wineglass stem stood next to her like an arrow protruding from the kitchen tile. Shards of glass sparkled from the light streaming through the mini-blinds. Sandra kneeled on the other side, wanting to straighten her dress, brush the glass away, and scrape the blood off her cheeks. But she knew the police were letting her do more than they should by even allowing her inside the house.

People often say that dead people look like they are sleeping peacefully, but Lizzie didn't. Lizzie looked like she was in pain. But she was, at last, at peace. Lizzie had been so worried about her future, her financial security, what was in store for her. If she had only known.

Sandra said a silent goodbye to Lizzie, nodded to Dennis Truman, and walked into the blazing sun where she waited next to the Jeep until Edgar came out. By the time she saw him, the tears had dried. She could again speak without her voice breaking. She asked him to drop her at her office. She needed to see her mother immediately.

"You seem upset," Edgar said as he started his engine. "You going to want to proceed with the examining trial?"

Since she didn't trust Edgar Saul and she knew him not to be an empathetic person, Sandra glanced at him sideways. What was going on in his little computer-like brain? "What are you getting at?"

He reached out, his hand halting before actually touching her, wavering above her arm. "You need a couple of days?"

"For what?"

He glanced at her face and jerked his hand back, grasping the steering wheel with both hands. "I just thought—"

"You just thought that if you could get me to agree to a postponement for a few days that would give you time to pin this murder on my client, too. Is that it?"

"Well, uh, if she did it . . . I guess I could always get her later."

"Yeah, I guess so. So, no, I won't take any continuances, by agreement or otherwise. You got anything else you want to discuss?" She shot him a look that would have shriveled a blooming flower and turned away for the rest of the drive.

Barely a ripple disturbed the clear, green Gulf of Mexico. An oil rig several miles out appeared to be only a hundred yards away. Sandra didn't see dolphins breaching, but so many mullet jumped that they looked like schools of flying fish.

Traffic was stop-and-go all the way back as tourists searched for parking spots on the seawall, blocking traffic when they found a space they thought they could squeeze into. Bathing suit-clad people jaywalked between cars. If it had been any other day, Sandra would have been happy to see that business was booming. Just a few years earlier, tourism had been down. But back then the city mothers and fathers had gotten the inspired idea of hiring a contractor to suck sand from offshore and dump it in the eroded beaches. "THE BEACH IS BACK" pictures had been plastered on billboards across the state. Tourism improved overnight.

When Edgar dropped Sandra off, the only thing she could think of was whether the bad news about Lizzie would cause Erma to have a relapse. After the events of the past few days, Sandra didn't know what she'd do without her mother.

Chapter Twenty-Two

Erma walked her client to the door and waved goodbye before kicking off her shoes back in her office. She stood on a thick rug and wiggled her toes. Goddamn, that felt good. One of these days she was going to switch to soft, flat shoes like nurses wore, but not yet. She liked the way heels made her legs look. She liked to be taller. She liked to feel younger. But man, did she pay for it sometimes with hurt feet. She wore a long, straight black skirt, a cream-colored rough-silk tank top, and her opera-length pearls. All she had to do was throw on her jacket and she'd be ready for a formal dinner. She and Phillip would have had their monthly dinner that night, had he not died. So, in his memory, a few days earlier, Erma had called Lizzie to dine with her. She'd gotten to dress up anyway. Lizzie had still been pissed, but Erma told her she was going to try to help her come up with a solution to her financial situation. Erma didn't know what Phillip had been thinking when he made such a minor provision for Lizzie. When Erma had tried to broach it with him, he had told her in no uncertain terms that the subject was not open to discussion. He had been her friend, but sometimes he could be an asshole. She told him so, frequently.

Patricia sat reading the newspaper at the serving bar in the kitchen. Erma got herself a cup of coffee and the last donut and sat next to Patricia. "That'll be a nice fee," she said.

"You're feeling better today. I'm glad," Patricia said.

Erma dunked her donut into the coffee and took a bite. The lemon filling oozed out. She licked it with the tip of her tongue. "Yep. You can't keep an old broad down, Patricia. You know that."

"Hey, I'm not anywhere near as old as you are, Missus Townley."

"Missus Townley. I wish you'd quit that Missus Townley bullshit. You've been with us what, a year?"

"Give or take. But you are the boss and I am the employee. It's only a sign of respect."

Erma patted at the white sugar on her lips and dipped her donut again. "I think we're more than that by now, Patricia, my darling. We've weathered a few things together. I think we've become a family." Erma swallowed some coffee and chased it with the donut.

"Why, I'm touched, Missus Townley. I really am." Patricia straightened up a little on the stool.

"Okay, okay. Here's what we'll do. You call me Erma except when there are clients around and then it's Missus Townley. Same as you do with Sandra." Erma smiled and patted Patricia's shoulder with the clean part of her napkin. "Deal?"

Patricia laughed. "Deal. Erma."

"Goddamn that's better." Erma laughed and finished off her donut and coffee. "Okay, I'm going to wash up and then get started on that estate. It's a couple of hundred thou." She smiled and slid off the stool, heading toward the restroom, a little bounce in her hobbled walk.

Sandra slipped her key into the deadbolt and threw open the door. "Work slow this morning?" she asked Patricia.

"It's just after noon, if you haven't noticed."

Sandra picked up the empty donut box. "What's this? Y'all taking advantage of my absence?"

Turning the page of the newspaper and smoothing it down on the counter, Patricia said, "You're in a mood."

"My mother here?"

"You know I am," Erma called from the open door of the restroom. "You parked next to my Lincoln and waited until you thought I left the room to come in."

"You don't miss a trick, do you Erma?"

"No, Sandra, I don't. You don't miss many yourself." Erma came out, tucking her tank top into her skirt. "And yep, we drank coffee and ate donuts. What are you going to do about it?"

Sandra dropped her briefcase on the counter and stalked to the refrigerator. "You know you aren't supposed to have all that sugar and caffeine."

"Who gives a flying fart? Not me." Erma laughed. Sandra just looked at her. "Something the matter?"

Patricia turned another page of the newspaper.

Sandra found a Dr Pepper, slammed the refrigerator door, and popped the top on the can. She took a swallow and held the can up to her forehead. "There's a storm brewing in my head." She swayed and reached for Patricia, who was the closest.

"Are you all right?" Patricia slid from her stool and helped Sandra to one of the chairs at the dinette table.

Erma said, "You getting another headache? Something happen at the examining trial?"

Sandra closed her eyes a moment. "I suddenly feel exhausted." She breathed deeply. "And I wish I wasn't an only child."

Patricia sat across from her. "Can I get you anything?"

"Something for this headache." Sandra rested her forehead on the table. She opened one eye and peered at Erma, who had sat in the chair next to her.

"What was that crack about being an only child about?"

After Sandra took the pills Patricia brought her, she said, "Mom. More bad news." She laid her head back on the table.

"Judge Perez found probable cause that Kitty murdered Phillip and bound her over to the grand jury?"

"No," Sandra said. "Worse than that. We're in a recess until tomorrow morning. I'll tell you about that later."

Erma looked at Sandra's tensed brow. She could see her daughter was in pain. "Want to talk about it? You could go into your office and put your feet up." She toyed with her pearls and watched Sandra's face.

Sandra's cheek was smushed on the table and her voice came out strangely, like she had a mouth full of candy. "No, got to tell you now. What are you all dressed up for, by the way?"

"It's my night for dinner with Phillip."

Sandra sat up and then grabbed the back of her neck.

"Oh, don't worry, Sandra, I remember he's dead. I'm taking Lizzie to dinner instead. Goddamn, I made a rhyme." Erma chuckled.

Sandra got up and went into her office. She plopped down in her executive chair. "Don't turn on the light," she said when Erma and Patricia followed.

They sat across from her. Patricia kept glancing from one to the other of them, like watching a tennis match, and not saying anything.

"No, you're not taking Lizzie to dinner. Lizzie can't go to dinner because Lizzie is dead."

"Dead?" Erma stared at Sandra, not sure she'd heard correctly. "Oh my God!" She grabbed Patricia's arm and squeezed it hard.

Patricia said, "You did take your blood pressure medicine this morning, didn't you?"

Erma swallowed and then began breathing deeply. She wondered if she had imagined that Sandra had said Lizzie was dead or had Sandra really said it. She'd talked to Lizzie a few days ago. Made plans for dinner. Calmed her down about her inheritance from Phillip. Dead?

They sat that way for several minutes. Sandra lay back in her chair with her eyes closed. Erma gripped Patricia's arm for dear life. Patricia was transfixed. It was like someone had punched the pause button on a DVD player. Finally, Patricia pried Erma's hand off her arm and retrieved the box of tissues. She pushed them at Erma, who had tears streaming down her face without even knowing it. The spell broken, Erma shuddered. She wiped her face and hugged herself. She sighed and in doing so, seemed to come back alive.

Sandra sat up and said, "Erma, is there anything I can do for you?" She got out of her chair and put her arms around Erma. Patted her back. Patricia went to the kitchen and made lemonade for all of them and brought it back on a tray.

"What the hell is this concoction?" Erma asked.

Patricia said, "Don't worry. It has vodka in it. I know it's not bourbon, but bourbon tastes funny with lemonade."

Erma took a glass. Poor Patricia was trying to be helpful. She didn't want to hurt her feelings. She swallowed a mouthful. Wasn't too bad.

Sandra started to wave Patricia away, but took a glass also and stood. "Are you going to be all right?"

Patricia set the tray down on Sandra's desk and proposed a toast. "To the survivors."

Erma said, "Damn straight."

They all took a drink.

Erma said, "I take it Lizzie didn't die of natural causes."

"No. Gunshot," Sandra said.

"Not self-inflicted, I trust," Erma said.

Sandra shook her head.

Erma nodded. "When did it happen?"

"Perhaps last night. They aren't sure yet."

"It could make a person nervous, knowing someone is picking off the people who were at that party," Patricia said.

"Yeah." Sandra looked at Erma. "You and I were at that party."

"Hell, a lot of people in town were at that party, not just us," Erma said.

"True," Sandra said, "but I think Lizzie must have known something. There had to have been a reason."

"What's Edgar Saul say?" Erma asked.

"Oh, he'd love to pin it on Kitty."

Erma wiped her nose. "Wouldn't he just."

After a while, the three of them moved back into the kitchen. Patricia made some sandwiches. The rest of the day, they sat in Erma's office, talking, discussing, and surmising. They took turns on the sofa, the carpet, and the chairs. They discussed the murders in a detached way, Erma thought. As if they didn't know the people involved. Patricia kept bringing them food and lemonade and coffee. Erma was glad that Kitty's case was continued until the next day. She wanted Sandra close to her for a while. If she could, she would have put her arms around her and pulled her close and never let her go. She didn't want Sandra to turn up like Lizzie. What had Lizzie known? And could Sandra also know it?

Sandra phoned Stuart later that night. She didn't want to be alone. She needed a distraction. She wanted him. He didn't ask any questions, just came right over. The sex was hot and fast and extremely satisfying.

Stuart was a blues devotee. Often before, during, and

after their lovemaking, he played one of his favorite blues CDs. He would insist on dancing, whether they were dressed or not.

Monday evening, post-lovemaking, Sandra stood over the wok, sautéing vegetables for dinner. She wore only a silk wrapper when he approached her from behind and pulled her into his arms. It hadn't been an hour, but she could tell he was feeling amorous again.

The feel of his bare chest against her back, the ripple of muscles in his arms, his lips on the curve of her neck, the pressure of his penis against her, all made her want him again. The feeling, the sudden passion, overwhelmed her. Different from what had been between them in the past. Not just the recent past, but during the entire relationship. Sandra wasn't stopping to analyze just then. That would come later. A fleeting thought of it having something to do with death flew through her mind. But it was displaced by Johnny Hartman's deep, bass voice, which seemed to permeate her soul as he sang of the tenuous nature of relationships. Stuart turned off the wok and led her to the living room floor. When she looked up, what seemed to be a long time later, she was surprised to see that the sun had just begun to set.

Reaching for her robe, Sandra brushed Stuart's cheek with her lips, leapt up, and headed for the shower. She was ravenous, but food could wait five more minutes. In spite of all the depressingly terrible things that had happened in the past few days, she found herself humming as she shampooed her hair. A few minutes later, she laughed with Stuart as he slipped into the shower with her. One more embrace, one more kiss, and she got out. She had wrapped herself in a bath sheet, her hair in a smaller towel, when the telephone rang. "Stu, the phone—I've put a fresh towel on the rack for you," she said loudly so he could hear her over the water.

"Okay. I turned the wok back on, Sandy, so watch it, will you?"

Sandra slid the door closed and ran to her bedroom as the phone rang a fourth time. "Hello," she hollered as she grabbed it off the nightstand.

"Sandra, it's Edgar. Sorry to disturb you at home, but listen, I thought I might as well level with you."

Droplets of water still sprinkled Sandra's shoulders. The air-conditioning blowing from the overhead vent chilled her. A shiver scurried around the back of her head and down her neck. "What are you talking about, Edgar? I feel like I came in during the third act."

"The gun that killed Lizzie. Dr. Michaels and the lab have been working extra diligently at my request. The bullets were from a .25 caliber pistol. Our computer says your client is the registered owner of a .25 caliber pistol."

Sandra gripped the huge towel around her as she sat on the edge of her bed. "Kitty and several hundred thousand other Texans, not to mention red-blooded Americans, Edgar. Shit."

"Yeah, Sandra, but several hundred thousand other people are not already suspects in the murder of a victim's shack-up."

"Don't talk like that about Phillip and Lizzie. They were respected members of this community."

"Get real. You know what I'm talking about. Do yourself a favor, go see your client tonight, and get me that gun. We'll check it. If there's no match, fine. We'll even let the judge on the Parker case know that. But don't kid yourself. I think we're going to find that little Miss Innocent Model is guilty as hell."

Sandra could feel her headache coming back. What was she supposed to do, tell Edgar that Kitty lost the gun? "Does it have to be tonight, Edgar? I was in the shower. Just getting ready for bed."

"Gimme a break, Sandra. Here I am trying to be up front with you. You want me to get a warrant? I was hoping I wouldn't have to do that, but I'm down here with Dennis. We can make out an affidavit and have it to a judge in thirty minutes and achieve the same results."

That's what he thought. Sandra knew it would be at least an hour. "Okay. Okay. I'll go talk to her and see if she owns a .25 caliber pistol."

"She does. I'm telling you."

"I said I'll go talk to her. You going to be down there with Dennis until you hear from me?"

"Am I going to hear from you?"

"Yes, Edgar. I swear. Does that make you happy?" She held the phone in the crook of her neck, drying herself.

"All right. I'll be here. Just don't take all night."

Sandra felt sick to her stomach. "Remember that I have to get dressed, and drive over there, and talk to her. Give me plenty of time."

"I'll be waiting right here. See you later." He hung up.

Sandra dropped the phone back on the night table and finished drying off. Throwing the towel onto the bed, she pulled underwear from her dresser and put it on as she went to the kitchen and turned the wok off. Stuart came out then. He had his Bermuda shorts on and picked up various pieces of clothing from around the apartment. He smiled at her. She again thought that they were like an old married couple, wandering around the house half-naked. Showering together. Well, maybe old married couples didn't make it on the living room floor.

"Will you take over here? I turned it back off." She held the wooden spoon out to him. "I have to make a phone call."

"Sure." He dumped his clothes into a pile next to the table and took the spoon from her, kissing her tenderly. "Who called?"

"I'll tell you in a minute. There's some leftover shrimp in the freezer if you want to dump some in with the vegetables." She went back into her bedroom and closed the door. While pulling on a pair of red and pink plaid shorts and a pink Galveston Island Proud T-shirt, she dialed Kitty's number on her mobile phone.

"Hi, this is Kathryn Fulton. Please leave a message at the sound of the beep."

Sandra sat down on the edge of the bed again and wondered whether Kitty was there and just screening her calls. "Kitty, it's me, Sandy. If you're at home, please pick up. It's imperative that I speak to you."

Putting on a pair of socks, Sandra waited a few moments to see if she'd answer. When she didn't, she said in a firmer voice, "Kitty, if you are at home, I have to speak to you immediately. Answer this phone. It's for your own good."

Again she waited. She pushed her feet into tennis shoes and tied them. Nothing. She would still go over there whether Kitty answered or not. She would prefer for Kitty to know she was coming.

"Pick up, damnit!"

"Hello."

"Kitty, you're home. Why didn't you answer sooner?"

"Are you alone, Sandy? Can you talk?"

"I was just coming over to talk to you about your gun. What's the matter? Why do you sound so strange? Are you okay?"

"I think I know who killed Phillip and Lizzie, Sandy."

That caught Sandra so off guard that she blurted out, "Who?" She finished tying her second shoe and turned around in search of her purse and keys. The door to her bedroom had been opened. Stuart stood watching her, the wooden spoon still in his hand, an intense, indescribably odd expression on his face. Sandra couldn't tear her eyes away for a few moments.

"I can't tell you over the phone, Sandy. Are you coming soon?"

"Yes, dear. I'll be right over." Sandra hung up. She had a terrible sickening sensation in the pit of her stomach. Her head buzzed. "I have to go out," she said. Quickly, she combed her wet hair back into a ponytail and wrapped a band around it. She dropped her cell into her purse as she brushed past him. "Go ahead and eat without me. I don't know how long I'll be."

"Where are you going?"

His voice even sounded weird to her. She had to get out of there immediately and get some fresh air, clear her head. She had no rational basis for her sudden feeling about Stuart. Nothing but gut. And that told her that she had to get away from him as fast as possible. Sandra didn't answer but concentrated on reaching the front door of her apartment.

He raced her there, his hand covering hers as she reached for the knob. He put his face close to hers. "I said, 'Where are you going?' "

Not knowing how much of her conversation he had overheard, Sandra didn't know what to answer. She took a chance. Gazing into his eyes, she said, "My mother's. She's not feeling well. I guess the shock of Lizzie's death has really gotten to her."

"Oh, I thought you might be going to see Kitty."

"No," she said, trying not to tremble. "I'm going to my mother's. What's gotten into you, Stuart? Let go of my hand. My mother needs me."

Stuart let go and leaned over to kiss her. Sandra took a step backward and then held her cheek up to him. “See you later.” She let herself out and walked calmly down the hall to the elevator, where she pushed the button. When the elevator doors opened, she turned and waved to Stuart, who stood watching her, the spoon still in his hand, only now he seemed to hold it like a knife.

Chapter Twenty-Three

After the elevator doors closed, Sandra couldn't get to her car fast enough. After she got to her car, she couldn't get away from the condo quick enough. She kept looking over her shoulder and in her rearview mirror, expecting to see Stuart following her. She felt like a seer. Suddenly she knew who had killed Phillip and Lizzie. She remembered some things that had never clicked before. Like the morning after Phillip's murder, something rough on Stuart's fingers caught on her silk blouse. He must have torn his fingernails when he smashed Phillip's face in with that brick, because the night before, his nails were not that way.

Then there were the phone calls from that weirdo. The cadence of the voice. Why had she been so dumb? He had simply dialed her on his mobile phone while he had been talking to her on his regular phone. He had been on two telephones at one time.

Sandra knew this, but how could she prove it? It would take time to get the records. Time was something she didn't have if he would be free until she had some proof. She and Kitty were very probably next on his list.

There must be some other things she'd been overlooking. Could he have slipped into the kitchen and put something in Officer Bradshaw's drink? Surely he hadn't been planning to kill Phillip that night and lucked out with the altercation between Phillip and Kitty.

Earlier, when she had mentioned that Lizzie was dead, he didn't say a word. He hadn't acted surprised. Was that because he already knew she was dead? Did he know because someone had told him or because he had killed her?

Lizzie. She would have let him into her house. She knew him. She trusted him. Had she known he killed Phillip? Is that why he killed her? Sandra was sure it had been Stuart who slept in the room next to Lizzie's the night Phillip had died. Lizzie must have figured the whole thing out.

But why kill Phillip? Stuart would have had such a bright future if he'd stayed partners with Phillip. Just as suddenly as the realization that Stuart was the murderer had hit her back at her apartment, the realization that she'd slept with a murderer struck her like a blow to her stomach. She gagged and stomped her brakes, almost causing an accident. She'd had sex with a murderer—twice in one day.

Sandra pulled over to the curb, jumped out, and ran down the seawall. How could she bear it? It made her sick to think that she had even enjoyed it. She leaned over the edge of the seawall and vomited her wine onto the rocks. To think that she had wanted it. How could she ever put it behind her, forget it? She'd screwed someone who had smashed another's face in, repeatedly, until that face was obliterated. She'd fucked someone who had come up behind a woman and put two bullets into her brain. She wanted an acid bath to get his germs off her. If only she could turn back the clock.

Sandra ran again without stopping until she remembered Kitty. Kitty waited for her at her home. Presumably alone. And Stuart. Did he know where she was really going? What if he got there first? Her heart raced so fast that she thought it would beat her back to her car. When she reached the Volvo, she realized that she'd left the keys in the ignition, the engine running, and her purse on the seat. Why it wasn't stolen was beyond her. Shifting into first, Sandra took off for Kitty's, hoping it wasn't too late.

Kitty flung open the door. "Where have you been?" she screamed. She slammed the door behind her and bolted it several times. "The phone has been ringing. I can't find Raymond anywhere."

For a moment, Sandra wondered whether Stuart had already killed Raymond. Surely not. "Stuart," she said to Kitty's back as she followed her into her living room.

"I know. That's what I wanted to tell you, Sandy, only I was scared to." She washed her hands in the air. "He took my gun. It had to be him. He came over for dinner Saturday night with Raymond. It was gone after he left. Raymond wouldn't have taken it. He's the one who gave it to me."

"How did he know you had one?"

"We were talking about it. Dumb. You're right, Sandy. I'm so dumb. I even talked about where I kept it." Like a little girl, she twirled a strand of hair around on her finger and paced back and forth in front of the sofa.

"Why do you think Stuart would want to kill Lizzie, Kitty?" Sandra stood at one of Kitty's front windows and stared out. In the dark, without much of a moon, she couldn't see but a foot in front of her face. She closed the draperies. She didn't want either one of them to give Stuart a target.

"Money. I'm sure it has something to do with money. And that trial. They were talking about an investigation into something having to do with that trial."

"I didn't hear about that." She checked all of the windows to make sure they were locked.

"Raymond told me that Phillip had yelled at Stuart for something to do with that trial."

"The asbestosis one, you mean?"

"Are you checking to make sure my windows are locked? I already did that. Do you think we should call the police?"

"And tell them what?"

"That Stuart did it."

"You got any evidence?"

Kitty looked at her blankly. "Oh."

"Everything we know is purely circumstantial."

"That means it's not enough?"

"Yes. We need more. If only we could put your gun in his hand."

"Well, what if he doesn't know that's all we have, then what?"

A phone rang. Kitty stared at her. Sandra checked her cell phone. It wasn't hers. "Are you going to answer?"

She shook her head. "It's been ringing almost since you called me." Kitty clutched at Sandra's arm. "I'm so scared."

Sandra counted aloud. After ten rings, it stopped.

Sandra's cell started ringing. Only a few people had that number. Her mother. Patricia. Her daughter. Jack Cartwright. And Stuart. She answered. "This is Sandra."

"Sandy, when are you coming back? Our dinner is getting cold."

Sandra felt as though her blood had curdled. All circulation seemed to have stopped. She nodded in response to Kitty's whispered question. "I just got here, but she's feeling better. I'll be leaving in a few minutes."

"Well, hurry up. I miss you, darling."

"You could eat without me, Stu. I wouldn't mind."

"Oh, I wouldn't want to do that. I don't mind waiting. Having dinner with you will be the perfect end to the perfect evening. See you in a bit." He hung up.

Had his voice sounded unnatural or did she just imagine it? Sandra punched in the main number to the police department. "Lieutenant Truman," she said when the desk sergeant answered. The police department recorder beeped in the background.

"Truman."

"Dennis, this is Sandra. Did Edgar call me from there?"

She heard him make an aside, "It's her."

"Are you on your way down here with the gun?" Dennis asked.

"No, she—"

Edgar Saul's voice, "Salinsky, are you coming down with that gun or not?"

Sandra glanced at Kitty who stood at her front door peering through the peephole every few seconds. "Edgar, I need to talk to you first. It's about Stuart."

"I don't want to hear a goddamned thing about anyone until I get that gun—"

"Edgar, listen to me! Stuart—"

"No, you listen to me. You either get down here with that gun or Miss Goody-two-shoes is going back to jail." The phone disconnected.

"Son of a bitch." Sandra stuck the phone back into her purse. "Kitty, I've got to go down to the police station. They won't listen to me. I've got to explain things to the lieutenant and Edgar Saul, and see if they can help."

Kitty gripped her arm. "You can't leave me here alone, Sandy. What if he comes after me? Raymond may not get here in time."

"Where is Raymond?"

"He went over to the mainland. He was supposed to be at his mother's birthday get-together. I don't know why he's not back."

Sandra didn't voice her concerns about Raymond. "Well, I've got to do something. If I don't get back soon, Stuart will come searching for me. I have a sneaking suspicion he already knows I'm here. We'll be safer if we split up. If he's outside, he'll most likely follow me. You lock yourself in. Take my gun." Sandra pulled her .38 snub-nosed revolver from her purse and handed it to Kitty.

"I thought you didn't believe in guns."

"I don't, normally. Listen, there's not much of a kick to that thing, but hold it with both hands if you have to fire it. Also, it's not that accurate because of the short barrel. Wait until he gets close, but not too close, and then pull the trigger."

"Okay. I can do that."

"Kitty, you have to pull the trigger over and over. It's a revolver, not an automatic. There's no safety, so just point and shoot."

Kitty reached for Sandra and hugged her neck.

"You'll be all right. I doubt he'll come for you if he thinks we both know. He'd want to get me first." She patted Kitty's cheek as she would a small child's. "If you hear anything, dial nine-one-one before you start shooting." Sandra went out the door and eyeballed the grounds before she closed it behind her. As she hurried to her car, she heard Kitty's locks click into place.

Quickly checking in, around, and under her car, Sandra jumped in, locked the doors, and headed for the police station. It wasn't that far away. Under normal conditions, everything on the island was no more than twenty minutes away, most places, ten.

She wondered if Stuart still had Kitty's gun. If he was smart, he would have gotten rid of it right after he did Lizzie. She wondered if he'd planned to get back into Kitty's house and plant it. Or did he figure on the police finding it at Sandra's office? That would be really clever of him, implicating her in an obstruction of justice situation. They would really question her credibility then.

Did he keep a gun in his car? She'd never seen him with one. And certainly there hadn't been one on him when they'd removed their clothing. If Kitty didn't get indicted, did he plan to kill Kitty too? Just how far did he intend to go with this killing thing? Would Sandra be next?

Sandra called Edgar at the police station. "I'm coming down there," she said. "I have something to tell you." Glancing into her rearview mirror, she saw a vehicle with no lights on behind her.

"Sandra, are you bringing the .25?"

Sandra turned around in her seat and saw the SUV more clearly. It looked like Stuart's, but when the lights came on in her eyes, she couldn't see a thing. He must have known all along that she was at Kitty's and called her on his mobile phone. She was sure it was his Ford Expedition when it bumped the back of her car. Her phone fell onto the floor and slid under her feet.

"Edgar, he's right behind me," she hollered, hoping Edgar could hear her. "It's Stuart!"

The vehicle pulled up beside her on the left; the passenger window came down. Sandra only lowered her window a few inches. Stuart beckoned to her and yelled, "Pull over, Sandra."

She drove east on the seawall. She needed to turn north to get to the police station. The trouble was, Stuart was in the left lane and she was on the right—on the water side, that being the side with nothing to stop her from going over the seawall if she lost control of her car. She jammed her foot on the accelerator and shot out in front of him. One thing about her Volvo, it had pickup.

Searching for her cell with one hand, keeping the other on

the wheel, and shifting gears intermittently wasn't all that easy. Sandra grabbed the phone and dropped it into her lap, squeezing her thighs together to hold it in place until she could get her bearings. Stuart's lights loomed in her rearview mirror. The closer she got to the street she needed to turn on, the worse tourist traffic grew.

She had pulled in front of him, but he had gotten into the emergency lane. He caught up with her and hollered "—talk to you!" He edged his Expedition over into her lane, forcing her to the right.

Sandra jerked the steering wheel to the left to dodge a parked car and gunned the engine again. She would not let him force her over the side of the seawall. She needed to get to the police station but couldn't get past him. Jamming her foot on the accelerator, she headed toward Cherry Hill, a two-mile manmade hill bordering four lanes on the seawall. There would be a lot less traffic. If she could speed up fast enough once she got out there, she could do a wide U-turn onto the hill and perhaps escape him.

Stuart blocked her turn all the way down in an attempt to get her to careen over the side. Sandra finally came to East Beach Road, which sloped down onto the beach on an unlit, two-lane, curvy, sandy, and lonely paved road. Not her first choice of destinations. She was forced to swerve to the right and down the ramp. Eventually she'd come to the condominiums—that is, if he didn't get her first. Over her shoulder, she saw Stuart make a U-turn. Moments later, he slammed into her bumper again. If he pulled beside her on the two-lane road, he risked a head-on collision, but that was only if someone else was driving on that dark little road. Picking up her phone, she said, "Edgar, I'm on East Beach Road. Help me!" She could hear some yelling, but she threw the phone down in the passenger seat so she could concentrate on her driving.

Stuart bumped her rear again as she sped toward the condos, clumps of beach sand spinning out from her tires. She could hardly tell where to drive in the dark and feared running off the road and into a sand dune. Stuart pulled even with her and moved into her lane. When they reached a level area, he managed to cut her off and sent her swerving from the paved road, over the curb, and into the soft sand, her tires losing traction. Sandra stopped just before her car hit a barricade made of railroad ties that stopped people from driving over the big dunes and down to the water. She grabbed her phone and scrambled out of the car.

Stuart backed up and plowed after her in his Expedition until he couldn't go any farther either. She could see the beach-front lights behind him as he got out and chased her on foot. Even though the sand dunes were covered with reeds, salt grass, dollar grass, and wildflowers, the sand made it difficult to get traction under her feet. Stuart drew closer. She could hear his voice behind her, but chose not to listen to whatever he yelled at her. The ocean crashed in her ears. She had hoped to get to the Islander East Condo for help, but it stood tall and almost dark in the distance. Stuart would catch her way before she could ever get there, his legs being longer than hers. Sandra held little hope that anyone in the condo would see or hear them in the dark. The only illumination came from the slice of moon above.

He leapt, grabbed her ankle as he fell, and she fell face forward. Stuart had a hold on her foot. Red and gold firewheels scratched at her face as he flipped her over.

"No, Stuart!" She hollered and kicked him in the face. He released her foot. Sandra pushed her heels into the sand and backed away. "Leave me alone, Stuart! Get away from me!"

"Sandra, I just want to talk to you!" He came at her on his hands and knees.

She kicked sand into his face and jumped up from the ground. "Just go away!" she called over her shoulder as she continued trying to run across the dunes toward the ocean.

"Come back, Sandra! I'm not going to hurt you!"

Sandra didn't look back. She didn't want to slow down long enough. Reaching the water's edge, she ran in. "Edgar, we're down East Beach Road. I'm going in. Help me!" she yelled into her cell phone before dropping it. The water felt warm as it came through her shoes. She could out-swim Stuart. He might be a runner, but he didn't like the water. Looking behind her, she could see him a few yards away. "No, Stuart! Stay away from me!"

Her feet dragged so she began unlacing her shoes while keeping her eyes on Stuart. She stumbled and fell backward into the water. She could taste the salt. Her eyes never left Stuart. He stood at the edge of the water and called to her. She could see him breathing hard. Slowly, she backed into deeper water. She would backstroke all the way to Cuba if she had to.

"Come back! I'm not going to hurt you, Sandy! You know how I feel about you!" He stepped into the shallows.

Sandra removed her first shoe and pitched it at him. Then she wadded up her sock and did the same. "No! I don't trust you! You'd better go away. The police know it's you!" she hollered. "I told them!"

"What do they know? What did I do? Why are you behaving like this? Come back and we'll talk about it!"

He took a couple more steps toward her, but she backed over the breakers several feet deeper than him. Not wanting the force of the waves to push her toward him, she backstroked farther away before she took off her other shoe. She figured he'd never come out as far as she did.

"You killed Phillip! They know you did it! You'd better

run, Stuart! They'll be here in a minute!" She yanked at her left shoe. The laces were knotted. She pulled and twisted until it came off her foot anyway. Holding it up, she pitched it at him also. It missed, but splashed him. Pulling her sock off, she just let it drift. Now lighter, but still heavy in her wet clothes, she backstroked a little easier into deeper water. The current was slight.

"I never meant for anyone to get hurt, Sandy!" he yelled. " 'Specially not you! I love you!" He glanced over his shoulder and moved from side-to-side in the knee-deep water as if trying to decide what to do. "You can't stay out there forever! Come in! We'll talk about it! You know I loved you!"

The past tense of his words was not lost on her. "Yeah, you were going to love me to death, weren't you Stuart Quentin?"

"Come back! You're going to drown out there, Sandy!"

"You want me? Come and get me!" She swam far enough away that she felt safe. Thank God he'd never let her teach him to swim. Hopefully he wouldn't pull a gun and start shooting. She treaded water, no longer able to touch bottom. She could stay out there for quite a while if she had to. "The police are coming, Stu! You'd better go now! Get away while you can!"

"Sandy, none of this had anything to do with you!" he called. "I can explain!"

"You can't explain killing Lizzie!" Flashing lights appeared in the distance. She hoped they were headed for them. "You could never explain that." Stuart must have seen the lights moments after she did. He glanced back at her. She couldn't read his expression in the dark.

"I swear I could have explained!" he said as he backed up a few steps. He didn't pull a gun. He stared in her direction. She wasn't sure he could still see her in the dark. He kept backing up, then suddenly turned and ran to his SUV. When he did a half-donut in the sand and drove off, Sandra swam toward the shore. Wading through the shallows, she found her shoes and stuck her wet feet in them. Her phone rested in the sand not far away.

Stuart's taillights grew smaller in the distance as he drove toward Apffel Park Road. They went up the slope to the seawall, but instead of turning left to possible freedom, he turned right. There was no escape to the right. There was only capture. The seawall ended at a two-foot-high concrete wall, followed by huge rocks and then water. His only other option would be to turn right at the end, but that road dead-ended at the water's edge several miles away.

Tiny in the distance, three police cars were visible as they followed him very fast. It dawned on her then that Stuart would not be captured. He sped up. The police kept pace with him in the beginning, but the distance between them widened. As Stuart's Expedition flew toward that wall, it was like a kamikaze pilot's plane as it zeroed in on its destiny. Under the distant streetlight, Sandra could barely make out his vehicle flipping forward. A loud clattering noise followed, as it hit the rocks.

Sandra felt cold on the outside and numb on the inside as she dropped down onto the sand, water from her soaking head streaming down her back. The man she had thought she loved had just committed suicide.

The police cars lined up three abreast, keeping well away from the vehicle in case of fire. Sirens came again from the west. Emergency vehicles. More police units. Sheriff's deputies. Beach patrol. All of them sped eastward, undoubtedly too late to be of any assistance to Stuart Quentin.

Dennis Truman and Edgar Saul found Sandra where she sat on the beach. Dennis pulled her to her feet and wrapped her in his arms for a few minutes. When he released her, Edgar even kind-of embraced her. Edgar Saul, who she never thought she'd be happy to see, and who she never thought would be glad to see her. They stared in the direction of the wreck and let out a collective sigh before getting into their vehicles and driving closer to the scene of Stuart's death to see what was left.

Epilogue

It didn't take the police much investigation to figure out what had been going on with Stuart once they knew who to look at and where to look. Searching his home turned up not only massive credit card receipts reflecting cards that were maxed out, but also shoeboxes filled with betting slips. A gambling addict, Stuart had lost thousands of dollars at the Gulf Greyhound Dog Track in LaMarque as well as at the casinos in Lake Charles and the Grand Coushatta Indian Reservation.

A bit more searching revealed that, among other things, Stuart was a methamphetamine user. His bedside table held bottles full of capsules. A further search turned up pills in his desk drawers, and even some in his suit jacket pockets.

Called speed in the 1960s, women went to diet doctors to get prescriptions for it because it would give them boundless energy and cut off their appetites. "Speed Kills," they used to say. Thirty or forty years ago kids thought that was funny. But it was true. No wonder Stuart could eat anything he wanted and not gain any weight. No wonder Sandra had so much difficulty getting a hold of him at times. He was going all night. He spent his evenings at the dog track. When he finished there, apparently he would drive to Louisiana and hit the gaming tables, returning in the mornings to practice law. The only times he didn't go on weeknights in recent months were when he was in the jury trial. Or with her. Authorities surmised that his debt level, coupled with the recent restrictions on his time, caused him to engage in aberrant behavior. Edgar's words.

And the reason he had endless energy when it came to their sex life was amyl nitrite poppers. Why hadn't she noticed? She drew the line at discussing their sex life with the cops. If they knew what poppers were for, they had the good grace not to mention it to her.

Sandra couldn't figure out how she had missed the indications that all was not right with Stuart, except that they both had been so busy. As she mulled that over at her desk late the next morning, her mother came practically bouncing into the office.

"What's buoyed you up?" Sandra's eyes followed Erma around the room as she bobbed to and fro. Erma acted like she was on speed.

"Besides the fact that all charges against Kitty have been dismissed?"

"Yeah, besides that."

"Besides the fact that Kitty just dropped off a very large bonus on top of her fee?"

Even that couldn't make Sandra smile. "Yeah, besides that, too."

"Edgar Saul called and said that Raymond told him that Phillip thought Stuart had tampered with the asbestosis jury."

"Yes, I suspected as much from something Kitty said last night."

Erma perched momentarily on a delicate antique chair that Sandra kept in a corner so that no one would sit on it. Erma knew that Sandra worried about it collapsing. Even that couldn't get her goat that day. "Well, Edgar says that's why Stuart killed Phillip. 'Cause if the verdict was thrown out, Phillip was going to get Stuart disbarred."

Sandra grunted.

"Want to hear what else Edgar said?"

"Yeah, I guess." Sandra's chest felt full. What she really wanted was to be by herself for a good long while. What she didn't want was to embarrass herself with any outbursts.

"He thinks Lizzie tried to blackmail Stuart and that's why Stuart killed her."

Sandra raised her eyebrows. "She must have known he killed Phillip. I figured Stuart was the one in the room next to hers. She must have heard him go out."

"Perhaps she even followed him," Erma said.

Sandra nodded and shrugged. "Makes sense."

"Yep," Erma said. "I always liked Lizzie, but she killed herself with her goddamn greed. Edgar's going to close that investigation, too."

"Why didn't you let me talk to Edgar?"

" 'Cause you don't want me to have fun anymore," Erma said. "He called. I answered the phone. We talked. It was that simple. I told him I'd tell you. Besides, you were in here moping anyway."

"Get off my chair." Sandra threw her pen at Erma, but even as slow as Erma was, she managed to catch the missile.

"So what's stuck in your craw, Missy? That you didn't get Kitty off? That you didn't have a big, public trial that would make you famous? That you didn't figure it out until it was almost too late?" Erma leaned on the edge of Sandra's desk as she hurled those words.

"Is the verdict in that asbestosis case going to get thrown out? It'd be a shame after a two-month jury trial."

Erma shrugged. "They'll have to have a hearing. The judge'll call each juror in. They'll be questioned. Raymond is the only one left of the three of them who was involved in the trial. He'll probably be the lead attorney, if it has to be retried quickly."

"Huh. Raymond's big break. He deserves it. He's a good kid."

"Not much of a kid anymore. He's dried-up behind the ears. Pretty soon he'll be married, with a couple of children to support and a beautiful, albeit rather dumb, wife."

"It's only right that Kitty be happy. What a beginning she had," Sandra said.

"Sandra, forgive Phillip." Erma came around Sandra's desk and lifted up her chin. "Kitty has."

Erma's motherly touch released a dam of tears. Tough women don't cry. Sandra had already done it once that week when she'd had to identify Lizzie's body. Erma clutched Sandra to her bosom as Sandra ranted and raved about how she'd almost died the night before, after she'd slept with a drug- and gambling-addicted murderer. As her grief subsided, Sandra wept some more. "I realized last night, as I was running from Stuart, that if he killed me the one thing I would miss out on would be seeing Melinda grow up." Lifting her head, she stared at Erma. "Do you think that's dumb?"

Erma shook her head and stroked Sandra's hair.

"I swore to myself that if I lived, I'd make everything up to her. Melinda is the most precious thing in the world."

Erma chuckled.

Sandra pushed her away, wet blouse and all, and reached for some tissues to wipe her runny nose. "What's so damn funny?" she asked, as she got up to examine her red eyes in the mirror.

"That's what I wanted to tell you. I've hired a young girl to work here in the office a couple of hours a day. She'll get school credit and it'll help her decide if she wants to be a lawyer like her mother and grandmother."

"No, you didn't!" Sandra said so loudly that her voice echoed back at her.

"I did! I did! I really did!" Erma danced around in a little circle like an evil elf.

"You didn't! You couldn't have! Not without consulting me." Sandra glared at Erma. "We are partners, after all. You wouldn't have made that decision all by yourself."

"Yes, she did! She did! She really did!" Dressed in a light blue pantsuit and carrying a shiny briefcase, Melinda waltzed into Sandra's office and gave her the beauty-queen wave. "Yes, I'm going to be working here from now on. So get used it, Sandra."

About the Author

Susan P. Baker is a former Texas District Court Judge, former criminal and family attorney, and a former probation officer. She is the past head of the Southwest Chapter of Mystery Writers of America, a member of Sisters in Crime, Private Eye Writers of America, and Authors Guild. She published her first mystery novel in 1989. She has published two short stories and two nonfiction books as well. She is married, the mother of two, and grandmother of six children. Read more about Susan at www.susanpbaker.com.